Praise for the Ice Cream Parlor Mysteries

"Fun! Fresh! Fabulous! Abby Collette has crafted a delicious addition to the cozy mystery world with her superbly written *A Deadly Inside Scoop*. Delightful characters and a puzzler of a plot kept me turning pages until the very end. I can't wait for my next visit to the Crewse Creamery for another decadent taste."

—*New York Times* bestselling author Jenn McKinlay

"A deliciously satisfying new cozy mystery series. It's got humor, a quirky cast of characters and ice cream. What more could you want?"

—V. M. Burns, Agatha Award–nominated author of the Mystery Bookshop Mystery series

"With an endearing cast of characters ranging from Bronwyn's close-knit, multigenerational family to her feisty best friends, this intricate mystery plays out with plenty of suspects, tons of motives and an ending I didn't see coming."

—*New York Times* bestselling author Bailey Cates

"With a host of quirky friends and family members, Abby Collette's new series is a welcome addition to the cozy mystery scene, and life at Crewse Creamery promises plenty of delectable adventures to come. Only one warning: *A Deadly Inside Scoop* causes a deep yearning for scoops of homemade ice cream, no matter the weather."

—Juliet Blackwell, *New York Times* bestselling author of the Haunted Home Renovation series and the Witchcraft Mystery series

"What do you get when you put together a tight-knit, slightly quirky family, a delectable collection of ice cream flavors and an original mystery? A tasty start to a new cozy series. *A Deadly Inside Scoop* is a cleverly crafted mystery with a relatable main character in Bronwyn Crewse."

—*New York Times* bestselling author Sofie Kelly

"This cozy mystery will leave you with a pleasant feeling when you read it, as you cannot help but love the characters that will steal your heart."

—Fresh Fiction

"The #OwnVoices debut novel of Abby Collette's Ice Cream Parlor mystery series is a breath of fresh air. . . . An enjoyable ride from start to finish."

—Criminal Element

"This setting is extremely appealing and the characters introduced are entertaining and memorable. . . . A promising start to a new series that will appeal to fans of foodie fiction."

—The Genre Minx

Berkley Prime Crime titles by Abby Collette

A Deadly Inside Scoop

A Game of Cones

A Game of Cones

Abby Collette

Berkley Prime Crime
New York

BERKLEY PRIME CRIME
Published by Berkley
An imprint of Penguin Random House LLC
penguinrandomhouse.com

Copyright © 2021 by Shondra C. Longino
Penguin Random House supports copyright. Copyright fuels creativity, encourages
diverse voices, promotes free speech, and creates a vibrant culture. Thank you for buying an
authorized edition of this book and for complying with copyright laws by not reproducing,
scanning, or distributing any part of it in any form without permission. You are supporting
writers and allowing Penguin Random House to continue to publish books for every reader.

BERKLEY and the BERKLEY & B colophon are registered trademarks and
BERKLEY PRIME CRIME is a trademark of Penguin Random House LLC.

Library of Congress Cataloging-in-Publication Data

Names: Collette, Abby, author.
Title: A game of cones / Abby Collette.
Description: First Edition. | New York: Berkley Prime Crime, 2021. |
Series: An ice cream parlor mystery; 2
Identifiers: LCCN 2020035710 (print) | LCCN 2020035711 (ebook) |
ISBN 9780593099681 (trade paperback) | ISBN 9780593099698 (ebook)
Subjects: GSAFD: Mystery fiction.
Classification: LCC PS3603.O4397 G36 2021 (print) |
LCC PS3603.O4397 (ebook) | DDC 813/.6—dc23
LC record available at https://lccn.loc.gov/2020035710
LC ebook record available at https://lccn.loc.gov/2020035711

First Edition: March 2021

Printed in the United States of America
1 3 5 7 9 10 8 6 4 2

Cover illustration and design by Vi-An Nguyen
Book design by Alison Cnockaert

This is a work of fiction. Names, characters, places, and incidents either are the product of
the author's imagination or are used fictitiously, and any resemblance to actual persons,
living or dead, business establishments, events, or locales is entirely coincidental.

PUBLISHER'S NOTE: The recipes contained in this book are to be followed exactly
as written. The publisher is not responsible for your specific health or allergy needs that
may require medical supervision. The publisher is not responsible for any
adverse reactions to the recipes contained in this book.

To my children, Kevan and Aaron.
Because it's a family affair.

chapter

ONE

A wave of discontent settled over the dusty, low-lit room. The momentary stunned silence crumbled by a low growling hiss.

"Booo." The jeer lingered as all eyes fell on the speaker. Reverberating from a back corner of the room, the sneer seemed surprisingly appreciated.

It was obvious he'd felt the disaffection his words brought. He ran his fingers through his summer bleached blond hair, pushing the stray strands back in place. The cheeky smile that had curled at the end of the lips when he first began to speak was put on pause as his eyes drifted to the place the word of scorn had emanated from.

"We're going to, uhm . . . to erect a mall." He swallowed hard. "A mini mall." Sputtering, he couldn't seem to find the right words, obviously disturbed by the reaction in the room. "A vertical mall on the square." He stepped beside the tabletop lectern, his eyes returning to focus on his audience. His voice ragged, the last words he'd read from the notes he'd now abandoned had spilled from his lips, hesitant and broken. They were out of character with the earlier poised, melodic tone he'd used with his words of introduction.

The second attempt at making his intended remarks went off no better than the first. It birthed a rumble across the room, low at first, the voices incrementally escalating. A ruckus soon ensued.

"Boooo!" The second call of disdain came from a man standing next to a seamstress's manikin draped loosely with material. He cupped his hands around his mouth and drew the word out, elevating his voice above the rumble, initially the only decipherable words made in the room.

"We don't have a square," Mrs. Cro, the owner of the Flower Pot, our town's flower shop, said, her voice raised, making her declaration known.

"It's a triangle," another person corrected mockingly. I couldn't tell who'd said that.

It was true, and anyone who knew Chagrin Falls knew that where most small towns had their downtown built around a square, ours was built around a triangle.

He didn't seem to get it.

Or maybe he didn't care.

Zeke Reynolds had entered the back room of Debbie Devereaux's clothing boutique in his navy blue skinny three-buttoned suit with the mien of a politician. He straightened his tie, tugged on his suit jacket and followed the mayor's lead as he gestured for him to take his place at the podium. An air of confidence and the woodsy sweet smell of musk followed him in, as did a woman.

The woman carried a large black vinyl artists' portfolio in one hand and an easel in the other. Once he stood in front of the lectern, he'd introduced her as Veronica Russell, a junior associate and his right hand. She bowed her head slightly at his acknowledgment, her bangs swaying with the tilt of her head, the rest of her hair pulled back into a tight chignon. She leaned the portfolio and tripod against the wall and stood there next to them at the back of the room, her hands at her sides, waiting, I guessed, for her cue.

Her hair color matched his. But her emerald-green eyes, bright even behind her black-rimmed rectangle glasses, gave off sparks of light and warmth, something he, at the moment, seemed void of.

"We're trying to help usher the Village of Chagrin Falls into the twenty-first century," he continued. He wiggled his fingers at Veronica and she jumped to action. She pushed her glasses up her nose with a flick of her finger then grabbed the handle of the portfolio with one hand, wrapped her other hand around the tripod and marched to the front, not wasting one moment in setting up.

The village business-district people were gathered for a meeting of the Shop Owners of Chagrin Falls Association. We called it SOOCFA for short. Well, it's what the members called it. I wasn't one. Yet. Although with my new food truck under construction and sliding off the assembly line soon, all shiny and spanking new, and the ice cream shop doing good business, I'd need to join. But today, I'd come to support Maisie, one of my best friends.

The room was sparsely filled. Old sewing machines, a long wooden table for cutting and a file cabinet—drawers hanging open, overstuffed with patterns and sewing materials scattered about. Ms. Devereaux had long abandoned the practice of dressmaking—designing and tailoring clothes. All the wares she sold in her boutique nowadays came ready-made.

There hadn't been an agenda circulated at the start of the shop owners' meeting, and after Maisie's plea for acceptance into the shop owners fraternity, everything had seemed to be winding down.

That was until Zeke Reynolds took the podium.

"Who is he, Win?" Maisie leaned in to me and pointed her finger.

I hunched my shoulders. "He said his name is—"

"I know what he said his name is," she said, not letting me finish. "But *who* is he?"

I shrugged. I was just as clueless as she was.

As clueless, it seemed, as everyone else.

I mean, I knew what he'd said—I'd heard what he'd read from his notecards, and so had Maisie. I think what everyone really wanted to know was why. Why was he here telling us what he was going to do to our little village? To us. How did he think he could?

I glanced back at the doorway where he'd entered twenty minutes earlier. Escorted by Kevin Greer, the mayor of our little village, and Amelia Hargrove, owner of the Around the Corner Bookshop.

Amelia had kept her eyes straight ahead, carried a small stack of colored papers. Expressionless, she sat at the front of the room. Hands in lap, she seemed placid and unperturbed by the speaker's words.

The mayor, however, seemed to have quietly slipped back out. He was nowhere to be seen.

Mayor Greer, whom I hadn't voted for in the last election because I was still in New York, was a good friend of my grandfather's. I'd have to be sure to ask PopPop what the mayor had been up to bringing in a man who would cause so much confusion at a SOOCFA meeting.

Had the two of them thought the crowd would be rowdy when they agreed to escort Zeke Reynolds in? I wouldn't want to be in their shoes when this was over.

I directed my attention to the others present and spied the reaction on their faces. Some of the faces I recognized, some I didn't know. All, though, except for Amelia, were upset.

"We've acquired all the necessary buildings but one, and there is still a plot or two of land we're working to gain ownership of." Zeke was back to talking. He'd built up a steady cadence, decidedly schlepping forward with his presentation. "It's amazing how they were sliced up into such small parcels." He drew in a breath and shook his head. "I'd hoped to come here tonight to get your support."

Veronica had pulled a poster board drawing out of her portfolio as he spoke, and placed it on the easel.

"Our support?" Maisie turned and looked at me, the red curls of her hair thrown to the side with the jerk of her head. "For which buildings?" She tightly clutched the back of the metal folding chair in front of her, the knuckles on her hand turning white. "Which of the buildings around Triangle Park? My building?"

I started to speak, but her curls, flipping the other way, gave notice she was no longer paying attention to me. She scooted forward in her chair, sitting on the edge of her seat, and eyed Zeke and his drawing board, intent on finding out what they meant.

"It's not really your building," Riya, sitting on Maisie's other side, leaned toward her and said matter-of-factly. "At least not yet." She gestured with a head nod toward the front of the room. "Or maybe ever." She raised an all-knowing eyebrow.

I gave Riya the most disapproving face I could muster, then mouthed, "What is wrong with you? Don't say that to her."

Riya's face showed not one glimmer of contrition.

Maisie glowered at Riya, then turned, her pleading eyes meeting mine. "But I am getting it," Maisie squeaked. "Right? Everyone here was in agreement I should get it and that's all the zoning committee cares about. Right?"

Maisie Solomon had come to the meeting because she wanted to expand her community garden using an adjoining vacant shop on the triangle. Such an endeavor was a feat for Maisie and was contrary to the way she usually did things.

Maisie never kept a job for long, or kept to anything for that matter. She'd get bored or disillusioned and would abandon projects, jobs or anything else just to come up with something new she wanted to try. She was usually good at her endeavors, whatever they were, even though they never held her attention for long. But the community garden had seemed to be a constant for her. She'd even grown spices for my ice cream recipes. That was why Riya and I, well, at least I, had come to support her.

Hearing Riya, I was no longer sure what she thought her purpose of attending had been.

Maisie came needing the shopkeepers' support to convince the village's zoning department to allow her to enlarge the windows, hook up sprinklers and lay plots in the building she wanted to purchase. She'd come bearing gifts—offering a community hall she had drawn into the plans as the meeting place for SOOCFA. She'd also use it, she'd told her rapt audience, for food drives and a fresh produce market in the winter months.

Her pitch drew smiles and praise, and ended in applause.

Then Zeke Reynolds took the microphone . . .

Riya leaned across the back of Maisie's chair and, I supposed, thinking she'd made her voice too low for Maisie to hear, said, "Did you hear he's buying plots, too?" Her voice strained to whisper. "Wonder if that's Maisie's garden he bought."

"My garden!" Maisie squealed and popped out of her seat.

"We're here to help," I scolded Riya.

"What?" She coiled back as if my remark had struck a nerve. "I *am* trying to help."

"Then be supportive," I said and gave a yank on Maisie's arm to try to get her back into her seat. That didn't work. I stood next to her. "Maisie." I bumped my hip into her. "You gotta sit down."

"I think he wants my community garden!" She wasn't trying to contain herself. She made known her feelings loud enough for the entire room to get wind of them.

"He wants all of our shops," someone yelled. "But he's not getting them."

"Talk about me? Hah!" Riya stood up next to us and leaned forward so she could see my face. "They're the rowdy little bunch," Riya said, jabbing her finger around the room at various people. "I"—now jabbing that finger at herself—"was trying to be reasonable."

Riya knew rowdy when she heard it. It was a major part of who she was.

"He's messing with our livelihoods." A man one row up and to my right turned to us, gesturing at Zeke still standing beside the podium.

"Whoa! I—rather, the company I work for is not trying to *take* anyone's shop." Zeke held out his hands, trying to calm the crowd. "We want to work with you. That's why I'm here."

"What does he think he's doing?" Maisie looked at the man who had spoken to us, then back at me.

"I think he's telling us that someone's building a mall on North Main Street," Riya said. "And it sounds like it's a done deal."

"And you're okay with that?" Maisie said to Riya, her voice going up an octave. She didn't give Riya time to answer before turning to me, her eyes suspiciously red and blurry. "He can't do that, can he?"

"How could this already be happening and none of us knew about it?" someone stood and asked.

My eyes went over to Amelia Hargrove again. I couldn't help but think that Amelia knew something about all of this—the buildings, the land being sold, or rather this company wanting to buy them. She had come in and made a beeline to her seat. A seat, now that I thought about it, that oddly seemed to have been waiting for her. I scanned the seat next to her. An older guy, maybe midfifties, dressed in a suit and a bow tie. He must have saved it for her. I didn't know who he was, but I had to wonder, was he in on it, too?

But why?

Her bookshop had been in Chagrin Falls as long as I could remember. Books stuffed in every nook and cranny, piled onto display cases and filling up bookracks, a family business like our ice cream shop. And as far as I knew, business was good.

"Look, I am not the one buying up the buildings." Zeke's face was flushed. He was getting weary of the jeers, it seemed. "I'm here because—"

"You work for the company." The interjector cut him off before he could finish. "Yeah, yeah, yeah. We get it. Now you go back and tell them for us that we're not interested."

"I do," he said, licking his lips. "I do work for them. For Rhys Enterprises. A smart and innovative company located in Dallas. And even though they're a good piece down the road, you'll find that they are the neighborly kind of folk and committed to keeping Chagrin Falls the quaint little village that it is."

"With a shopping mall right smack in the middle of it?" That woman's voice was so strained it squeaked.

"You're not proposing anything good for our little village!" Another dissenter squawked.

"On the contrary," Zeke said. "Urban revitalization is a good thing. Even I'd agree with that."

"We don't need revitalization," someone yelled from the audience. "There's nothing wrong with Chagrin Falls."

"It's not revitalization," someone else yelled out. "It's gentrification."

"We're not a blighted area."

I knew that voice. I swiveled from the waist and cast my eyes toward the rear of the room. Standing near where Miss Green-Eyed Junior Associate Veronica had just vacated was my brother Bobby. The activist. Standing next to him was my grandfather.

Someone must have spread the word because neither of them had been there when the meeting first started. Now, the back of the room, since the last time I looked, had become standing room only.

"We've been named Tree City USA for twenty-five years running," PopPop said. "We've got the falls, the trees and our shops. We don't need anything else."

"That's right," I heard several people say. "Yes! We don't need anything else," came the chorus.

"We're not going to stand for this!" Ms. Devereaux said and stepped forward. Even dressed in a dainty pink summer sweater with three big bows down the back and a pair of loose-fitting jeans, she seemed ready for a fight. Though she was usually glittery and gem encrusted, the only sparkle I noticed now was the one in her eye that I was afraid would flicker into a flame. At nearly seventy, I hoped she wasn't thinking of forcibly ushering the man out of her shop. She was known to be a little feisty.

"You're coming here trying to mess up things that aren't broken." It was Squeaky Voice speaking again—she seemed willing to join in the fight if that was what Ms. Devereaux had planned. I didn't know which, if any, shop she owned.

"I'm not—we're not—" Zeke Reynolds stopped what he was trying to say and let out a nervous chuckle. "Please," he said, raising his hands to control the crowd, "I'm just here to assess and send in a report. And"—he stopped to take a sip out of his bottled water—"keep you informed of how things are progressing."

"We don't need your progress reports," Ms. Devereaux said. "And we don't need *or want* you here."

"That's right!" Maisie pumped a fist in the air, choking out the words. "We don't want you here." The threat of tears emerging spilling out in her voice.

"Get out!" Riya said and with that hurled her shoe.

As it went spinning over the heads of the sitting shopkeepers and toward the podium and Zeke, a hush came over the room, and all heads turned toward Riya.

"What are you doing?" I screeched, my mouth agape, my eyes big.

"Being supportive," she said, as if it were obvious.

"Hey!" Zeke Reynolds shouted defensively, ducking out of the way of Riya's projectile. "Don't shoot the messenger!"

chapter

❧❧❧

TWO

"Someone shot Zeke Reynolds!" Maisie hustled into the ice cream shop, out of breath. She wiggled into a cardigan to cover her bare arms—we kept it pretty cold in the kitchen of the ice cream shop—then put an apron over her head. "Can you believe it?" she asked, cheeks flushed, eyes wide.

"Shot him?" My mother repeated her words. "Is he okay?" She'd grabbed the plastic bags Maisie had brought in with her, full of mint, and walked over to fetch a knife from the counter rack.

"He's dead," Maisie said with a nod. She stood tying the apron strings behind her, shaking her head.

"Oh my God," my mother said. She dropped the knife and slapped her hands over her face. "Not again. This can't be happening again."

"This isn't the first time he's been shot?" Maisie asked, her brows furrowed.

"I'm sure she meant not another *murder*," I said, shuddering at the memory of the first one our little village had seen. One that had had my father as the prime suspect and me caught up in the killer's claws. "And how do you know something happened to him?"

"Ms. Devereaux told me," she said, as if it was an obvious answer.

"When did she tell you that?" I asked, glancing up at the clock on the wall.

"Just now. On my way in." Maisie swung open the door to the commercial fridge and stuffed the crook of her elbow with cartons of cream. "He'd been staying at her sister's bed-and-breakfast. He and Veronica."

"Together?" Riya asked.

Maisie gave an exaggerated nod, waggling her eyebrows.

"Is that where it happened?" my mother asked, covering her heart with her hand. "At Dell's bed-and-breakfast?"

"Nope." Maisie shook her head, her curls flopping from side to side. "Ms. Devereaux told me they found him in the alley. Behind the shops." She pointed, indicating the shops across the street from us.

I inhaled hastily and wished I could cover my ears, blocking her out. It was five a.m. and much too early to hear the news she came bearing. I'd had enough of murder.

"Who is this Zeke Reynolds, anyway?" my mother asked. She retrieved her knife, seemingly somewhat recovered, and rocked it back and forth over the mint leaves, mincing them, the aromatic fruity scent escaping and wafting through the room.

My semiregular ice cream cooking crew—my mother and two best friends, Riya and Maisie, were making quick work of the morning. Out of the three of them, no one was on the payroll but Maisie. The other two showed up because this business had always been about family, even though I had staff. It was summer, and that meant we were going to need buckets and many, many scoops of ice cream. We had our work cut out for us.

Today on the menu were drink-inspired ice cream concoctions: We were serving smooth cool mint mojito coffee, creamy churned buttermilk and peaches, and steeped black tea folded into buttery crumbs of shortbread. All three were going to have a vanilla bean ice cream base.

"Zeke Reynolds was the guy at the shop owners' meeting last night," Maisie said. "Didn't you hear? He was trying to take my community garden and my building."

"We don't actually know *which* buildings he was trying to buy," I said.

"Oh," my mother said with a grunt. "PopPop came in last night talking about that guy. He was telling Graham the whole story. But I didn't listen—I knew I had to get up early this morning so I went to bed." She took the side of her knife and scooped the mint leaves into an aluminum bowl.

It was surprising to me that my mother wouldn't stay up a little later to hear what my grandfather was telling my dad, since she was always one to succumb to gossip. "He was the guy trying to turn Chagrin Falls into Michigan Avenue, right?" she said without lifting her head up from her work.

"Right." Maisie gave a nod.

"Employee of Rhys Enterprises," Riya said, her hands dripping with the juice from the peaches she was dicing. "But I guess now you don't have to worry about them taking your life's dream from you, Maisie."

Was she being sarcastic? I gave her a stern look. She shrugged and mouthed, "I'm being nice."

I was beginning to think that having Riya's support might not be a good thing.

I realized I'd gotten chilly, too, and plucked a sweater off the peg coatrack on my way to grab a couple of pots to fill with water for the tea and coffee.

My family's ice cream business had been around a long time. We'd been in the same spot for fifty-six years, built directly atop the Chagrin River falls in 1965 by my newly northern trans-planted grandparents, Aloysius and the late Kaylene Crewse. My father's parents had the only black-owned shop in a predom-inantly white neighborhood—it had been a personal as well as a business adjustment for them.

Now, just one of a string of small boutiques and shops—some with awnings, some not, some new, some not so new, but all owner occupied—on North Main Street. Our village shopkeep-ers had always fought back against people like Zeke Reynolds and his employer, Rhys Enterprises. We'd been immune to the beckoning of strip malls, big stores, conglomerates and fran-chises.

Well, until now . . .

I found it hard to believe that anyone in our town was will-ing to sell out and let those high-end, upscale entrepreneurs move in.

Sure, our shop had gone through transitions of its own—the riots of the sixties, inflation of the eighties, Grandma Kay get-ting sick—but we'd never been anywhere near the verge of sell-ing it. Managed by different family members over the years, the last one being my father's sister, Aunt Jack, who had put our business on thin ice. Our brand staple had taken the back burner and Crewse Creamery was slowly, but surely, becoming a novelty shop.

Then Aunt Jack left, following her newfound internet love, and my grandfather turned the management of it over to me. Reopening with me at the helm had more bumps in it than a double dip of rocky road—building delays, then opening day coinciding with a snowstorm and a frozen body right outside our wall of windows. But everything eventually thawed—except for the ice cream, which, after people got a taste of our frozen creamy concoctions at the local university's President's Dinner and I helped solve the murder (and of course, the falls outside our window, a Chagrin Falls staple attraction), started selling like hotcakes.

"Did I hear someone knocking on the door?" my mother asked.

But even hotcakes didn't start selling this early in the morning...

I looked at my mother, who had her ear trained toward the front of the store, her eyes wide with concern. Then I looked toward the door.

"Who'd be stopping by this early?" she asked, glancing my way. "It's hours before we start serving."

"I don't know," I said and turned the eyes off on the stove. "Only one way to find out." I swiped my hands down the front of my apron and headed toward the door.

"Don't go out there!" my mother yelled, startling me. "What's wrong with you? There's a murderer on the loose."

"I don't think the murderer is going to knock," I said.

"You never know," she warned.

"Mom."

"Don't 'Mom' me. You never know," she repeated. "If you're going to go, take a knife with you." She thrust the one she'd been using to cut the mint in my direction.

"According to Maisie, Zeke Reynolds's killer used a gun," I said. "Don't think that"—I nodded my head at the twelve-inch chef's knife she was holding—"will do me much good."

"Riya," Maisie ordered, "you go with her."

Riya shook her head. "Even my black belt in tae kwon do can't stop a .38."

"Oh good lord," my mother said. "We'll all go." She blew out a breath and placed her knife on the stainless-steel countertop. "I'm sure it'll be fine."

Hadn't she been the one to start the whole killer-on-the-loose thingy...

I glanced once more toward the front of the store before I ventured that way. The 1950s motif with cobalt-blue seating and a stainless-steel counter was partitioned off by a plexiglass wall. I had it installed when I remodeled the store. I wanted to see the customers and make it so they could see me. But with it being pitch-black in the front room of the shop and outside, I couldn't make out who had come a-knocking.

My mother flipped on the lights as we went to the front. I saw Felice, our resident white Persian cat, already perched in her usual spot on the window seat. I hadn't even seen her come down. She usually made such a fanfare of her arrival in the morning from the upstairs apartment where she lived—acting like royalty prancing through the kitchen, waddling on her short chubby legs, her plumed tail swaying back and forth.

"Who's there, Felice?" I asked as if she could answer. She

didn't, nor did she seemed interested in what I was asking. She stretched and yawned and, rolling over, snuggled down for another interval of beauty rest. Her Royal Highness didn't seem alarmed, so I figured neither should we.

I glanced back at the door. The figure peeking through the glass became recognizable.

"Detective Liam Beverly," I announced.

My mother threw up her hands. "A face I don't want to see or hear anything from." She did an about-face and marched back into the kitchen. Riya and Maisie stuck close by.

I flipped the lock on the door and pulled it open.

"Morning," he said.

"Good morning." I smiled. "If you've come for ice cream, you're a little early." We stood in a half circle around him in the middle of the black-and-white-checkered floor.

"A lot early," Riya said.

"Not here for ice cream, unless you need me to sample anything you got going." He stepped inside and drew in a deep breath through his nostrils. "I can smell all that goodness already."

"Ice cream doesn't have a smell," Riya said, and she squinted her eyes. "I can't understand why everyone says that."

"We're still prepping," I said.

Liam Beverly had eyes the color of pistachio ice cream even down to the flecks of gold. This morning, though, they looked melted and tired. Still I could sense from them that his visit was all about business.

I hadn't seen him in a while. Thank goodness there hadn't been a need to. The last time I'd seen him, it had been cold outside and each time he'd worn a leather jacket, more in line with a biker than a cop, and an apple cap—but today he wore a nice crisp light green shirt that matched his eyes and tan pants. I wondered was that the official summer uniform for the CFPD.

"You come about Zeke Reynolds?" Maisie said, folding her arms across her chest. I guess she sensed the same thing. "Because we don't know anything."

I looked at Detective Beverly and wondered would that statement appease him and send him on his way.

I could only hope.

He stepped closer into the little arch we'd formed around him, leaning back on his bowed legs. (I remembered that about him, too.) He was always invading other people's space. "You know something?" he asked, one eyebrow arched.

"She just said we didn't," I said.

"I think you do." He smiled as if he could charm an answer out of us. "You want to tell me what it is you know?"

"He's dead," Maisie said, taking a step back from him and toward me. "Somebody shot him."

I elbowed Maisie. Sometimes she could be surprisingly gutsy.

A lopsided grin crawled up one side of the detective's face. "And what do you know about that, Ms. Solomon?" He took another step toward Maisie.

She shook her head. "Nothing." Her tone defiant.

It was much too early in the morning for her to start trouble.

"Is that why you stopped? To . . ." I didn't finish my sentence. I thought I'd let him fill in the blank. I just needed to stop Maisie before she did any more talking.

"I stopped by to let you know what happened." He looked at the three of our faces. "And to see what you knew about it."

I saw from the corner of my eye Maisie start to speak. I jerked on her arm, wrapping my hand around her wrist, hoping she'd get the message to stay quiet. "Like Maisie said, we don't know anything."

"How do you know he'd been shot?" he asked, turning to me.

"I don't know anything about that." I probably should have added, *Except for what Maisie told me.* But I wasn't volunteering any information. The last murder had family members involved. This one I was sure had nothing to do with me.

"Ms. Solomon?" He turned to Maisie.

Maisie pursed her lips and looked at him as if deciding whether she was going to share what she knew.

"Ms. Devereaux told her," Riya volunteered, being helpful again, I guess. "Maisie saw her when she came in this morning."

He nodded, but the spark that came into his eye said he was filled with more questions. "And what can you tell me about what happened last night?" he asked. "At the shop owners' meeting. I understand the three of you were there?"

"And how do you know that?" Maisie asked.

"Same way you know he got shot," he said. "Someone told me."

I wondered how many people he'd talked to already. I glanced up at the clock on the wall. It was 5:40 a.m. He'd have had to awaken practically everybody. Besides the staff over at the bakery, no one else was at their shop this early.

"We haven't heard anything," I said and pointed toward the kitchen. "We've been here making ice cream. We don't know a thing."

"I see your mother back there," he said. "Ailbhe, isn't it?" Like he'd forget after he tried to take my father away from her and send him to death row.

I turned, glanced at her. "She doesn't know anything either," I said. "She wasn't there."

He pulled out a small spiral notebook from his pants pocket. First time I'd seen him with one. Last investigation he interrogated me about, he never made one note. Flipping through a few pages, he said, "No, doesn't seem she was." He flipped the notebook closed. "At least not from what I know so far."

I gave him an "I told you so" look.

"What did the three of you do after you left the meeting?" he asked.

"We went home," we said in unison. It couldn't have sounded more rehearsed.

That seemed to amuse him. "All to the same home?"

"No," I said, shaking my head. "Different ones."

"Our own homes," Riya added.

Maisie was still being defiant and didn't offer anything more.

"I see," he said, nodding slowly.

I shrugged. "Okay. If there isn't anything else, we've got to get back and finish up. Otherwise, I won't have any ice cream to sell today."

"Nope. Nothing else." He tilted his head to the side. "But if you find out anything, Bronwyn, you'll let me know?"

"I'm sure there won't be anything that I'll find out."

"You might," he said. "Maisie, same goes for you. And . . ." He looked at Riya. "Have we met before?"

"This is Riya Amacarelli," I said. "*Doctor* Amacarelli." I placed a hand on her shoulder. "She's a medical doctor." I liked giving the impression there was a modicum of decorum to Riya when I spoke of her. If I let her actions speak for her, most times people wouldn't think she had any polish or urbanity about her.

"Who moonlights at an ice cream shop?" He pointed at her apron.

"On occasion," I said, not letting his skepticism detour me.

"And is she the same Riya Amacarelli who threw a shoe at Zeke Reynolds last night?"

The three of us looked at each other, then at the detective. Okay, so he did stump me with that response. After stumbling over how to answer, I asked, "How do you know that?"

He patted his pants pocket where he'd stuck the notebook. "I have my ways."

Seems he'd heard a lot about last night.

"It was nothing," I said.

"It slipped," Riya said.

"She has trouble controlling her temper," Maisie said. We offered all of our answers in tandem.

"And," Detective Beverly said, wrapping his fingers around the doorknob, "that might just be the reason we've got another murder on our hands. Someone having a problem controlling their temper."

chapter

∽♡∽

THREE

"He's cute," Riya said after Detective Beverly left. We walked single file back into the kitchen area. "Is he single?"

"What did he want?" my mother asked as we went back to our stations. She narrowed her eyes, acting as if the detective was up to something himself instead of investigating someone else who was.

"He wants us to solve the murder," Maisie said, her eyes wide and twinkly.

"No. He does not want us to solve the murder," I said. "And, Riya, keep those crazy thoughts to yourself."

"What?" Riya said and chuckled. "You don't think that detective is cute?"

"I can tell you what *I* think about him," my mother said, assaulting the mint leaves as she spoke. "He's a thickheaded, dim-witted, no-good son-of-a—"

"Mommy!" I cut her off.

"Gun," she said. "I was going to say son-of-a-gun."

"I think he does," Maisie said, nodding her head, still having the conversation I thought sure I had put an end to. "I think he wants us to help solve this murder like we did last time."

"I know he doesn't want that," I said, my voice a little more haughty than it should be. But I wanted to nip her little idea in the bud. Heck, our last investigation had nearly gotten me killed.

"Who doesn't want what?" PopPop asked. He'd swung open the back door, letting a whoosh of the morning sunlight and warm breeze into our frozen kitchen tundra. He stood with his hands in the pockets of his khaki-colored pants.

PopPop had a penchant for plaid shirts, no matter the season, he wore one with long sleeves. Except for when he went to church, which, since my grandmother died, hadn't been as often—there he always wore white.

Tall, he was where my father got his height. Both showed no signs of going bald, keeping their hair cut low. The only difference, my grandfather's was nearly all white.

"I wasn't the only one upset with *that* man," Maisie said, the tension in her voice matching mine. "And Detective Beverly seems to know that. That's why he needs us. We've got inside ears."

"Who needs you?" PopPop was standing there with a confused look on his face, wondering why we were all up in arms.

"That detective!" My mother pointed her knife at PopPop, not answering his question. She was having a completely different conversation. "That's who!" she said and slammed the knife down on the tabletop, making the small bits of mint bounce around.

I went over and moved the knife away from her.

"What are inside ears?" Riya asked, giving Maisie a confused look.

"Okay. So now, what detective?" PopPop asked.

"Liam Beverly." I offered the answer to PopPop. There were three conversations going, all directed at me.

"Oh," he said.

"He wanted info on Zeke Reynolds," Riya added. "The guy at the SOOCFA meeting last night." She drew in a long breath and shut her eyes. "And I don't care what you say, Win, that detective is so good-looking."

"Zeke Reynolds," PopPop muttered and shook his head. "The Devil himself. Wouldn't mind if someone ran him over with a bus."

"Someone shot him dead instead," my mother said.

PopPop looked at my mother. "What you say, Ailbhe? He's dead?"

"Yep," my mother said. "So you won't be needing that bus."

"Who shot him?" he asked.

"Don't know," I said.

"But Detective Beverly asked us to find out," Maisie said. Again.

And that was the way the rest of the morning went. Maisie insisting that we start up another sleuthing investigation. Riya wanting to know if I had Detective Beverly's personal phone number and my mother taking her anger out on having to see him again on every item—food or otherwise—in the kitchen.

CREWSE CREAMERY WAS one of the few shops that sat in the block right before the town's center where the falls cut through the town. Most of the other shops sat around the village triangle.

I was curious, though, although I'd never mention it to Maisie, just how Detective Beverly got so much information about us so early in the morning.

I had just reopened the ice cream shop after going through an extensive renovation when I'd met Liam Beverly, the village's only homicide detective. I was unsure, though, how he'd gotten that job. We'd never had a murder, at least one that I could remember. And while I had warmed up to him, I would really rather not have to run into him again so soon. Or at all.

I sat in the window seat at the front of the store with Felice. My mother and Maisie were in the back. It was almost noon, we'd only opened at eleven and we'd already had fifteen or more customers. Business usually picked up after lunch, so I knew we'd be swamped. But there was a lull now, and I was taking a breather.

Looking out the window of the shop at the cloudless sky, I could feel the warmth of the late August day. The weather had changed so much since I had spent most of my time outdoors growing up in our suburb. Now we were having ninety-degree weather in September and snowstorms in October. But if the world's climate was taking a nosedive and murder was a common occurrence in Chagrin Falls, it was still the only place I wanted to be.

I had left a good job in New York at one of the largest ad agencies—Hawken Spencer—because I missed home. I missed my family. Not because I couldn't take it or wasn't up to it. It was just time to come home.

I had spent most of my childhood hanging on to my Grandma

Kay's apron strings. Running a family-owned business had made us a close-knit family and my Grandma Kay had been the glue. She was short and scrappy, willing to stand up to anyone and anything for what she loved or believed in, and she had a heart of gold. Anyone who knew her loved and respected her. And as a family we wanted to hold on to the traditions and beliefs she'd instilled in us. And one day, it had just happened. Sitting at my desk, basking in a big account I'd just landed, I realized that my achievements just didn't seem the same without my family being a part of them. I knew then that even the lure of the big city, and using my overpriced MBA to secure a good lifestyle, wasn't going to be able to keep me away from what I knew to be the foundation of who I was.

In the last years of her life, Grandma Kay suffered from Alzheimer's. She'd wander off and forget what the keys she'd picked up and held in her hand were for. But she never forgot us—my three older brothers, James Jr., Lew and Bobby, or me.

I had gotten sick. Turned out to be something minor. But with three brothers in the medical field, and my dad a well-recognized orthopedic surgeon at the renowned Lakeside Memorial Clinic, to get well I knew there was no place like home.

My Grandma Kay wasn't around anymore, but I missed being around the things that mattered to her. The things that she taught me. And I was happy to run the ice cream shop she and my grandfather had started because it meant I was helping to keep her memory alive.

I was going to make sure we never forgot about her either. She would live on through the ice cream business she helped start.

I heard the bell ring over the door and whispered to Felice that I had to go. "We have a customer," I told her.

"Erreow."

I guess she knew that already.

"Welcome to Crewse Creamery," I said, standing up and placing the cat on the window seat.

"Good morning."

"Oh, Amelia," I said, surprised to see her. Her bookstore was just down the street, but I couldn't remember her stopping by our family's shop since we'd reopened. Now, after taking notice of her last night, I was seeing her again. "How are you?"

She ran a hand through her ear-length dark blond hair. She had a small stack of colored paper in her hand—it looked to resemble the stack she had the night before. "I'm good," she said. "How is business?"

"Business is great," I said, which prompted her to look around the store. I guess she noticed there was no one there but the cat and me. "Just taking a short breather before the afternoon rush," I added.

I went around the counter and washed my hands in the sink.

"These look good," she said. "And different." She'd walked up to the display case and was perusing what was inside.

I grabbed a paper towel and dried my hands. "Which one would you like to try?" I asked.

"How about the tea and shortbread?" she said and smiled. "That seems appropriate for brunch, if it is ice cream I'm going to have."

I scooped her up a sample spoonful and handed it across the counter.

She took it with a slight smile and I wondered was there another reason, other than trying to pick a flavor of ice cream good for a morning snack, that she was there.

"Mm-mm, that's good," she said. "You can taste the butter in the shortbread and the savory brewed taste of tea." She had a look of approbation on her face. "But it's smooth and creamy"—her eyes widened—"and delicious! I like it."

"I'm glad you like it," I said, smiling proudly.

"Can I get it to go?" she asked. "In a cup maybe?"

"Sure," I said. "You want a pint?"

"No," she said. "A cup is fine."

"Okay," I said and went about scooping it up for her.

"I was wondering, Win . . ." she said hesitantly.

"Yes?" I put the top on her cup and handed it over the display case.

"I have some flyers here." She held up her hand. The one holding the stack of colored papers.

"Flyers?"

"For the sidewalk fire sale the shops are having."

"Oh?" I said. I hadn't heard anything about any such event. I walked over to the cash register, alerting her that there was a charge for the ice cream. She followed.

"Yeah. I was going to pass them out last night. But . . ." She sighed. "It just didn't seem like the right time."

"Has there been a fire?" I was being sarcastic. I wasn't sure what she was up to.

"No." She chuckled. She set the flyers down on the counter and dug into her purse for money. "How much do I owe you?"

I told her, she paid me and then she continued with what I now assumed was the reason she came in. "Some of the stores are getting rid of some inventory and we are having a, I don't know"—she swayed her head back and forth and shrugged—"a collective sales event." She picked up one of the flyers and handed it to me. "I was wondering if I could hang this in your window?"

I let my eyes run over the flyer. The bookstore, the art gallery, the souvenir shop and the Blue Moon clothing boutique were all listed as participants. I wondered why I hadn't heard about it before now. It did seem like something that would have been mentioned at the SOOCFA meeting. Didn't they want other shop owners to participate?

"You're cutting it close," I said. "This is in three days."

"Yeah, just something we decided to put together last minute." She pushed up her glasses. Perched on her nose, it was easy to see that they were bifocals.

I glanced back down at the flyer I was still holding in my hand and wondered if that was true. They were going to have food, stay open past their regular business hours and hold a silent raffle. Very coordinated.

I passed the flyer back to her. "Sure," I said, smiling. "You can hang it in our window." I was thinking maybe I'd get in on it without letting them know by offering coupons for future visits or reduced prices during the time they were having the sale. "You need some tape?"

"No," she said. "I brought my own." She patted her purse.

I handed her the receipt, told her to have a nice day and watched as she posted her flyer in my store window, but before she left I couldn't help but comment on the goings-on of the previous night.

"I'm sorry about what happened to your friend," I said.

"My friend?" She turned and looked at me, a question on her face.

"Last night. You know, Zeke Reynolds. I was sorry to hear about that."

"Oh," she said. "Thanks. But he wasn't really a *friend*. He'd been in Chagrin Falls maybe a week. I only talked to him maybe a few times."

"I saw you come in with him ..."

"Excuse me?" she said.

"Nothing," I said. "Never mind." I offered a polite smile. "It's just bad to hear news like that."

She nodded and finished taping up the advertisement. After she left, I walked over to the flyer. I couldn't see the writing on it from the inside—she'd posted it so the writing faced the street—but I knew what it said.

"Strange," I said and looked over at Felice. "I thought the idea of a shop owners' association was to share information like this."

"Brreeow." Felice evidently agreed, but it wasn't anything that kept her interest. She initiated her usual cleaning ritual after her nap—she licked her paw and swiped it across her face.

"You don't think it's strange that only four shops are involved?" I asked the cat.

"Brreow." She swished her tail to the other side and held up her head. It was the pose she held when she wasn't sleeping, which she did most of the time. The one that made most customers think she was a doll. She yawned, noting, I guess, she was done with that boring conversation.

"Well, I think it's weird," I said. "And interesting."

FOUR

Ooooh! It's freezing down here." I knew the voice I heard behind me. "I'm so glad you have on a sweater."

It was Rivkah Solomon, Maisie's grandmother, our upstairs tenant and owner of Felice the Cat. At seeing her, Felice glided off the window seat and scampered over to Rivkah.

"There's my baby," Rivkah said. "Come to Mama. It's a good thing you have fur," she said, scratching behind Felice's ear and kissing her on her wet nose. "Otherwise you'd be one of the frozen treats Win sells down here."

Rivkah was the only grandmother-like person I still had after mine died. I, like Maisie, called her Savta, the Yiddish word for grandmother.

She was also the owner of the Village Dragon Chinese Restaurant, the only one of its kind in Chagrin Falls.

"What are you doing here?" I asked, looking up at the clock on the wall. "You're not at the restaurant?"

"I had to make a shiva call today," she said, taking her slender finger and pushing a strand of her gray hair out of the way. She wore her hair pulled back, braided and wrapped around in a bun, and there were always wisps falling down around her face.

"Who died?"

"Frank Seidman. Maybe you know him." I was sure I didn't, but I nodded just the same. "He used to come to my restaurant all the time and order tofu. Trying to eat healthy." She waved a hand. "A lot of good it did him—he died from a heart attack."

"Oh, that's sad," I said.

"I took food," she said, telling me the story I knew I wouldn't get out of hearing. "People were bringing trays of cookies and dairy."

"But not you?" I asked.

Juggling Felice, she shifted the cat to the other arm and tugged on her sweater, pulling it closed. "My heart was so heavy. I don't think anyone at the house can cook."

"Anyone? Like who? His wife? Did he have a wife?"

"Yes," she said. "He had a wife. A sweet woman. A little loud sometimes."

"Why don't you think she can cook?"

"If she could cook"—Rivkah shrugged—"why did he eat at my place all the time?"

I chuckled. "Maybe he just liked Chinese food."

"No one likes Chinese food that much," she said.

"So what did you take? Some tofu?"

"*Pfft*. No." She placed the palm of her hand on her cheek, pushing the wrinkles around. "I took chicken and a side dish."

I raised an eyebrow. "Is that all?" That didn't sound like her.

"It was probably three side dishes." She hunched a shoulder

as if she didn't remember. "And creamed herring. And potato knishes. Not too many."

"Anything else?"

"I may have dropped off a tuna casserole for the *seudat havara'ah.*"

"What's that?"

"The first meal after the burial."

"That's a lot of food, Savta."

"And of course, some hard-boiled eggs." She was still going down the list.

I tried to contain my amusement. Rivkah loved to feed people. "And that's it?" I asked.

She shrugged. "What does it matter? Everyone there will eat it up. There were twelve people sitting shiva and all the visitors. There'll be nothing left for Elaine."

"His wife?"

"Yes. Elaine is his wife." She shook her head. "I'll have to take food again when the mourning period is over."

"All this talk of food has made me hungry," I said.

"Don't worry," she said. "I kept a plate for you."

chapter

FIVE

Afternoon!" Wilhelmina ambled into the store for her shift. She had on lip gloss, a light dusting of too light powder for her dark-skinned face and her signature reddish-brown wig.

Rivkah groaned. I chuckled.

When Wilhelmina first started, she'd had a crush on PopPop, which made him nervous. He'd bounce up and out whenever he saw her coming. But she was a good employee, which I was sure came from her time as a Walmart greeter. Always pleasant, smiling and attentive. She handled all the customers, big and small, with care.

Rivkah, like PopPop, hadn't liked the whole crush thing. I wasn't quite sure what, if anything, my PopPop and Rivkah had going. I knew that with my old grumpy grandpa, there weren't a lot of things that made him smile. Except for me. And Rivkah. We, it was easy to tell, were his favorites.

Maybe it was because Rivkah had been friends with my

Grandma Kay and he liked having someone to share memories with. Or maybe he just liked Rivkah.

Either way, to keep PopPop from acting jittery every time Wilhelmina was at the ice cream shop, and to keep her on payroll, I had to have a sit-down talk with her.

"What is she doing here?" Rivkah whispered to me.

"She works here," I whispered back.

"Hmph." Rivkah walked back toward the kitchen and disappeared only for a second. She came back, walked to the window seat and picked up Felice. "Come, Baby, Mommy's taking you home." She disappeared through the kitchen again.

"What was she doing here?" Wilhelmina whispered after Rivkah had disappeared.

"She lives here," I whispered back.

"Hmph." Wilhelmina walked over to the sink and washed her hands.

I smiled. All of that over a man. Love never grows old.

"Welcome to Crewse Creamery," Wilhelmina said just as the chime jangled over the door.

I looked up to see the Dixby sisters coming in.

"Win," Delilah said, huffing as she came over to the counter. "We heard you were our new competition."

I raised an eyebrow.

"Don't play coy with us," Delilah's sister, Daubie, who was just as round as her twin, said. "Are you selling tea and coffee?"

"Nooo," I said slowly. I glanced at the counter behind me, hoping their eyes would follow mine. "No coffee or tea here."

"Good, because we thought we may have to take you out if

you were trying to compete with us," Delilah said, her face serious.

Take me out?

Wow.

I looked at Delilah's twin, she had the same expression on her face. One that said "Don't mess with us or our business."

Delilah and Daubie Dixby were the owners of the Juniper Tree Coffee and Tea House. Had been for years. Way before coffee shops became popular. Their shop was cozy, had plants hanging from the ceiling and always the sweet aroma of something brewing. Not necessarily a trendy hangout, but in Chagrin Falls, it was all we had.

"Uhm . . ." I looked at them, flabbergasted, not quite sure what to say to that.

"We're just kidding," Daubie said and laughed. "I think we really had her going."

"I think we did, sister," Delilah said.

I looked at Wilhelmina, who'd been standing there, not saying a word, then back over to the sisters.

"We came in for that coffee ice cream we heard you had."

"And the tea one, too. What else is in it?"

"Shortbread," I said.

"How clever," Daubie said.

"And British," Delilah said.

They both thought that was funny and almost doubled over with laughter.

"Sorry, Win," Daubie said. "We just couldn't resist when we heard you were serving *our* drinks in your ice cream."

It sounded as if they thought they had the tea and coffee market cornered.

"I'll dip them up some," Wilhelmina said.

"Oh good," Daubie said and followed Wilhelmina over to the far end of the dipping case. "I want to try the tea and crumpet one."

"It's tea and shortbread," Wilhelmina corrected.

The sisters were short and stout just like a teapot. They wore matching oval-shaped bifocal glasses, had the same coffee-stained teeth, and both wore their gray hair short and parted down the middle. "Did you hear about that awful mess last night?" Delilah asked. She hadn't mentioned any ice cream she wanted.

"What mess?" I asked.

"With the mall and the murder, Madness!"

"Yes," I said, not wanting to delve into the gossip.

"Sometimes we have to protect our own," she said. "My sister and I have been in this town a long time. It's our home. People must know that outsiders coming in won't be tolerated."

"I guess not," I said, my voice going up at the end. I didn't have an answer for that.

"Everyone has to be on the same page."

I didn't even want to ask which page that was.

"Sister, are you getting ice cream?" Daubie called over to her twin. She wrapped her hand around the double scoop of ice cream piled high on a sugar cone and held it out toward her. "You must! This is delicious. You have to try this!"

"I'll get my own," Delilah said and walked down to the end of the counter. "What kind did you get?" She bent forward and peered through the glass case.

"Tea and crumpets!" Daubie said.

"Shortbread," Wilhelmina said.

Delilah tapped her nail on the glass case. "I want to try this one. Mint mojito coffee." She stood up and looked at Wilhelmina. "Please."

I cringed when she chose that one. It had alcohol in it. Rum to be exact. And with her hyped-up attitude, I wasn't sure if that was a good idea. There was a sign that stated its contents. She'd been close enough to it.

Delilah Dixby reached over the counter and took the taster spoon from Wilhelmina. She stuck the tip of her tongue on the ice cream, which she then rubbed against the roof of her mouth. I saw a smile cross her face. "This is good," she said. "Your grandmother would be proud of you."

"Thank you," I said, beaming.

"Give me two scoops," she said. "On a sugar cone." She turned and looked at me. "Not so sure how she'd feel about you selling alcohol, though. Don't you need a license to do that?"

"I have one," I said. "We're all legal here."

"Good," she said. "Because I'll be back for more."

When Wilhelmina handed Delilah the cone, she ran her tongue around the ice cream then turned to her sister. "It isn't as good as our tea and coffee . . ."

"But it *is* a very close second," Daubie said. And with that they toasted each other, touching the tops of the cones.

They paid, and went out licking and chatting and throwing me a wave as if it was an afterthought.

"That was strange," I said.

"Don't they own the coffee shop?" Wilhelmina asked.

"Yep."

"They must have been drinking too much green tea."

"What?"

"It makes you kind of crazy. Hallucinations and such. Really not good for you. I've heard it can make you do crazy things."

chapter

SIX

Maisie and I were headed out to get her food at Dave's Cosmic Subs. It was the opposite way compared to most of the other shops. She hadn't wanted the plate of food her grandmother had saved for her. I ate mine. Rivkah, after all, is a good cook.

But as we walked down the street, I questioned why I'd agreed to go out with Maisie. She was back to talking about her Acorn sleuthing shows and how we could solve this murder.

"They've got a new show," she said. "*Queens of Mystery*."

"Uh-huh," I said, ambling along next to her, my mind somewhere else.

"The amateur sleuth has three aunts who write mystery books, and the four of them solve murders together." She grinned at me. "That could be us."

I raised an eyebrow. "*Us* as in who?"

"You, Riya and me!"

"That's only three people." I held up as many fingers.

"I didn't mean exactly like them."

"Good," I said. "Because I don't think I could juggle writing mystery books, solving murders and running the ice cream shop all at the same time."

"There probably won't ever be another murder around here. So it would be just this one time. And Detective Beverly did—"

I held up a hand. "Don't say it."

"You know you heard him say—"

"Uh-uh." I shook my head. "I'm not listening."

"Don't you want to know who shot him?"

"No."

Unlike Maisie's television shows, I was pretty sure that people in real life (other than her) didn't actually investigate murders on their own or try to track down a killer. Wouldn't self-preservation step in and grind those kinds of thoughts to a halt? It did for me. I didn't want to chase murderers.

"And I've been thinking, if he was in the alley, how did Ms. Devereaux know he'd been shot? Did she find him? Is she the one that called it in?" She smacked me on the arm. "Is she the one who did it?"

I blew out an exaggerated breath.

"At first I thought she knew because he was staying at her sister's bed-and-breakfast." We went to turn the corner onto River Street, but she stopped. "But if he wasn't killed there, there really wouldn't be a reason for Ms. Devereaux's sister Dell to know. So how did Ms. Devereaux find out?"

She was excited formulating her theories and precipitous revelations. Talking fast, eyes fluttering, hands gesturing. I could almost see the smoke rising from the questions burning through her brain.

"I'm sure Detective Beverly will figure that all out." I started walking so she'd follow suit.

I got her feet to move while her mind churned, and we made it to the sub shop without anything else from her. But that didn't last long. She grabbed the yellow-painted screen door and swung it open. Standing in the doorway she looked at me. "I don't know why you're so averse to *us* finding it out."

"What?"

"You said Detective Beverly would figure it out. But we could do it." I started to shake my head. "No!" She placed a hand on my cheek. "Stop saying no. We could do it. We solved the last one. And if I remember correctly, which I do, you were all gung ho to do it."

"The last one involved my father."

She pushed opened the wooden psychedelic-painted door. "This one could involve you." She gave me an all-knowing look.

"Me?" I chuckled. "I don't think so."

"Yep. You. And me. And Riya." Her eyes got big. "Maybe your grandfather and even your brother Bobby. All the people you care about."

I frowned. "How do you figure that?"

"We were all there. We all had a motive."

"I didn't have a motive to kill that man," I said. "*If*, and that's a big if, he was killed based on what he was doing here in Chagrin Falls, it didn't affect me or my family's store. So that would leave out Bobby, PopPop and me as suspects. *We* had no reason to hate him or what he was doing. At least not enough to kill him over it."

"You think me or Riya could have done it?" Maisie stopped and turned to face me. "Really?"

"I didn't say that." I shook my head. "And of course I don't think you or . . ." I thought for a moment before I added Riya's name—she was such a firecracker, still I had to stick up for her—"or Riya could do such a thing." I hunched my shoulders. "And that proves my point. None of us did it. So that means you and I"—I wagged my finger between the two of us—"have no reason to go around sticking our noses in trying to solve it."

"No reason other than the fact Detective Beverly—"

I covered my ears. "I'm not listening."

She gave me a smirk and got in line to get her sub. There was a crowd of people waiting to order or for their food to be prepared.

Since the remodel, we had yet to have this many people in the ice cream shop all at once . . .

I sat at one of the two round tables at the front of the small store, next to the windows, and surveyed the joint. The walls were painted, like the front door, in bright colors—yellow, blue, pink—with peace signs and squiggly lines all over them. Mounted were framed pictures of 1960s rock 'n' roll artists, posters and musical instruments. The ceiling, depicting a blue sky with white clouds, was hand-painted like the Sistine Chapel—only these paintings were of the music gods—Jimi Hendrix, Jim Morrison, Elvis Presley and Frank Zappa, among others.

I looked at the faces of the people waiting for their food. They were young. Half the people in line wouldn't even know who the people on the walls and ceiling were. I wasn't even sure how I knew who they were.

It couldn't be the atmosphere that brought them to the sub shop, could it? I looked around at the walls again and up at the ceiling. Ours was all classic 1950s soda fountain.

Maybe I picked the wrong motif . . .

"You want anything?" Maisie had made it up to the counter to order. She turned and looked at me.

"No," I said and gave her a half smile. "I'm full."

"There wasn't that much on those plates," she said.

How would she know, I thought, *she didn't even unwrap hers.* "I'm fine. If I need anything else I'll just eat some ice cream when we get back to the store." A couple people turned and looked at me. I smiled.

She gave a half-throated chuckle. "Okay. I can share my sub if you get hungry."

"I'm fine," I said.

Maisie hung out around the counter until they called her name, then she got her food and walked over to me. "I'm ready," she said.

I stood up and we headed out the door.

"Look!" Maisie said, grabbing my arm and shaking it with urgency. "It's Ari." She took to whispering.

"Aren't you guys speaking?" I asked. "He couldn't still be mad that you quit working for him."

"Shhh!" she said, gesturing for me to lower my voice. "He wasn't ever mad," she said and waved her hand.

"Why are we whispering?"

"Because. Think about it," she said so low I had to lean my head into her to hear. "He wasn't at the meeting last night."

I blinked my eyes and thought about it. "Oh. I guess not. But that still doesn't explain why we can't talk louder."

"Maybe he wasn't there because he was waiting on Zeke Reynolds out behind the stores. In the alley."

"What?" I said. I frowned and stepped away from her.

She grabbed my arm and pulled me closer. "He could be the killer."

"Oh. My. Goodness," I said. My shoulders drooped. "Really, Maisie? Really?" I started marching off, back in the direction of the ice cream shop.

"What?" she said, trotting to catch up, as if she didn't know what I meant.

"Didn't you have him pegged as the last murderer?"

"I think he's capable."

"Oh brother." I closed my eyes and let my neck roll around.

"Let's go and talk to him," she said, excitement and determination locked in her voice. "Find out where he was last night."

"Let's not."

"Why?"

"I thought you didn't like him. You said you were never stepping foot in his restaurant again."

"I'm not going in the restaurant. I'm just going down the street to talk to him." She grabbed my wrist, wrapping her fingers around it tightly, and started dragging me along. "C'mon. The detective would want us to." Before I could protest, she raised her other hand and waved. "Hey! Hey, Ari!" she shouted. "Wait up!"

chapter

SEVEN

That sub smells good," Ari said after we made our way to him. "You got it hot, huh?" He pointed to Maisie's sub and I could see his muscles ripple under his white button-down shirt. I couldn't understand how Maisie could think someone so handsome could do something so heinous.

But that was Maisie. She was a lot like a banana split, not knowing exactly what to be so she tried to be a little bit of a lot of things. But when she did set her mind to something, it was next to impossible to get her to change it. She turned into a DQ Blizzard—even if you turned her upside down and gave her a good shake, you couldn't get her to move. And proving Ari Terrain was a cold-blooded killer just seemed to be one of those things that she was stuck on.

Ari smiled that big wide, easy smile of his, and his scent—a cool breeze—wafted up my nose.

He squinted to keep the sun out of his brown eyes, and his long dense lashes made it nearly impossible to see the sparkle in them.

"How are things over at Molta's?" Maisie asked. Small talk. I guess that was her interrogation tactic of the day.

"Everything is good. Why?" He shot a look at me, mischief in his eyes. "They're not treating you right over at Crewse Creamery?"

"No," she said. "It's just like being with family all day."

"Well, if you change your mind about working there"—he winked at me—"you're always welcome back at Molta's."

Maisie let out a cough and I knew exactly what she was thinking: *She'd never work for a murderer.*

Although, she had yet to prove he'd ever committed one.

"And we're just heading back to work," I said and gave Maisie's arm a tug.

"What was on the menu last night?" Maisie asked, pulling her arm away from mine. "Anything scrumptious?"

"Maisie, you know that's all we serve. Eye-appealing, skill-fully prepared, scrumptious food." He chuckled as he stroked his closely trimmed goatee with his thumb and forefinger, and stuck his other hand in the pocket of his brown trousers.

That didn't tickle Maisie at all.

"What exactly was it?" she asked, her face stern. She was determined to find out his whereabouts. "You remember? Or weren't you there?"

"Of course I was there," he said. He looked upward and stroked his beard again. "I think it was lamb."

"You think?" Maisie said.

"We should probably go," I said, fully prepared to pick her up and carry her away if it would stop her.

"Why didn't you come to the shop owners' meeting last

night?" she asked him, changing her approach and ignoring me and my plea.

"Oh, I heard about it—" he began.

"You heard about it?"

"Yes. Happy to donate money for what you are trying to do."

"Is that why you weren't there?"

"Because I want to donate money for your cause?" He blinked his eyes, seemingly trying to process what she was saying. He glanced over at me. I hunched my shoulders. "I don't understand," he said.

"Because you knew they were going to build a mall, didn't you?"

"A mall?" He seemed to be getting more confused by the minute. "There's going to be a mall?" He tilted his head. "In Chagrin Falls?" He looked around as if trying to imagine it. "No." He shook his head. "Couldn't be." He looked at Maisie. "There's not going to be a mall." There was conviction in his voice.

"There *isn't* going to be one?" Maisie asked, leaning in and turning her head like she wanted to be sure to hear every word he said. "Why? Because you made sure of that?"

"What?" His nose scrunched up.

"She's hungry," I said and yanked her arm so hard she nearly leapt off the ground. I twirled a finger close to my temple. "Her sugar is low and she is just talking out of her head." I dragged her off down the street. "Bye!" I waved as I got behind Maisie and pushed her up the street and around the corner onto North Main Street.

"What is wrong with you?"

"That man is sneaky."

"He is not." While I didn't know Ari Terrain all that well, what I knew about him I liked. Even after I found out he might have done some not so legal stuff with the last murder victim we had, like robbing pharmaceutical warehouses. I had decided everyone needed a second chance. And he was doing well with his.

"He is too. He's trying to protect Molta's."

"Protect Molta's from what?"

"Remember when Riya said that everything is going upscale?"

"No. I don't remember." I did remember her saying it, I just didn't want Crewse Creamery labeled like that. We were just a family ice cream parlor. "But Molta's *is* upscale," I said.

"And every other shop around here is a mom-and-pop establishment."

"So?" I said.

"So he wouldn't want an upscale mall going up around here because then he wouldn't stand out anymore. People wouldn't come to his establishment as much."

"So?"

"Sooo ..." She drew the word out that time. "He doesn't want any competition."

"So he killed Zeke Reynolds to stop him from building a mall?"

"Yes!"

"Zeke Reynolds wasn't building the mall," I said. "Remember? 'Don't shoot the messenger'? He only worked for the people who were—are—building the mall."

"Rhys Enterprises."

"Right," I said, hoping I had convinced her that she had it all wrong about Ari.

"He probably planned on killing them next." She let her eyes drift off. "The whole lot of them."

"Who?" I asked cautiously.

"Ari," she answered resolutely.

I slapped my forehead. "I can't. I just can't."

"What?" she said. She gave me a sideways glance then smiled. "Okay. So maybe it wasn't him who killed Zeke Reynolds."

I couldn't do anything but shake my head.

"Walk with me to check on the building," she said, doing a one-eighty about-face.

"Check on the building?" I had to think for a moment about what she meant, she changed subjects so abruptly. "Oh," I said. "*Your* building."

"Yeah. I'm worried about it."

"What about your food?" I pointed down to the bag. "It'll get cold."

"I won't be able to get it down, hot or cold, if I don't check on the building."

"Don't worry." I frowned to show I felt for her. "Maybe Rhys Enterprises won't want to put their new mall in such a crime-ridden town and withdraw the offer."

"How can they come in and buy my building anyway?"

"You don't know that they have," I said. "So don't jump to conclusions."

"That snake of a mayor would know."

"Oh goodness. Why is the mayor a snake?"

"Didn't you see how he slithered in and dropped off that building-stealing messenger boy and then slithered right back out?"

I laughed. "Yeah, I did see that."

"Even though he's sneaky—"

I cut her off. "I thought it was Ari who was sneaky and the mayor was a snake."

"The mayor's even sneakier than Ari." She gave a firm nod. "A sneaky snake. And even though he is, he was probably rooting for the mall to come here."

"I'm sure there's a point to that assessment."

"There is. It means the mayor is probably *not* the killer."

"Oh brother." I blew out a breath. "I'll walk with you to check on your building if you promise not to talk anymore about whodunit."

"Wasn't my idea for us to start looking into it in the first place."

"Ah. Ah. Ah." I held up a finger to stop her. "Deal?"

She lifted an eyebrow, saying she wasn't sure if she could make that promise or not.

I sucked my tongue. "C'mon," I said. "By the time you eat that sub, it'll be cold." I shook my head. "Didn't do you any good to get it hot."

"Yes, it did," she said. "I got to cross one suspect off my list. I found out that Ari Terrain didn't do it."

"Oh my lord!" I gave her a push. "C'mon, Agatha Raisin, let's go!"

chapter

EIGHT

We crossed to the other side of the street after leaving Ari near the town hall and landed in front of the hardware store.

Our village's hardware store was a thing from the past. It had three different sets of windows and all were filled with displays. Some hardware-like, some not so much.

That was when I saw Myles Mason.

He was down on his luck these days, and it seemed that people had started to avoid him. He was an artist by passion, but to make a living he had sold life insurance for years, including a five-hundred-dollar policy to my grandparents that hadn't covered a thing when my grandfather had to bury Grandma Kay. But my grandmother loved him. When she was alive he'd come once a month to collect the premium and end up spending the afternoon "chewing the fat" with her.

Even after she took sick, he'd still come and sit with her on her bench. That gave him a special place in my heart.

"Hello, Mr. Mason," I said.

He turned to look at us. Initially a blank look on his face, then it brightened. "Win," he said. "Hi."

"You remember Maisie?" I asked. "She's Rivkah Solomon's granddaughter."

"The Village Dragon."

"Right," I said and nodded.

"Did he just call my grandmother the village dragon?" Maisie leaned over and asked.

"He was talking about the name of her restaurant."

"I talked to your grandmother yesterday, Win," he said.

"You did?" I said and smiled. He was down on his luck, but I'd never known him to talk out of his head.

"Yep. Sure did." He gave me a lopsided smile that showed me the two or three teeth he had left. "You want to know what she said?"

"I sure do. What did she say?" I asked.

"She said she was real pleased with the way you was running her ice cream shop." He nodded his head as he spoke, as if it were a fact.

I grinned and blushed despite knowing he couldn't talk to the dead. Sure, he went over to the cemetery, I'd seen some of his paintings from there. He could actually make the tombstones and landscape look beautiful—hauntingly beautiful.

"Were you there painting?"

"Oh no." He hung his head and started rubbing his right arm. That was when I noticed he held it funny, like it was weak. "I don't do that anymore. Those people are nothing but a jack of spades."

I didn't know what that meant, but I knew how much he enjoyed painting. I was sorry to hear he wasn't doing it anymore. "That's too bad," I said. "You're so good at it."

"If I were painting," he said, "I'd get that." He turned and pointed to something in the window of the hardware store. I leaned in and peeked around him.

"A tackle box?" I asked.

"No, next to it," he said and smiled at me.

I looked and saw he was talking about a gun. An old-time revolver that was part of a cowboy display. "You don't need that." There had been enough shooting. "Why don't you get the tackle box? You have paint to keep in it, don't you?"

"No." He grinned again. No shame in being toothless. "I threw them all away," he said. "You know what else I saw?" he asked, changing the subject without warning.

"What else did you see?" Maisie asked.

"I saw a red ball bouncing down the alleyway." He pointed toward the street that ran behind the shops.

"A red ball?" I asked.

He nodded. Still grinning.

"We have to go, Mr. Mason," I said, not sure how to interpret that comment, or any of the things he'd said. "You come by the ice cream store sometime and get yourself a scoop."

"Will do," he said and tipped an imaginary hat.

"You see why I have to set up my community center," Maisie leaned into me and whispered. "To help Chagrin Falls residents like Mr. Mason."

"I think he needs help more from someplace like my brother Bobby's clinic." I turned back and looked at him still standing in front of the hardware store peering in. "He seems to be eating okay, at least from the way he looks." My heart went out to him. "Don't know how he's making money if he's not painting anymore, though, so I don't know how he's living. And why would he want a gun so he could paint? That makes no sense."

We had to pass my ice cream shop to get to Maisie's building, as well as the other shops that resided on the leg of the triangle where the proposed mall would be built. There were currently five occupied, and the empty one that Maisie wanted. It was located next to her community garden. To the back of it was another grassy plot of land.

As we passed each building, Maisie read out the shop name and announced, in her opinion, whether its owners were guilty of Zeke's murder based on whether they had been present at the meeting or not.

"Blue Moon," she read off the sign as we passed the boutique. "Who owns that?" she asked.

"I don't know," I said. I glanced in the storefront window as we passed. "They've only been there a year. I was too wrapped up in renovations all year to go and introduce myself. Plus, they're Ms. Devereaux's competition. My grandfather would hold me out as a traitor if I befriended whoever owns that place."

"Do you think the owner was there last night?"

"I wouldn't know, Maisie, seeing, like I said, I don't know who the owner is."

"So, there's another possible guilty proprietor," she said.

"Or not."

"Are you going to be a naysayer through this whole investigation? Because we'll never find anything out with that attitude."

"Did you know that Blue Moon . . ." I said, ignoring her comment and tilting my head, "and all these shops"—I waved my finger toward the buildings in the block we were walking—"are having a fire sale?"

"Has there been a fire?" she asked.

"I asked the same thing," I said. "Although I was being sarcastic when I asked, it appears that the answer to that is no. It's just the name they came up with for this big sales event they're having."

"Did you know about the big sale?" she asked.

"Not until this morning when Amelia Hargrove came in and asked could she post an advertisement for it."

"So, what, you want to go to it?"

"No," I said and scrunched up my face.

"Participate?"

"No, I mean, I might come up with some special or something to get people into the store while it's going on. I just wondered why I hadn't heard about it."

"Maybe it's a conspiracy."

"What?" I said, my eyebrows wrinkling.

"Zeke's murder." She was matter-of-fact. "Maybe the shop owners involved in the fire sale *all* killed him, and now they're selling off their wares and leaving town because they don't want to get caught."

"That makes absolutely no sense," I said. "Wasn't he only shot once?" I looked at her and raised an eyebrow. "Wouldn't that mean they couldn't have all been involved?"

"Uh . . ." she started, but I interjected.

"I thought your premise was that if the shop owner wasn't there, they're not a suspect."

"Yeah," she said. "Right. That's what I think." She gave me a firm nod. "So?"

"Well, Amelia Hargrove was there. At the meeting. And she's taking part in the fire sale." I pointed over my shoulder to her shop, which we'd already passed.

"Oh." Maisie clucked her tongue. "Still," she said, undeterred, "I probably should make a list of the shops, their owners and their attendance at the meeting."

"Why?" I asked. Geesh! Hadn't I just proved her shaky theory wrong?

"For my suspect list."

I groaned. "Didn't we have a deal?" I looked at her. "No Miss Marple or Hercule Poirot talk. We're supposed to be going to check on your building."

"And I could go over the list with your grandfather." She was still running the logistics of corralling her suspects through her mind. "I could ask him if the owner of each shop was at the meeting last night." She nodded like that was a good plan. "He would know."

"Why do you think he'd know?" I asked.

My grandfather was as big of a wannabe sleuth as Maisie. I found out he'd been following me around while I tried to investigate the last murder on my own like he was an old-time gumshoe. Said he was trying to protect me. He was seventy-nine years old—what did he think he was going to do if someone attacked me? Help me scream? Then he came up with people he wanted me to question. His own little suspect list.

Although he did help, getting him involved again probably wasn't a good idea. I'd have two "Maisies" on my hands.

"Why don't you ask *your* grandmother who the shop owners are?" I said. "She'd probably know just as well as my grandfather."

"Savta?" She pursed her lips and shook her head. "She may know all of them, but she probably doesn't like any of them. She'd color my investigation."

Color her investigation? *Oh geesh.*

"First, Maisie, you're not investigating anything," I reminded her.

"Black Market Paper," she said.

"What?" That wasn't a proper response to my stop-trying-to-get-involved nudge.

She pointed to the shop we were passing. "Black Market Paper. I know who owns that." She tilted her head. "Their names are on the tip of my tongue."

"Fine Art." I read the wooden sign. "It's owned by Baraniece Black and her husband."

"Right!" she said. "But he has a different last name, doesn't he?"

"Yeah. It's something like Rykov or Rynok or something like that." I shrugged. "Not sure, but I know it means 'market' in Russian."

"It's their last names? I wondered how they came up with the name. Black Market." She gave a nod of understanding. "It sounds kind of scandalous for an art gallery."

"Your mind is always on something criminal," I said. "You should probably be banned from Acorn TV."

"If I didn't watch my shows, how would I solve all of these murders?"

"We've had *two* murders." I held up two fingers. "No one in

Chagrin Falls is on a killing spree. I don't think there'll be more bodies to come. We're not in Cabot Cove."

"Where?"

"Jessica Fletcher." I pointed at Maisie. "*She* was a mystery writer turned amateur sleuth just like your Queens of Mystery, on TV, but a long time ago. She lived there."

"Oh, *Murder, She Wrote.*"

"Yep."

"Someone was always getting killed there," she said, and I thought I saw a gleam in her eye.

"I think practically everyone in her little town was killed," I said. "They had to have her travel to find more victims."

Maisie let out a sinister little chuckle.

"Don't get any ideas, Maisie."

"About what?" She feigned innocence. "The Juniper Tree," she announced next.

She didn't catch me off guard that time. I knew what she meant. "The Darling Dixby sisters," I acknowledged. "Tea and coffee purveyors."

Maisie chuckled. "Yes. And I know for a fact that they weren't there."

"So they are not suspects. And they're not on that fire sale flyer either so that clinches it. They didn't do it."

"Well, you can't sell off tea and coffee inventory at a sidewalk sale . . ."

"True," I said.

"And their shop is right in the middle of the shops that are involved."

"That is a marketing opportunity," I said. "If they're smart, they'll stay open past their usual seven p.m. closing time. Catch all the customers passing by going from store to store."

"I think they go to bed at six thirty," Maisie said.

I laughed. "Maybe all the coffee and tea they sell filled with caffeine might keep them awake until all hours of the night."

"Yeah, like during the time Zeke Reynolds was shot," Maisie said.

"I didn't mean that."

"I'm putting them on my suspect list," Maisie said.

"I thought we just decided since they weren't at the meeting, they aren't suspects," I said. "Didn't we clear them?"

"It's just a feeling I have," she said.

"Like the *feeling* Ari did it?"

"That wasn't a feeling. I know he's sinister."

I closed my eyes and drew in a breath. "Maisie, I really don't think any of the shop owners are murderers."

"Then who shot him?" Maisie asked.

I stopped walking. "I don't know. And it's not for me—or you—to find out."

"Wouldn't you want to know if eighty-year-old twins killed a man because he wanted to take their little shop? Something they've had forever." She pointed at the Dixby sisters' teahouse.

"Who says he was trying to take their coffee shop?" I asked.

"Stands to reason."

I didn't ask whose reasoning.

"Win, if Rhys Enterprises were building a vertical mall, one of the anchor stores would have to be Java Joe's. No doubt. Every mall has a food area, and coffee is a staple. Java Joe's is the number one coffee shop in the world."

"I don't know."

"Right. We don't know." She nodded and raised an eyebrow.

"If Rhys Enterprises is building a mall, eventually everyone will have to sell. I'm sure everyone understands that and would kill to stop it."

"Those Darling Dixbys could never compete with Java Joe's." She stood in front of the window and peered in. "They'd lose their only source of income."

"Did you hear what I just said?"

"Yes," Maisie said and glanced at me. "I heard what you said."

"And I'm sure they have retirement money saved up. They would be okay."

"If they did have a nest egg," Maisie said, "you think they'd still be trying to serve up scalding hot coffee and tea with those shaky hands of theirs? They would have retired by now."

I laughed. "Their hands don't shake." I stood next to her and, following her stare, glanced through the window. My heart skipped a beat. I had caught a glimpse of the back of a girl with wild red hair. In my life I'd only seen a mop of hair like that on one other person.

Rory Hunter.

Rory was a colleague and good friend from New York. She was part of my team at Hawken Spencer, the ad agency where I had worked, and was an awesome graphic artist. Shoot. Artist period.

I scrunched up my face. There was no way she could be in Chagrin Falls. I stepped closer to the glass-paned shopfront.

The woman I saw was petite. Her thick red hair couldn't decide if it wanted to be curly or straight, and she didn't try to help it decide one way or the other. Black leggings covered shapely legs, a sleeveless yellow silky top was draped above them and as my eyes slid down to her feet I noticed those red-bottomed shoes. They weren't her usual ones, but they were her signature.

My gaze shot back up to her face. That had to be her.

"Rory?" I mouthed.

Then I saw her stick a piece of gum in her mouth and I knew it was her. Rory always said, "You have to cleanse your palate before you inhale your coffee." Morning coffee was an experience in itself to her.

I turned and looked at Maisie. "You go," I said. "I need to stop here."

"To question the Dixby sisters? I'm game!" she said and grabbed the handle to open the door.

"No!" I grabbed her hand from the knob. "I think I see someone I know," I said. "I'm going in to say hi."

"You *think* you know someone?" We both glanced through the window.

"I'm pretty sure it's her, but she belongs in New York. Not here."

"So let's go see." She gave a head nod toward the door.

If that was Rory, I wouldn't be able to keep an eye on Maisie and I wouldn't put it past her to try to interrogate Delilah and Daubie Dixby while we were in there. I couldn't let her go in with me.

"No. You go ahead and do a walk-past of your building," I said. "I'll meet you back at the ice cream shop."

"No," she said. "I'll go in with you."

"No. You need to get back to the store and . . ." I had to think of a reason quick. "Re—uh, relieve my mother," I said. "I think she has an appointment."

She squinted her eyes at me.

"Or something," I said. "I'm sure she has something." I held on to her arms and nodded, trying to get her to mimic my head gesture. "And Riya probably has to get back to the hospital. I might be a minute."

She raised an eyebrow, seemingly not in agreement with me. "Okay then," she said, her voice reluctant, but my mind was relieved. "I'll catch up with you back at the ice cream shop."

I watched her walk down the street to make sure she went on her way. I was going to have to find a way to talk her down from wanting to solve Zeke Reynolds's murder. But not now.

I swung open the door to the Juniper Tree and walked up to the redheaded girl standing at the counter.

"What do you mean you don't have a skinny latte either?"

The Dixby sisters were standing at the counter. Their servers had taken a step back and were observers to the ensuing showdown, both Rory and the twins standing their ground.

Looking like they had this morning when they stopped for ice cream except now they had donned colorful smocks—one pink and one lime green—over their summer dresses. Both had placed their hands on their hips and twin scowls on their faces.

"Rory?" I said, almost afraid to step into their face-off.

She swung around, the frown on her face dissipating when she saw me.

"Bronwyn!" She wrapped her arms around me and squeezed tightly. "Hey, girl!"

Her mop of hair smelled like coconut and lavender. It made me smile. "What are you doing here?" I asked.

"Right now I'm trying to get a decent cup of coffee." She swung around and glared at the sisters. "They don't seem to know what that is."

One hissed at her, lips upturned, wrinkled nose flaring, two front teeth showing like a cat. The other said, "Perhaps you can go elsewhere to buy your coffee."

"They're not Java Joe's," I leaned in and whispered. "Or New York."

"You're telling me," she said, not lowering her voice. "The rudeness level seems to be about the same, though." She turned and hissed back at the sisters then swung back to face me. "After I got my shot of caffeine, I was coming over to your ice cream shop to see you!" she said. "I can't wait to see it."

"But that's not telling me why you're here."

"Oh"—she waved a hand—"I came to talk you into coming back to New York." She gave me a decisive nod. "Peter sent me. But first . . ." She looped her arm in mine and led me toward the door. "You gotta tell me where I can get a good cup of coffee around here."

chapter

NINE

"Wait! What?" I said. My eyes narrowed and I could feel all the wrinkles folding in my forehead. "Talk me into doing what?"

"We need you," she said, hands together. She bent her knees like she was going down on them to make her plea.

"You don't . . . Hawken Spencer does not need me." I stood firm.

"After you left, they promoted me."

"That sounds like a good thing," I said, giving a half smile. The way she said it, I just wasn't sure.

"It is," she said. "For the most part. But now I'm not doing what I want to do."

"What do you want to do?"

"I want to paint." She spread her arms as if she could take flight in the moment. "I want to draw. I want to immerse myself in art and everything about it."

"O-kaaay." I grabbed her arm and put it at her side. "Aren't you doing that at Hawken Spencer?"

"Not anymore," she said. "That's why I volunteered to come and persuade you to come back."

"Why?"

"I don't want to do your job." She tensed, making her whole body tight.

A mission to get me back to New York, no matter how it made Rory feel without me there, sounded a little crazy. "Because you don't get to draw?"

"Exactly!" She grabbed me by my arms. "I used to go to work and draw. Create! I got to do what I love." She smacked me on one arm. "Now I don't."

"Oww!" I rubbed my arm. "Sorry."

"Yeah?" She tilted her head. "Are you really?"

I didn't say anything.

"You have to come back." She nodded unapologetically.

"Rory . . ."

"Okay. Okay." She held her hand up in surrender. "I didn't want to spring it on you like this." She sucked in a gulp of air and blew it out. "First, let's visit." She looped her arm in mine and then smiled at me. "I've missed you."

"I've missed you, too," I said.

"It's not the same in the office without you."

"When did you get here?" I asked.

"Oh . . ." Her eyes roamed up the street, seemingly taking in her surroundings. "When did I get here?" she said, her voice drifting off.

"Don't you remember?"

She opened her mouth to speak, but nothing came out.

I chuckled and looked at her out of the corner of my eye. "You okay?"

"I'm fine." She turned back to me, straightened her shoulders and gave me a smile. "I just got in. Just pulled off the highway, and only wanted to grab a cup of joe before coming to surprise you."

"Well, you surprised me."

"Good," she said. "Now"—she smacked her lips—"is there anywhere else to get coffee?"

"There are no other coffee shops in Chagrin Falls."

"That," she said, jerking her thumb toward the Juniper Tree, "is not a coffee shop. It's like a haven for an old ladies' society. Watered-down, murky soaked beans and liniment-scented doilies."

"Molta's has good coffee," I said. "Ari is Middle Eastern." I shrugged. "Or North African. Whatever." I waved a hand. "But a cup of coffee from there reminds me of being in New York."

"Well, then that's where we need to go." She reached inside her bag and opened a new piece of gum, folding the one she'd been chomping on into the wrapper. "Show me the way before I go into withdrawal."

I glanced at my watch. "It's not open yet."

"Really? O-M-G, Bronwyn." She let her neck roll back and stomped one of her high-heel-clad feet. "How do you live in this godforsaken place?" she whined. As soon as her words left her mouth, she slapped her hand over it. "Peter said no Chagrin Falls or Ohio bashing, at least until I got you to agree to come back."

"I'm not coming back." My words came out slowly, to make

her understand. "And there isn't anything you could say bad about Chagrin Falls. Or anything about anything here that would make me want to leave." I gave a curt nod to show I meant what I said. "You know I left New York because I *wanted* to come back home."

"I know that's what you think, but wait until you hear what they authorized me to offer you."

"That won't matter—" I began.

She waved a dismissive hand interrupting me. "We'll talk about it later. Now, I want to see this ice cream shop of yours. I need to know my competition." She squeezed her eyes and shook her head. "There I go again. It must be coffee withdrawal." She pulled me. "You've got to help me."

I shook my head at her. "Okay," I said. "And I've got just the thing for you at my shop."

"You've got coffee?"

"I've got something even better."

"OH MY GOD! This is so good!"

Rory stuffed another mouthful of her double dip of my mint mojito coffee ice cream into her mouth. She licked the spoon after every bite and smacked her lips. Knees buckling, my grandfather had offered her a chair twice.

"You made this?" she asked, mouth full.

I was blushing, face as red as it could be on my dark skin, and was grinning from ear to ear. "It was a group effort."

"But all Win's creation," my mother said, proudly. "She's added a recipe or two to her Grandma Kay's menu."

"Her grandmother would be proud." My grandfather said

that. I knew he was pleased with all I'd done. Especially turning the sales around after opening on a snow day.

But that was my niche, marketing. I hadn't gotten an MBA in it for nothing. All I needed was a good product, and that definitely was the ice cream made from my Grandma Kay's recipes and sold in our little family shop.

Maisie and my mother had taken right to Rory, both giving her a hug. PopPop was always nice to my friends. They'd even included her in the gossip. Talking about the mall. How all the shops were up in arms because they wanted to move our village into the twenty-first century. The murder. Only briefly, though, my mother didn't want to discuss it, especially when she noted Rory's face going pale. Guess they were trying to be polite.

But if they knew what she was up to, the reason she'd come, I wasn't sure how my Crewse Creamery crew would have taken to her.

I was serving a customer, hand over the counter with a triple dip of chocolate, chocolate chip and butter pecan, when I saw out of the window a car that looked just like PopPop's. I glanced over and saw my grandfather. He'd gone back to his usual bench and was sitting there concentrating on winning a game of backgammon he was playing against himself.

It wasn't his car.

I only knew of one other person who owned a car that looked like that and would pull up and park in front of our door.

Aunt Jack.

What was she doing back in Chagrin Falls?

The door to the ice cream shop was pulled open with such force, I thought it might break from the frame. Everyone turned toward the door and watched as Aunt Jack, with a huff and a couple of puffs, came barreling through.

A matte red lipstick covered her large full lips, and her brown wig sat on top of her head like a hat. Aunt Jack was a large woman with a booming husky voice, thick fingers and big ankles. She always seemed to be out of breath, huffing out the smell of peppermint from the candy she was always sucking on, with the rest of her smelling like Chanel No. 5.

"Surprise!" she said and stood with her arms spread.

I guess she expected us to rush over and hug her. She hadn't even been gone all that long. And my mother didn't think much of her. At least not enough to be happy she was there.

"Jacqueline!"

Oh, but yes, she was my PopPop's only daughter, although the only two girls I knew for sure that put a smile on his face were Rivkah Solomon and me.

He scooted out of the bench and walked double time over to her.

"Daddy!" she exclaimed. She kissed him and gave him a big hug. "I'm home."

"Yes, you are," he said. "And I'm glad to see you." He turned and looked at the rest of us still staring at Aunt Jack with blank looks on our faces. "Look what the wind blew in."

"I don't remember there even being a breeze today," Riya said. She knew how I felt about Aunt Jack.

Everyone who knew me, knew how I felt about Aunt Jack.

I frowned at her before coming from around the counter and giving her a hug.

"Hi, Aunt Jack," I said. "Good to see you."

"I know it must be." She looked around the ice cream shop. "Things sure look different." She walked around in a circle, taking it all in. The large cobalt-blue accent wall behind the well-lit display cases. It was the same color as the vinyl cushions on the white metal ice cream parlor chairs and the benches on the wooden booths. Then her eyes spotted the full glass wall I had had placed to give a full view of the falls. Our store sat atop it, the only one in the village. And from all the oohs and aahs I'd gotten from customers, I would say it had been a hit.

Of course Aunt Jack didn't like it.

"Why would you put all that glass back there?" she said. "What if someone falls through it and into the river?"

"It's double pane," I said. "They'd have to fall through both of them."

"Then you'd be doubly liable."

I didn't think being liable twice for the same thing was a possibility.

She looked back at PopPop. "Daddy, looks like I came back just in the nick of time."

"What does that mean, Jack?" my mother said. "Everything is going great around here."

Aunt Jack smiled. "That wouldn't be what I heard."

"What—" my mother started.

"Ailbhe," my grandfather said, interrupting what he knew was going to be the start of insults slung around, all the while with fake smiles plastered on their faces and hurled in sweet singsongy voices. "Call Graham and let him know Jack's here."

"He's in surgery, I'm sure."

"Jack, how long you staying?" my grandfather said, ushering her back to his seat.

"I'm back to stay!" Aunt Jack said and tugged on her wig. "Don't know why I left in the first place." She patted PopPop on the back as she looked around. "Bet you're happy about me being back."

"Of course I'm glad you're back, Jacqueline. I like having my children close by. What happened with that fellow you went chasing after?"

"I didn't chase him, Daddy. He pursued me. Don't know why, though," she mumbled and tugged at the side of her eye. "He didn't need me."

"Oh, Jacqueline," he said.

"But I see you guys need me." She stood up straight and brushed her hands together. "No worries. I'm back to help." She nodded.

"We don't need your help, Jack," my mother said. "We're doing just fine."

"Win, get your Aunt Jack some ice cream." PopPop didn't give Aunt Jack a chance to respond. He pointed her to a seat, not the bench where he'd been sitting. She probably wouldn't have fit. He sat her in one of the parlor chairs. "What kind you want, Jacqueline?"

She cocked her head to one side and glanced over at the display case. "What kind you got?" she asked, popping back up and heading over to take a gander.

Maisie jumped behind the counter and started naming them

instead of just pointing up to the sign. I was sure she didn't remember that it was always better not to say too much to Aunt Jack, because Aunt Jack always had something not too nice to say back.

"My goodness, Bronwyn," Aunt Jack said. "Can't you just make up your mind what flavor of ice cream you want to serve?"

chapter

TEN

Rory and I left the ice cream shop and walked over to Molta's. I needed to calm my nerves after Aunt Jack blew in and started a commotion. She hadn't been there ten minutes and already she'd made my mouth turn dry and my stomach cramp up. My mother left soon after her, I was sure she was having a parking lot moment. Whenever she was stressed or depressed, she'd pull over into a parking lot and sit. Sometimes for hours. It didn't matter where the parking lot was, just whatever was close when those feelings took over. My father said it was probably a good thing to have her off the road.

Maisie graciously stayed to man the store.

I was glad to have Rory for a distraction.

"So what do you do here?" she asked.

"Here, as in Chagrin Falls?" I asked.

"Yes. Chagrin Falls." She glanced in the window of the shops as we passed. "I mean, I know Cleveland is literally just down the street, and it is bursting with stuff to do, but this place seems so far removed."

"We're a suburb of Cleveland," I said. "And no, we're not New York City, but it's home. It's a great neighborhood. A great place to live. And I have my business here."

"Do you?" she asked.

"What is that supposed to mean?"

"I'm just saying"—she held up her hand defensively—"your Aunt Jack seems to want to take the shop back."

"She won't do that," I said. "I've taken over management of the shop. She left. My grandfather turned it over to me."

"In case you didn't notice, she's back," Rory said.

"Of course I noticed," I said. "But that doesn't mean anything."

"You don't think your grandfather will give her the shop back? That is his little girl."

"She is fifty-something years old," I said, annoyed with the conversation. "She is no one's little girl."

"Don't get huffy with me," Rory said. "I'm just an observer."

"An observer with an agenda."

"Yes. I admit to that," she said. "I have an agenda. I'm here to cart you back to New York, to your job and your office."

"I didn't have an office. I had a cubicle."

"Not anymore. Not if you come back." She lifted her eyebrows, letting me know it was part of the package Peter had put together to woo me back.

"Not interested."

"Okay." She said it like she was just placating me. Like she'd win me over in the end.

We walked in silence for a while. I had to admit, it felt good that my ad agency wanted me back. But it also made me wonder what was going on there that they needed me. And why send Rory? I glanced over at her. She was inspecting every store window we passed. I wonder what she was holding back.

And as for my Aunt Jack—well, I was sure she had her motives for coming home and I was sure they were selfish. Peter and Aunt Jack. I blew out a breath. Whatever their reasons, decidedly they weren't doing anything good for me. All they were doing was interrupting my life.

A life I was quite satisfied with.

"Apart from your ice cream shop," Rory said, breaking into my reverie, "this town seems a little behind the times."

I chuckled, looking around at our surroundings. "We prefer 'quaint.'"

"Good word," she said and smiled. "See. You can still market anything."

We rounded the corner onto West Orange Street where Molta's was located. I nudged Rory and made her take notice of it.

The restaurant was new and chic. Architecturally modern in form, it had clean straight lines and resembled two boxes, one larger than the other, attached together. An entryway made up the smaller square structure. It had big dark wooden double doors with huge wrought-iron handles. The second square, in the back and to the right, made up the interior of the restaurant. The building was covered in a whitewash stucco. The trim and wrought-iron fence that delineated the porched-in eating area were black.

"You want a little piece of New York, Rory?" I smiled and pointed. "How about that?"

"It looks nice." She chuckled. "Food good?"

"Yep," I said. "And so is the coffee."

I pulled open the heavy door and we walked inside, the cool air and the smell of roasted meats and exotic seasonings invading our senses.

"Smells so good in here," Rory said. "I forgot I hadn't eaten since yesterday."

I frowned. "You got on the road this morning with nothing in your stomach?"

"What?" She turned, a confused look on her face. "Oh . . ." She closed her mouth and opened it to say something else, but nothing came out.

"You okay?" I asked.

"Just hungry." She smiled. "And dumbfounded about something so upscale sitting right in your quaint village. We're still in Chagrin Falls, right?"

"Yes," I said. "We only walked around the corner."

"Just checking," she said.

Rory's comment about Molta's again reminded me of Riya saying that the village was going upscale. She'd said it the day I reopened the ice cream shop back on that snowy, cold day, saying that me serving flavors like cherry amaretto chocolate chip was ushering Chagrin Falls into gentrification. Looked like Riya may have had a portent of what was to come.

Gentrification.

That word had been used the night before at the SOOCFA meeting. Something all the shop owners present apparently resisted. Our village had stayed small and quaint because that was the way we liked it. It had been one of the reasons I'd come back home. Not because my life was spiraling on a course I couldn't control and not because I had left chasing a dream I wasn't able to achieve.

I wasn't Aunt Jack.

I came back home because I wanted to be here.

I didn't know if gentrification, or revitalization as Zeke Reynolds put it, was a bad thing, or not. But if moving our quaint little village up to the twenty-first century, like he said, meant that murder was invading our boundaries, me and my family's ice cream shop wanted no part of it.

"Follow me, please." The hostess greeted us with a smile and, clutching two menus, led us to a table against a colorfully tiled wall. "Your server will be right with you," she said.

"You have to order the coffee," I said, shaking out my cloth napkin and placing it over my lap. "You'll enjoy it."

"I'm good," she said, mimicking my actions. "We'll grab my car and drive over to Cleveland. You know where a Java Joe's is, right?"

"I do," I said. "But you have to try a cup here. I know you'll like it."

"Okay," she said reluctantly. "But don't be surprised when you have to resuscitate me from going so long without my fix."

"You ate a ton of ice cream," I reminded her.

"That was because it was soooo good." She drew her shoulders together and wiggled in her seat, squeezing her eyes shut. "I know it goes against my mission, but your little shop is so cute and the ice cream will make you crave it even if there was a ton of snow outside."

I laughed. "I don't know about that," I said.

"Trust me," she said. "I know when word gets out about it, you'll have a line going out the door."

"Actually, your snow theory has already been tested."

"How?"

"The day I opened, it snowed."

"What? Get out of here!"

"Yep. Snow and a dead body tripped me up on opening day. Literally."

Her whole expression changed. Rory's skin was a beige color with red undertones and freckles scattered about, but with my words her face lost all of its color. "Oh my," she mumbled.

"Can I get your drink order?" The waitress showed up with a bright smile before I could ask Rory what was wrong, her question cutting in on my concern.

"I'll have water with lemon, please," I said and waited for Rory to answer, but she seemed to still be distracted. "She'll have coffee." I ordered for her. "Cream and sugar."

"Maybe a shot of expresso," Rory said. She looked up at the waitress and I noticed a little color coming back to her face. Her voice hadn't yet seemed to regain its full volume, though.

"You okay?" I asked. "You had me worried there for a minute."

She cleared her throat. "Just feeling a little dizzy." She shook her head. "That's all withdrawal." She gave me a weak smile. "I'm good."

"Probably fatigue from the drive this morning and the lack of coffee."

"Here's your coffee"—the waitress was back—"and your water." She smiled. "Do you still need time to look over the menu, or are you ready to order?"

"No. We're not quite ready," I said, realizing Rory hadn't even opened up her menu. "Give us another minute, please."

When I looked at Rory, I noticed she was frowning down into her cup.

"Now what's wrong?" I asked. "You haven't even tasted it yet."

"I'm afraid to."

"Drink the coffee," I said. Her frown intensified, and she was blinking rapidly, combating, it seemed, watery eyes that emerged just from the thought of having to taste it. "You'll like it. Ari isn't the Dixby sisters. And he isn't even from Chagrin Falls."

"Who?"

"The guy who owns the place. Ari Terrain. He's from a place that knows coffee."

"I can't imagine where that would be, but I do know he landed here. That couldn't mean anything good."

"I'm from here. And New York," I added, "and I like his coffee." I raised an eyebrow. "You trust my judgment, don't you? I know a good cup of coffee."

She blew out a breath and picked up the cup. She took an exaggerated sniff, put the cup to her lips and looked at me over the rim. Her frown still prominently displayed.

"Oh my," I said. "Don't be so dramatic. Take a sip."

Her nose crunched and her lips tightened as she took a sip, but as soon as she had, her eyes brightened. "Oh man, this is good." She smiled at me and licked her upper lip. "Almost as good a cup of coffee as your scoop of ice cream."

I grinned. "Thank you, and I told you so."

She set the cup down and let her eyes drift. "So what did you mean when you said you literally tripped over a dead body?"

"That I tripped over one," I said matter-of-factly.

"How can you say it like that? That is so . . ." Her words trailed off. She looked at me, biting her bottom lip, seemingly searching for the right word.

"So what?" I prompted.

She shrugged. "Scary. Devastating." She stared down into her coffee cup. "Life altering."

I laughed. "It wasn't that bad. And it wasn't the dead body so much that made it scary. It was *who* the dead body turned out to be."

"Who was it?" She leaned in, attentive, like I was telling a scary story.

"It was a man who had wronged my grandmother. A man my family hated and a man who was killed by a drug that was only used in surgery."

"Okay, you want to explain that answer?"

"Long story short, my father was the number one suspect."

"Oh," she said, realization washing over her face. "He's a surgeon?" I nodded. "Your grandmother—his mother?"

"Exactly."

"Oh wow. So what happened?"

Looking down at my napkin, I smiled. Trying not to blush too much—it really was a serious thing—I said, "I solved the murder and cleared his name."

"You did not!"

"I did." I beamed. "Well, Maisie and I did."

"Maisie? The girl I met in the shop today?"

I nodded.

"How in the world did you do that? I mean, put all the clues together and everything."

"Believe me, we just stumbled our way through. Maisie watches Acorn TV—"

"Acorn TV?" she interrupted.

"It's a British television streaming service that has all these amateur sleuth shows."

"Oh. I get it." She laughed. "She thinks she's Nancy Drew or somebody."

"Yes. But don't laugh, because we did it."

"You didn't get into any trouble?" she asked.

My mind flashed into that stairwell. The white walls. Green doors. That great big painted number "1" showing my way out, and all that fear I felt that day made me shudder.

"None to speak of," I said, my voice barely above a whisper.

"I'm impressed." Rory bowed her head to indicate mock reverence. "Purveyor of ice cream extraordinaire and emerging impromptu amateur detective."

I chuckled, tossing those memories out of my head. "Let's order," I said. "I think you're getting light-headed again. You need food!"

chapter

ELEVEN

I did see one place in your little village I'd love to visit, though," Rory said before stuffing another forkful of the breaded chicken stuffed with spinach and cheese into her mouth. "I saw a gallery." She took her napkin and dabbed at the edges.

"Sure," I said and nodded. I swallowed my bite of red snapper before continuing. "Black Market Paper. We can go there. And I think I saw that the village is having an art exhibit over at the visitors' center. We can check that out, too."

"You have a visitors' center?" she asked, leaning over and lowering her voice like repeating it was saying something dirty. "In this tiny little place? Why?"

"There is a lot going on in our little village," I said. "And already, we have two things that pique your interest."

"There is definitely a lot more to this place than I imagined," she said, letting her gaze drift off again.

"What does that mean?" I asked, thinking she might be being negative again. But her face belied something more.

Sitting up and straightening out her napkin, she turned her attention back to me and gave me a slight smile. "For instance, everyone keeps coming back."

"By everyone, I'm assuming you mean my Aunt Jack?"

That brought my mood down.

"Yes. You. Your aunt Jack." She scooped up some of the jasmine rice and speared a piece of asparagus. "She's as intrusive as a hurricane."

"She is," I said.

"Looks like I came with Peter's offer just in time."

I raised an eyebrow. "What are you talking about?" I put my fork down. I had ordered the whole snapper, which I had been thoroughly enjoying until Rory brought up my aunt. Again.

"The mall coming is sure to take out your ice cream shop if your aunt doesn't get to it first."

"I'm not worried about my aunt. My grandfather put me in charge of it."

"Oh, but you are worried about that mall."

"No." Then I realized I hadn't thought much about it. Not anything about what would happen to our ice cream shop if a mall was built. I wasn't sure how it would affect it. People would still eat my ice cream, there would just be competition. I looked at Rory and puffed out my chest. "I'm not worried about a mall either."

Rory chuckled. "I like that brave face you just put on. Reminds me of the one you used to wear when you were going into Peter's office to get the green light on one of your off-the-wall ad pitches."

"I always came back out with what I wanted."

"And that's why they want you back," she said.

"Not interested," I said.

"You'll get an office, your old team back, and anyone else you want to hire, and a twenty percent raise."

"Twenty percent?"

"Yep," she said and took a sip of her wine. "Unless you want more?"

"You're not authorized to offer me that, I'm sure."

"Don't be so sure." I saw a sparkle in her eye.

"Money can't woo me."

"Why?" She tilted her head and gave me a smirk. "Because how much money are you making here?"

I laughed. She got me on that one. If it wasn't for my taking money from my savings, I probably would have had to move back in with my parents. Between paying back the construction loan, plus my student loans, and revamping our family business, I didn't have, as my Grandma Kay used to say, two nickels to rub together.

"Are you finished?" I said as she bent over her plate scooping up more rice.

"Mm," she grunted, trying to keep the rice from falling back out of her mouth. She pointed to my plate with her fork. "You're not."

"I am," I said. I put my napkin on top of my plate and glanced at my watch. "Didn't you want to see the gallery before they close?"

She nodded eagerly and gulped the rest of her wine, washing down any remnants of food. She swiped the napkin across her mouth. "I would love to go there."

I signaled for the waiter. "I got this," I told her and reached for my purse.

"No," she said and stretched her hand across the table. "Peter gave me an expense account. Don't spend your money when we can spend the company's!"

I chuckled. "Okay. Now, that I'll go along with, I'll let Peter treat us." My face brightened. "I should have ordered dessert!"

The waitress took Rory's company Amex card, and as we waited, I saw Ari. He was showing those beautiful teeth of his going from table to table greeting his customers. I was sure he wouldn't want to talk to me, not after the earlier confrontation with Maisie. But his eyes locked with mine and he beamed. He headed our way.

"Here comes the owner now," I said to Rory and discreetly pointed to Ari. "I can introduce you."

"Where?" she said, turning her head. When she saw him, though, her face went pale.

"What's wrong?"

"Nothing," she said and started fidgeting in her seat.

"Hi, Win." Ari made it over to our table, his smile even wider. I was glad he didn't hold Maisie's craziness against me.

He turned to speak to Rory and recognition sparked in his eyes. "We meet again."

"Hi," she said, not looking up, keeping her head tucked.

"You find whatever it was you were looking for?"

She cleared her throat like her words had gotten stuck and nodded.

"Good," he said. "I'm Ari." He stuck out a hand to Rory. "This is my place."

"Rory. Rory Hunter," she answered and placed her hand inside of his.

"Nice to see you," he said. "Again. Kind of scary meeting strangers in the dark, I know."

"You met before?" I scrunched up my face.

"But you can see—" Ari stepped back, still talking, and gestured down his body. "I'm one of the good guys. Aren't I, Win?"

I chuckled at his comment. Good thing he was asking me that question and not Maisie. "Yes, Ari. You're one of the good guys."

"Win, was the fish okay?" He pointed down at my plate. "You didn't finish."

"It was delicious, Ari." I glanced down at it. No need to tell him that I'd lost my appetite because everyone was trying to disrupt my life with murder investigations, job offers and the invasion of fly-by-night relatives. "And filling." I rubbed my stomach.

"As long as you enjoyed it."

"I did."

"I can tell Rory Hunter enjoyed hers." He smiled down at her, but she had yet to look up. "Her plate is clean."

At that, Rory abruptly popped up. It was like she had just gathered up enough combustible energy to do it and it was coming out at once. "We have to go" spilled out as she pushed her chair back and took off for the door.

Ari and I stared after her, then he looked at me. I shrugged. "We're trying to get to Black Market Paper before it closes."

"Oh," he said, one eyebrow arched upward.

"Ma'am!" It was our waitress. Rory had left so quickly, she'd forgotten her credit card.

"I better go catch her," I said, excusing myself. "That's a company credit card. I don't want her losing her job over a half-eaten red snapper and some jasmine rice."

Ari laughed. "I wouldn't want that either."

"Ma'am!"

The waitress was still chasing Rory.

There was definitely something going on with her.

chapter

TWELVE

W hat is wrong with you?"

Rory had made it all the way to the door before I caught up with her. I got her to sign the check—didn't want the server to have to chase her up the street—and ushered her out the door. The sun had started to set and it wasn't as hot out as it had been earlier, but Rory was sweating.

"Are you okay?" I asked. She nodded and started up walking again. "Look." I grabbed her arm. "You have to tell me what's going on with you. You are not okay."

"I am," she said. She sucked in a breath and blew it back out through her mouth. "Really, I'm fine."

I glanced back toward the restaurant. "I don't believe that. But I'm guessing you'll tell me when you can." I tried to soften my eyes, make her feel more comfortable. She looked tense. "How do you know Ari?"

"I don't," she answered a little too quickly.

"Then what was the whole in-the-dark-but-now you-see-I'm-not-so-scary thing?"

"I don't know."

"Okaaay." I didn't know what to make of her. She'd always been a bit high-strung and sometimes even moody. But I'd always attributed it to her being the creative type. I knew sometimes to us "unartistic" folk, artists could appear to be a little weird.

"You still want to go to Black Market Paper?" I asked.

"Yes."

"Okay," I said. "And you're sure you're okay?"

"I'm okay," she repeated.

"Okay, good," I said.

"I'd be better if you'd agree to come back to New York and take your job back," she said and bumped her body into mine.

"You are so weird," I said. "I forgot how much so. You're worse than Maisie."

"Is she weird?" Rory asked.

"After spending the day with you, I'm thinking I should rethink that assessment of her." I shook my head. "I think you might win the prize."

"Is that any way to treat company?" She smacked my arm. "I'm good, I tell you. Just probably, you know, I'm tired from the drive and I've got my mission on my mind."

"So c'mon, then. Let's give you some art intervention. Maybe it'll help you feel better."

BLACK MARKET PAPER was bright and had a good vibe with the recessed lighting, stark white walls and contrasting shiny dark wood crown molding. The store was narrow and long and seemed to go on forever. Every inch of the walls was covered in paintings and prints and sketches, whether they were framed or rolled up and stuffed into little cubbies stacked along the walls. The floor had easel after easel scattered about the space, with just enough room to squeeze by to get to the next picture just beyond. And the AC was set to "freezing."

When we walked in, the place seemed deserted. No one came to greet us, but the faces and landscapes of the pictures seemed to welcome us. Warm brushstrokes, vibrant watercolors and chalked figures beckoning us to come on in and have a look.

"They have a really nice collection," Rory said, her eyes wide with delight and wonder. She had walked over to me and whispered her declaration.

"I see you're surprised."

"After the coffee debacle this morning, and all the . . . uhm . . . *quaint* shops"—she smiled at me—"I really didn't expect much from Chagrin Falls."

"You should be more open-minded."

"Maybe I will, but I'll never be open-minded enough to ever want to live in this itty-bitty place."

"Not even with this awesome gallery?"

"This *is* an awesome gallery." A man with a Russian accent had walked up behind us. "It is awesome, because we are awesome."

"Don't harass our customers." A woman's voice, deep and throaty, came out from the back. Rory and I turned to look at her. "Hi," she said and offered a limp hand. "I am Baraniece Black, and this"—she did a head nod—"is my husband, Ivan Rynok." She shook hands with each of us.

Rory looked down at her hand, then ran her other one over it. "Paint," she said. I looked down at mine. I had red streaks on it, too. We've must have interrupted a painting session.

"We are the owners." Baraniece, not seeming to care that she'd used us like a canvas, not even apologizing, spread her arms wide as if she was going to take flight. Rory and I couldn't help but to let out a chuckle.

"I know you." Baraniece pointed one of her talons at me. Her nails were long and painted in a shiny black. I didn't know how she painted with nails that long. "You're Aloysius's daughter . . . family . . . or something. You put the glass wall up in his store."

"Our store," I said and, following her lead about being the owners, I almost spread out my arms when I spoke. "It's a family business."

"Did you come for art?" she asked, ignoring my correction.

"I came—"

"To admire your art." Rory took over talking for me and gave me the eye saying let her handle this. "You have quite a collection here."

"We do, don't we?" Baraniece said and smiled. "We have art from all over the world and from every period." She clasped her hands together. "What is it that you want to see?"

Baraniece Black didn't have a trace of an accent, but the way she spoke seemed foreign. Her face was saggy, but it looked as though she tried to keep it in place by piling on makeup. She had dramatic smoky eyes and cherry-red lipstick. Her hair was shoulder length, but its height and curls didn't move. I wondered if I touched it whether it would be hard and sticky from hair spray.

"There are so many things I want to see," Rory said, her gleaming eyes roaming the small boutique-style gallery.

"If you need anything, just let us know," Baraniece said. "We'll be moving to a new location soon. Prices will be good." She hunched her shoulders. "Almost like a fire sale."

"A fire sale," Ivan said from behind us. It made me jump. I had forgotten he was there. He hadn't said a word since his wife had made an entrance.

"I'm going to do a little research," Rory said when we left the art gallery. "I saw some things I really like."

"Are you going to buy something?"

"I don't know," she said. "I might." She had a thoughtful smile on her face. "I need to go back."

"Why?"

"A couple of reasons. There was a section of Russian art that I'm very familiar with, but didn't have a chance to check it out. I'm guessing from his accent Ivan is Russian. It'd be fun to have a look at it, then have a discussion with him about it."

"He's Russian, but what is she?"

"I know, right?" Rory said, her eyes brightening. "What was that accent?"

"I would guess 'made-up.'" We both chuckled. "But they are both very nice," I said. "I've never bought anything from them. Too expensive. But I believe if they say they'll give you a deal, they will."

"Good. I'm definitely going back."

"What's the other reason you mentioned?"

"I just want to make sure I'm paying a good price." She bit her bottom lip. I could tell she was excited about her consideration.

"Some things I saw were priced about right and some things I wasn't sure of."

"Like what?" I asked.

"Like the paintings they have by the Florida Highwaymen." I could hear the excitement creep into her voice. "I'd really love to have one of those. I've never seen any for sale before. So I know I have to act quickly."

"The Florida who?"

"Highwaymen," she said.

"I don't think I've ever heard of them."

"They were black artists known for painting Florida landscapes from, like, the 1950s through the '80s," she explained. "They sold the paintings door-to-door and from the trunks of their cars."

"Door-to-door? Why did they do that?"

"You know it was the fifties and because of racial barriers some galleries wouldn't accept their work." She shrugged. "But their selling techniques worked. They painted a couple hundred thousand pictures over the years."

"That's a lot."

"Yeah, and at first they were selling them for, like, twenty-five dollars apiece. Sometimes the paint wouldn't even be dry when customers purchased them."

"Twenty-five dollars is certainly affordable," I said. "If they have some you should get you a few."

"They were inexpensive *then*." She emphasized the word. "I don't know how much they go for exactly, but I know they cost more now. Nowadays, I'm thinking, they could sell as high as tens of thousands."

"Whoa. Isn't that over your head?"

"Those are, but there are some not so expensive."

"Oh. Okay. Did you see one you like?" I asked.

"I did," Rory said, her eyes lighting up. "Maybe more than one. They were by Alfred Hair."

"They had more than one in there?"

She nodded. "And that is so exciting to me. Just think, I could start my own little collection."

"That would be nice," I said. "Something to take back home from Chagrin Falls."

"Taking you and a Highwaymen painting back to New York." She gave a low whistle. "That would make this trip more than worthwhile."

I laughed. "You probably should have picked up one," I said. "It might not be there later, and I wouldn't want you to go home empty-handed."

"Oh, I will convince you soon enough." She laughed. "But, I didn't want to get one because I think I recognized another one of the signatures of the artists, but I'm not sure."

"How will you find out?"

"I'm going to check to see if I can find a catalogue raisonné."

"What's that? And where would you find it?"

"It's a comprehensive annotated catalog of an artist's work," Rory said, speaking passionately. "I should be able to find one online. What it is, is a book, or booklet, that shows pictures and lists the locations, if known, of an artist's work. But more importantly, it'll give me an idea of their worth."

"So you'll know what to offer?"

"Right." She nodded. "They had a price listed and I'm thinking that it was a really, really good deal."

"How much?"

"Eight thousand."

"Whoa! Do you have money like that?" I grabbed her arm and stopped her from walking. "To spend on a picture?" I asked, my eyes wide. I knew how expensive it was to live in New York and I knew what Hawken Spencer paid.

"It's not a *picture*," she said. "It's a Florida Highwaymen *painting*." She sucked in a breath. "And I was thinking I might draw from my 401(k)." She started walking again.

"To buy it?" She nodded. "Wow," I said, following behind her, "you'd spend your retirement money on that?"

"It's an investment," she said. "Probably in twenty years, or forty years when I'm old enough to retire, I could sell it for three times as much. Maybe more. And like you said, they're having a sale, so I might get it cheaper."

"Ivan did say he'd give you a deal."

"Yes. He did," she said. Then I saw a smirk emerge on her face. "You still have your 401(k)?"

"Nope," I said.

"And what did you spend *your* retirement money on?"

"The light bill. My cell phone bill. Rent." I listed the things I paid to live. "Bread. Milk. Microwavable popcorn." And what I needed to eat.

She chuckled. "See, that's why you should take Peter's offer. How are you going to live when you reach retirement?"

"Same way I'm living now," I said. "I'll make ice cream."

chapter

ം⁃ഗഠനം

THIRTEEN

After we left the gallery, we walked aimlessly down the sidewalk in front of the shops and boutiques, and chitchatted. By the time we made it around, it was late. Rory had said she was going to check in, and I thought I'd go back by the ice cream shop, but before I could, I saw Maisie bounding toward us.

"Where are you going?" I said, checking my watch again although I knew exactly what time it was.

"I came to check on my building."

"Didn't you just check on it at lunch?" I said.

"It likes to be checked," she said. "Hi, Rory!" She flapped an arm at her.

Rory gave a polite smile. "Hi."

"Where you guys coming from?" Maisie asked.

"Who's minding the store?" I said. "That's the question."

"PopPop and your aunt Jack."

"Aunt Jack?" I reiterated this as a question. That was surprising—no—disturbing news. "I thought she'd left."

Maisie shrugged. "She came back."

"Oh my," I said and swiped a hand across my forehead. I could feel my red snapper coming back up my throat. "You let her behind the counter?"

"You know your aunt," Maisie said. "I didn't *let* her do anything."

"Where was my mother?"

"She'd left before your aunt came back."

I glanced over at Rory, she seemed to find the whole thing amusing.

"Told you you were going to need a job," Rory said.

"You go buy your painting from Black Market Paper and let me worry about my livelihood."

"Black Market Paper?" Maisie said, her face going flush. "Why didn't you tell me you were going to interrogate suspects?"

"What?" I said, scrunching up my nose. "We didn't."

"What did they say?" she said, shrugging off her book bag and scrambling through the stuff inside. "Did you find out his first name? The husband?"

"What is she talking about?" Rory asked.

"Nothing," I said.

"The detective that's working on the murder we had here asked us to help." She stopped rummaging through her bag and looked at Rory. "Did you know we had a murder here? It's the second one."

"She knows," I said.

"Oh wow," Rory said. "Are you really going to help with this murder, too?"

"No," I said resoundingly. I wanted to convey that message to Rory and Maisie.

"Yes," Maisie said at the same time.

"I'm not," I said with a brashness I'm sure Maisie didn't expect.

"I am," Maisie said, matching my tone.

"She's not either," I said, shaking my head and pointing my thumb at Maisie.

I wasn't going to follow Maisie down that rabbit hole. And I decided I was going to have to keep her from going down it, too.

Yes, sure, I had helped to solve the last murder, the only murder we'd had in Chagrin Falls, but that was because my father was a suspect. I had been dragged into that fray reluctantly. There was no need for me to help in this investigation. I was sure Detective Beverly did not mean that he wanted us to go purposely snoop, he just meant if we had any ideas or heard anything we should help.

Maisie had her small notebook opened and a pen hovering over it to take notes. "Tell me everything they said."

"Who?" I asked.

"The suspects." I gave her a blank look. "The owners of the art gallery."

"They're suspects?" Rory asked.

"Yes," Maisie said.

"No," I said.

"Why do you think they are the ones that killed the guy?" Rory asked.

"Maisie thinks everyone who wasn't at the business meeting is a suspect."

"Is that why?" Rory asked, as she raised an eyebrow at Maisie. "Yes."

"That's your only evidence?" A look of disbelief emerged on Rory's face. "I've watched enough *Law & Order* to know that that's not enough to convict anyone of anything."

"That's why it's called being an *amateur* sleuth," I said.

"We have to start somewhere," Maisie said.

"I see you found the red ball!" Mr. Mason had one of his big toothless grins. He walked over to us, dragging his right foot in a limp that I didn't remember ever seeing before. But that didn't stop him from getting to us, nodding his head and pointing to Rory with his left hand.

Good thing he showed up and broke the tension. I was going to have to find some way to talk Maisie off that amateur sleuth ledge.

"This is my friend from New York," I said, turning to smile at Rory, but she had stepped behind me like she was trying to hide. "Rory." I tried to get her to greet Mr. Mason. "This is Myles Mason. He's an artist, too. You two probably have stuff in common." But she wasn't listening and wouldn't budge from her hiding place. She stayed planted firmly behind me. Her eyes focused on the ground.

She couldn't be afraid of him, I thought. There were plenty of down-on-their-luck residents in New York City. I'd seen her give them money and even food a time or two. "What's wrong with you?" I asked her.

"I gotta go," she said and took off. Just like that.

Mr. Mason watched Rory leave, bobbing his head up and down, up and down, just as if he was watching a ball bouncing.

A big red ball.

"What was that about?" Maisie asked, turning to me after seeing Rory leave. "Is she okay?"

"I've been wondering the same thing," I said.

"That's the red ball," Mr. Mason said, focusing his attention back on me. He had lost the grin and was pretty serious about what he was telling me.

"Rory?" I asked. "You think she's a ball?"

I looked back in the direction Rory had disappeared then at Mr. Mason. He was confused, and I was getting somewhat concerned over the things he'd been telling me. I blew out a breath. Just like I was concerned about Rory. I took in Mr. Mason. His clothes were relatively clean, although maybe he was wearing too many of them for the warm weather we were having, and other than needing some dental care, he appeared to be relatively clean, too.

I had one brother, Lew, who was a dentist, and another one, Bobby, a nurse practitioner, who ran a community clinic in the village. There was some reason I'd run into Mr. Mason twice today, and I was sure it had nothing to do with bouncing red balls. My Grandma Kay would have seen to him. She was all about family and community.

I decided I'd help him out and make sure he was okay.

"Mr. Mason," I said. "Come over to the ice cream shop tomorrow. I want to talk to you."

"Your grandmother's ice cream shop?" he asked.

"Yes," I said. "I'm sure she'd want you to come by and see it and have a little taste of what we have."

There was that rotten-tooth grin again. "She always gave me ice cream."

I was sure in those days he was able to buy it, but I knew what he was getting at. "I'll have some ice cream for you," I said.

And, I thought, *an appointment with both my brothers.*

chapter

꩜

FOURTEEN

I padded down the hallway wondering who in the world could be at my door. The little red-numbered alarm clock on my bedside table said 10:04 p.m.

As I got farther down the hallway, I cringed at the thought that maybe someone was dropping by to tell me there had been another murder. I couldn't figure out how my hometown got to be so dangerous. I even thought about stopping by my kitchen and grabbing one of those twelve-inch chef knives my mother had been wielding earlier in the day. But decided if it were that kind of news, they—whoever it was—would have called.

I shook off the thought and shook my head. How could that be what I was thinking about anymore? Sure, we're parked right next to Cleveland—a big city with big-city problems—but that wasn't Chagrin Falls.

"Hi," I said, pulling open the door and talking through the screen. Rory was standing there with her Dooney & Bourke overnight bag in hand, her purse in the other, and dejection written all over her face.

"Hi," she said back and nothing else.

We stood there in a stare-off for a long moment. Not sure what to say to her, she seemed to be having the same problem.

"Can I come in?" she asked.

I pushed open the screen door and stepped out of the way, gesturing with a hand sweep. "Sure," I said, trying to sound chipper. I didn't want her thinking I minded her stopping by. "Come on in. I live up here." I pointed to the steps and, after locking the door, led the way up to my apartment. At the top, we hooked a left into my living space and I pointed to a chair for her to sit down. I sat on the couch across from her.

"You okay?" I asked. Seemed like that was all I ever said to her.

"I need a place to stay," she said. "Can I stay here?"

"Of course you can," I said, feeling bad that I hadn't offered it to her earlier. I hopped off the couch and went to the linen closet. "I only have the one bedroom and one bed," I yelled over my shoulder as I grabbed a couple of sheets, a pillow and a case for it. "You're welcome to take half my bed and sleep with me, or"—I appeared back in the doorway with my arms full—"you can bunk out here on the couch."

"The couch is fine," she said quietly. "I don't want to be any trouble."

"Don't be silly," I said. "We can have a sleepover anytime as long as we're limited to polishing nails, doing hair and talking about boys."

She chuckled. The first sign of life I'd seen in her lifeless eyes since she knocked on my door. "What about if I want to talk about Peter and his offer?"

"Then I will promptly kick you out."

She shook her head. "Fair," she said. "But tomorrow I'll get a room because I drove those four hundred–plus miles to talk about Peter and his offer."

"That's fine," I said. "But I should warn you, just because you talk about it, doesn't mean I'll listen."

"Yeah," she said, pulling her legs up into the chair and crossing them. "I've noticed that. But that was before I had help."

"Help? You've got help?"

"Aunt Jack." She said it as if it were obvious.

I threw up my hands. "No! Please! Let's not talk about her either."

"You see how as soon as you left the ice cream shop—"

"She slithered back in?" I finished her sentence.

"You're in trouble, girl." She pointed her finger at me.

I picked up one of the throw pillows from the couch and threw it at her.

"Don't be mean to me," she said, catching the pillow. "I might just end up being your rescuer. Here in the nick of time with another job for you."

"I really don't want to have to send you and your Mary Poppins Dooney bag scrambling out the door as I chase you with my umbrella."

"Sorry!" she said, clutching her chest in mock sorrow. "Not another word about it from me. Promise." She hooked an imaginary lock to her mouth, turned the key and tossed it over her shoulder.

"What happened with your room?" I couldn't imagine she'd come all the way from New York and hadn't arranged for a place to stay. I'd imagine it would be the Ritz-Carlton in downtown Cleveland or something on that scale. I looked at her out of the corner of my eye. "What is going on with you?"

"Nothing!" she said animatedly as, uncrossing her legs, she scooted to the edge of the chair and dug down in her overnight bag, pulling out a comb. "She said I was too late to get my room."

"Who said you were too late?"

"The lady at the bed-and-breakfast." She pointed over her shoulder.

I followed her finger—although it indicated the wall behind her, I knew what she meant. "You made a reservation at Rose Cottage. Dell told you you were too late?"

"Is that her name?" she asked. She made a small part in her hair and, grabbing a section, she twisted it.

"She owns it, yeah."

"Okay, then Dell told me." She shook her comb at me. "Can you believe that? Too late to get my room. In this little bitty city." She held up her hands. "Tell me. Honestly. How many people are actually coming here and needing a room? I'm sure not many."

"When did you get there?"

"When I left you," she said, parting off another section of hair.

I wanted to say, *When you ran away from me.* But I didn't.

"Remember," she was saying, "once we finished at the art gallery, my car was still parked in front of the Wicked Twin Witches' fake coffee shop. And I drove right over."

"I hadn't thought about your car," I said and glanced out of the window. "Did you drive it over here?"

"I couldn't have gotten over here without it." She sectioned off another part and twisted it. I always wondered how she got that half-wavy, half-curly do she wore. "I put your address in the navigation system. Thank goodness I had it."

"You could have just called."

"I was so frustrated."

"Maybe I could talk to her." I stood up. "Let me get my phone."

"No. Don't," she said, waving her hands back and forth like windshield wipers on a car. "I'm good if you are."

"I already told you, no problem. You can stay as long as you need."

"Thank you," she said, finishing up her hair. "I came here to save you and you're saving me."

"It's just a place to sleep, Rory." I waved a hand. "It's nothing. Really. In spite of your 'mission'"—I did the air quotation marks—"I'm really happy to see you." I put a smile on my face. "I'm happy to have you."

"Good," she said, and she stuck her comb back down in her bag. "Because I'm happy to be here." She got up and took the linens off the couch where I'd placed them.

"You good?" I asked, thinking I should leave her alone and get back to bed.

"Yep," she said absently. Taking one of the sheets, she unfolded it and with a flick of her wrists let it fly over the couch and float back down, covering it.

She made busy readying her bed. Instead of going back to my room, I stood and watched her. With that last question, I wasn't asking if she was "good" making up the couch, what I was really wondering was what was wrong with her in general. She been acting weird all day. Moody. Distracted. Seemingly more was on her mind than talking me into coming back to Hawken Spencer.

But she was in another zone. A zone that didn't include me. Her words trailing off, I decided not to bring it up.

"Hey, do you have a laptop?" she asked.

"Sure," I said. "You need it?"

"Yeah, I wanna see if I can find an online catalogue raisonné, like I told you. I'll look for one for the entire Florida Highwaymen collection, although that'll be big. I might be able to find one for either one of the two artists that they have at Black Market Paper Fine Art, though."

I pointed to a corner table. "There it is," I said. Once she got it fired up, I put in my password.

"Thanks," she said.

"Okay. Well." I looked around to see if there was anything else. "I'm going to bed. I usually get an early start."

"How early?" She stopped what she was doing, stood up straight and eyed me.

I laughed. "On mornings I make ice cream, I'm up by four thirty."

"Oh good lord," she said. "Do you have to make ice cream tomorrow?"

"No," I said.

"Thank goodness," she said. "Does that mean we can sleep in?"

"Yes," I said. "We don't have to get up until six."

"Six! I don't ever get up that early, and I have a real job."

"So do I," I said, walking out of the room and down the hall to my bedroom.

"Not for long," she shouted behind me. "Not if your aunt Jack gets her way."

I knew I should have thrown her out right then and there.

chapter

FIFTEEN

It seemed like I had just dozed off when I heard her. She was standing at the door speaking so softly to me it made me think she was trying not to wake me. But if she was talking, she must have wanted me to hear her.

I sat up in bed. "You okay, Rory?"

"Do you mind if I climb in the bed with you?" she said, still whispering. "I just can't seem to fall asleep."

Without a word, I scooted over to the edge of the bed and then patted the side I'd just vacated, telling her to come on in. "I don't know how you'll be able to sleep in here," I said, barely moving my lips and adopting her way of speaking by lowering my voice. "I snore."

"Couldn't be any worse than my mother." She climbed in the bed. I snuggled back into my covers and closed my eyes. "I just don't want to be by myself," she said after a long moment.

I don't know why Rory said she was having trouble sleeping. Once she got in bed with me I heard soft, even breathing coming from her side of the bed, letting me know she went to sleep almost as soon as her head hit the pillow.

EVERY MORNING I would walk to work, good weather or bad, and stop in to see my grandfather on the way to the shop. A habit I picked up from him—he walked everywhere. A ritual that served me well while living in New York City. There you walked, or you took the subway or an Uber.

This morning I had Rory with me, and I thought I'd skip going to PopPop's. But before we could get on our way, my mother was calling and inviting us over for breakfast.

At five a.m.

I wasn't even sure how my mother knew that Rory was at my house that early in the morning. Probably the gossip mill. Dell told Ms. Devereaux, who told somebody, who told my mother, or something like that.

My grandfather's house was the in-law suite of my parents' large home. The house had been the one that my grandparents had raised their children in, then passed down to my parents to raise us after the house got too big for my ailing grandmother. My grandfather had taken care of my Grandma Kay's every need in that little apartment suite until the day she died.

PopPop had his own entrance. Most mornings I bypassed my parents' front door to head around back to him.

It was closer to six thirty when we walked through the front door of my parents' home. PopPop was sitting at the kitchen table with my mother, though he didn't often venture over to the main house. My father was at the stove cooking.

"He's a surgeon and a chef?" Rory whispered.

"And he's really good at both," I whispered back.

"Morning!" my mother said after we came down the front hallway and stood at the doorway to the kitchen. She hopped out of her chair. "I hope you brought your appetites with you."

"Mom, no one eats this early." I felt safe to speak for Rory as well as myself. She complained about getting up at six. I got up, but I usually didn't eat anything until around nine.

"We do." The three of them said it at nearly the same time.

"We always eat early," my mother said.

"No one under fifty is what I should have said."

"You'll live long enough to get there," my father said. "Then you'll see." He wiped his hand on the tea towel he had slung over his shoulder. "And this must be Rory."

"Yes, it is." I smiled to make the formal introduction. "Daddy—I mean, Graham Crewse—this is my friend from New York, Rory Hunter."

"Glad to meet you," he said and shook her hand. "New York City. I love that place. How long you staying?"

"I just got in yesterday," she said, "but how long I stay is up to Win."

"Win dictates my life, too, don't you, Pumpkin," my daddy said.

I smiled at my father. My daddy. Dr. James Graham Crewse, orthopedic surgeon at the world-renowned Lakeside Memorial Clinic. He was tall and fit, with perfect posture, was thoughtful and methodical, and had a dry wit. He had a calmness about him and never faltered even when there was a lot of craziness going on around him. That was probably how he stayed with my mother for nearly forty years because she was all about the craziness.

"Mr. Crewse," Rory said, heartily shaking his hand. "Nice to meet you, too. I've heard so many good things about you."

"I give hugs," my mother said and squeezed Rory.

"You met her yesterday," I said.

"I can still hug her," my mother said.

"Good morning," PopPop said to her—he'd met her yesterday, too, and was acting accordingly. "You helping out at the ice cream shop this morning?"

"I don't think I'll be much help." Rory shook her head. "How do you psyche yourself up to work this early in the morning?"

We laughed.

"Kaylene," my grandfather said. "She'd have everyone up and ready to start the day before the sun could make its way overhead. It's just part of our ritual now."

"That's my Grandma Kay," I said, explaining to Rory who Kaylene was. She'd heard me speak of her enough, but not by that name. "And I don't mind getting up, but I can't eat."

"We're all eating this morning," my mother said, her usual cheerful self when she was around my father. That was when she was her happiest. They were soul mates and it was easy to see their "honeymoon" stage kind of love had lasted throughout the years.

"Pass the orange juice," my mother said. We had sat down at the table. My dad had whisked up eggs Benedict and a side of bacon (because I guess the Canadian bacon wasn't enough) and fresh strawberries and blueberries.

My mother grabbed the handle of the pitcher, poured a glass

full then grabbed my dad's glass to fill his, too. "Did you hear that Veronica and Zeke had a fight at Rivkah's restaurant and she left crying? Ran right through the kitchen out the back."

"Who?" my father said. He crunched down on a piece of bacon. "Who are Veronica and Zeke? Are they some of those reality stars?"

I knew who she was talking about, but how that conversation seemed to go part and parcel with "pass the OJ" just went to show the hold the gossip mill had on my mother.

"Mommy!" I said. "Are we talking about that at breakfast?"

"I agree with Win. That is not appropriate breakfast conversation, Ailbhe," my grandfather said. "Talking about the dead."

"I didn't know there was an appropriate time to discuss the dead," my mother said, spreading margarine on the extra English muffin she had grabbed.

"Who are we talking about?" Rory asked.

"No one," I said and gave a dismissive pass of my hand. "My mother likes to gossip."

"It's not gossip," she said. "It's the truth." She took a bite of her muffin and pushed it into a corner of her jaw so she could keep talking. "I don't mean a knock-down, drag-out fight. It was just an argument."

"Who are Zeke and Veronica?" my father asked again.

"Zeke is the guy who was trying to buy up property to build a mall," my mother said.

"His business was, not him personally," I corrected.

"The guy you were telling me about, Dad?" my father asked.

"Yeah. The one who turned up dead in the alley yesterday."

Rory went into a coughing fit with those words.

"Are you okay?" my mother asked, as she hopped out of her seat and went over to pat Rory on the back.

"I'm fine." She choked out the words. "Just something got caught in my throat."

"See, Mom, what happens when you talk about dead people at the breakfast table?"

Rory's face went pale, and she let out another cough.

"Here, drink some juice," my mother said.

"Are you okay?" my father asked. Always the doctor.

Rory, swallowing hard, nodded to let him know she was okay.

"Okay, then I need more food," my father said and looked back at the stove.

"You only made enough eggs Benedict for the five of us, didn't you?" my mother said.

"I scrambled eggs for PopPop," my dad said. "I knew he wasn't going to eat any of the fancy stuff I wanted to impress Win's friend with."

"I appreciate that, son," PopPop said. "Like I always say, I just need my morning coffee—" he started.

"A newspaper and a couple of eggs." My parents and I finished his sentence for him. We'd heard it enough from him.

"You have coffee?" Rory sputtered out.

"I had mine before I came over here this morning. Those two"—he pointed at my parents—"don't understand the importance of a good cup of joe first thing in the morning."

"I understand it perfectly," Rory said.

"You had a cup at my house," I protested. "Before we left."

"I could use another cup," she said sheepishly and eyed Pop-Pop.

"What's wrong with her having another cup, Win?" my mother said. "You have to be accommodating to your guests."

"I wasn't saying she couldn't have . . ." I shook my head. I could tell by my mother's look, she wasn't going to understand what I meant. "I'm sure PopPop will be happy to share some of his with you. Or," I said, "we could stop by the Juniper Tree on the way to the ice cream shop."

"Oh God, no!" Rory said. "I couldn't drink a cup of that even if that was the last coffee shop for the next hundred miles."

"You've never tasted their coffee," I said.

"I met the owners," she said. "That was enough."

"The Darling Dixbys?" my mother said. "Did they say something to you?"

"No," I said putting up my hand, wanting to put a halt to that conversation.

"Come on over to my place," PopPop said, scooting his chair back and standing up. "I'll brew you a cup."

"Sounds good," Rory said.

"We have to go to the ice cream shop," I said.

"You go," my mother said. "I'll bring Rory when I come down."

"Before we go, though," PopPop said and handed his plate to my father, "I'll take some more of those eggs if you have any left. Win works me down at the ice cream shop. I need all my strength."

"PopPop." I tilted my head. "All you do all day is sit at your bench. Taking up space for the paying customers."

"You don't do a thing," my mother said.

"What are you talking about?" my grandfather said. "Who ran that shop yesterday when everyone took off? It was me and Jack."

My mother waved a hand at him. "That is just not the truth. You may have helped out yesterday, but that's a rare occurrence."

PopPop laughed. "I do help, though."

"Not all the time. Or often. Talking about me bringing up the fight at the Village Dragon, which really happened, but you can't sit around and say things that are just made up."

"There's a difference in kidding around and gossiping," my father said, coming back to the table with his and PopPop's plates.

"I wasn't gossiping," my mother protested.

"Yes, we know, sweetie," my father said and gave her one of his we'll-just-let-you-think-what-you-want smiles.

"Why don't you go and tell Liam Beverly your little tidbit of truth," PopPop said. "Maybe he'd appreciate it."

"I wouldn't tell that man to move out the way if I saw a semi headed his way," my mother said.

chapter

SIXTEEN

The sun had long made its appearance in the bright blue sky and birds were chirping somewhere up among the lush green trees that lined the curb and large yards as I walked down to the shop after breakfast with my parents. Streets were all hilly in Chagrin Falls, and if you grew up here, it was probably true that as a child you walked to school in the snow, uphill both ways.

I was worried I was going to start feeling sluggish after eating so early. It was a good thing I didn't have to make ice cream. I had made enough the day before. My original plan had been to make ice cream at night, but I was so used to getting up early—and it was the way my Grandma Kay had done it—that I started making it in the mornings.

Rory had stayed with PopPop and his coffeemaker. She definitely wasn't going to get a Java Joe's kind of cup from his ancient coffeepot, but she didn't seem to mind. I was happy she got along with my parents. Maybe we could all go to dinner or something...

Then I thought about how it would affect me. Rory hadn't ever told me how long she was staying. If her only mission was to woo me back to Hawken Spencer, she could leave anytime that day. I wasn't going back.

But I knew she wanted to go back to Black Market Paper and I definitely wanted to take her to the art festival at the visitors' center.

Maybe immersing her in art would help whatever it was that seemed to be wrong with her. She was getting weirder by the hour.

I wondered if I could help her . . .

Then I wondered who was going to help me because as soon as I rounded the corner from Carriage Hill Lane where my parents lived onto North Main Street, taking into view the yellow-and-baby-blue-striped Crewse Creamery awning I'd had installed, I saw my aunt Jack. That big ole ancient car of hers was parked right in front of the ice cream store and she was sitting on my Grandma Kay's bench.

My grandfather had put that bench out front of the ice cream shop when my grandmother first took sick. Family members took turns sitting there with her, keeping her company and keeping her from wandering off. I kept it even after I remodeled because it reminded me of her. I had spent so much time there with her that having it made me feel like she was close by.

"Geesh." It gushed out in a huff, and as soon as it did, Aunt Jack looked my way. I knew she couldn't hear me. I was too far away. Maybe it was just the bad vibes I was having about her being back that had bounced over to her like sound waves. She stood up, signaling to me that she'd been there waiting for me.

"Hi," I said when I finally got to the store. "What are you doing out so early?"

"My key didn't fit," she said, pointing back at the door and not answering my question.

"It's a new door," I said, following her finger and letting my eyes land on the full plate glass door I had had installed during the remodel. "A new lock."

"Well, I'm going to need a key," she said.

"The lock on the side door didn't change," I said. "Your key will still fit that. That's the way we go in anyway."

"I don't use that door," she said. "I don't like going down that alley in the dark."

I looked up at the bright blue sky and then back at Aunt Jack.

"It seems like there are a lot of people getting murdered around here," she said. "You can't be too careful."

"Two," I said, unlocking the front door and letting her in. "Compared to Cleveland, that's not a lot."

"Any murder is too much. And that's two more than there was the whole time I lived in Chagrin Falls. Which, by the way, was my whole life."

She walked in the door behind me, out of breath from just the few steps and carrying a large cloth bag with her.

"What's in the bag?" I said. I stopped and stroked Felice on the top of the head before going in the back. She let out a soft purr. The little pompous cat was up and ready to start her day, too.

She followed behind me. "Just some things I thought we might need for the store."

We?

That was what I wanted to say to her, and I wanted to add that she wasn't a part of any "we" if there was one. But I sucked in a breath and edged away from going down that road with her.

Okay. She *was* part of the "we" because we were a family business. Aunt Jack, no matter how edgy her return was making me, was part of the family.

"What kind of stuff?" I asked.

She put her bag down on the stainless steel prep table with a thud. I was thinking maybe there were bricks in there to throw at my glass wall overlooking the falls that she didn't like.

She pulled out a stack of catalogs.

"I called the lottery sales rep," she said. "They said they could have us set up by next week."

I raised an eyebrow. "Set up for what?"

"To sell lottery tickets. And my candy guy." She tugged on her wig, straightening it out. "I've put in a call to him. We did really well when we sold candy. Especially licorice." She patted her hair down in place. "They let me request different-flavored ones. I came up with flavors people loved."

"People love my flavors of ice cream," I said.

"No one's ever heard of ice cream made from tea or buttermilk." She clucked her tongue. "You need to make some changes," she said. "I can help you."

"Did you try them?" I asked. "The tea or buttermilk ice cream? Because they are really good. The customers love the flavors I come up with." I looked at her. "Most of them are Grandma Kay's recipes."

I thought me telling her that they were her mother's ideas might soften her some on the idea of the new flavors. It didn't.

"They'll like the candy better, Bronwyn." I didn't like when she called me by my full name, she made it sound like she was scolding me. "It's tried and true. And the lottery tickets will bring people in here who don't want to buy anything."

Why would we want people in the store who aren't buying anything?

I tried to shake off my confusion. "I don't think we need candy," I said, trying to sound respectful, but I was getting annoyed with her conversation.

"If you want to get any customers in here, you do! This place is as empty as a mausoleum."

"We're not opened yet, Aunt Jack."

She slapped her hands on her hips and pursed her lips. "I don't think you'd get anyone in here even if the door was flung wide open and you were giving that stuff away."

I started getting ready for the day, walking around Aunt Jack, reaching over her head and avoiding even glancing at her mound of catalogs.

She stood in the middle of the floor for a while watching me work, then started walking around inspecting everything. I didn't know what she expected to find, but I knew if she found something she didn't like, I'd hear about it.

"Why is this cat always in the window?" she yelled from the front of the store. She acted as if she'd just noticed Felice. Hadn't she seen her when we came in the door and I sat there on the window seat with her? "She doesn't even look real," she was saying. "You'll probably scare the customers away with it. She needs to go."

I didn't respond. Felice never left that window seat. Never bothered anyone. In fact, all the customers that even noticed her liked the cat, too.

I sighed. The only one I thought that needed to go was . . .

"I'm going to get breakfast," Aunt Jack came into the kitchen and announced. I was sure we hadn't been there any longer than twenty minutes. Already she was ready to go.

I exhaled a sigh of relief. That made me happy.

"Okay," I said, smiling as sweetly as I could. "Have a good breakfast!"

After she left, I went to the front of the store and turned on the jukebox. It sat on the far wall all red, silver and shiny.

"You want a little music, Felice?" I said, crossing the room. "It'll calm our nerves after our morning with Aunt Jack."

There were fake vinyl 45s that sat inside the glass front, and between songs, there was a clicking sound like the records were changing. But it was all preprogrammed. A customer couldn't choose what they wanted to hear, just what I had programmed, and that was all Grandma Kay's kind of music.

There wasn't a Pandora or music streaming in my grandma's day. But there was always music. She used to bring a portable turntable and play her albums all day long. Customers always asked what she was playing.

And she would always say music that was good for the soul. She loved jazz and rhythm and blues. And singers like Dinah Washington, Brook Benton and Ray Charles, and because of her, so did I.

And my grandmother liked trying new ice cream flavors. She had a whole recipe box full of them. A box that my grandfather had kept hidden until I took over the ice cream shop. He said he knew my grandmother wouldn't want anyone else to have them but me.

Maybe Aunt Jack didn't like the recipes my grandmother had come up with, or the jukebox I had installed to play her music. But I did. I liked everything about what my grandmother had done. She was still alive and smiling in my heart.

And even though Mr. Mason might be going through some kind of mental health issues at the moment, I knew that what he said wasn't too far off from what my Grandma Kay would have said if she was still around. Like he had said, my grandmother *would* have been proud of what I'd done with Crewse Creamery.

I was always going to keep her memory alive in the ice cream shop she started, and Aunt Jack with her lottery machines and candy catalogs wasn't going to change that.

And as if in agreement, "Hit the Road Jack" by Ray Charles came on the jukebox.

"I hear you, Grandma Kay!" I said, looking upward. "That's exactly what I was thinking."

I busied myself with checking inventory, washing down the display case and pulling out the ice cream from the walk-in freezer.

"Morning!"

My mother came in the side door with Rory and PopPop in tow.

"Hi," I said and glanced at my watch. "That was a long cup of coffee." I raised an eyebrow.

"You know how your mother gets," PopPop said. "She pulled out all of the family albums."

"Rory, sorry," I said. "My mother made you suffer through my baby pictures."

"She showed her everyone's baby pictures," PopPop said.

"No?" I said and looked at Rory.

She nodded, saying it was true.

"She enjoyed it, didn't you, Rory?" my mother said.

Rory looked at me and nodded again. Then she smiled.

"It's nice to meet one of your New York friends," my mother said, not noticing the looks Rory and I were passing to each other. "I'm going to take her to my jitterbug class later. I've already told my instructor I am bringing a guest." She pointed down at Rory's heels. "But she's going to have to get rid of those."

I laughed. "Rory had plans to go to the art gallery this morning," I said. "Black Market Paper Fine Art. Didn't she tell you?"

"It's okay," my mother said. "My class is later this afternoon. She'll have time to do both."

I shrugged. "I tried," I said to Rory.

She smiled. "It's okay. I'm sure I'll enjoy learning how to jitterbug."

"A talent you'll probably use often in your life in New York," my grandfather said with a smirk. "I'm going up front to my bench." He held up his backgammon game. "I've got things to do."

"I'll go with you," Rory said. "I want to check on the catalogue raisonné I ordered."

"I thought you were looking for an online one," I said, remembering that was what she was doing when she borrowed my laptop the night before.

"No. I found a site for one, but it was unavailable online. Seemed to have been some kind of problem. I got to chat with a Becky, and she said she'd try and send me one. Funny, she said that I was the second person that called and asked to have one sent to this zip code."

"Others interested in the Florida Highwaymen?" I said. "That was good you reached a real person."

"Yeah, it was. And hopefully"—she held up her cell phone—"she'll call and tell me she'll be able to get one here in time for the sidewalk fire sale."

"A sidewalk fire sale?" my mother asked.

"Yes, for some of the artwork at the gallery," Rory said.

"You didn't notice the flyer in the window?" I asked my mother.

"No," she said. "I'll have to check it out."

"Then," Rory said, "I have to figure out how I'm going to get the money to buy something."

Rory walked out front with PopPop. I could tell my mother waited until they were out of earshot.

"She doesn't have money and she wants to buy something from Baraniece and Ivan's shop?" She shook her head and turned up her nose. "They are expensive over there and what they sell isn't even appealing."

"They're having a fire sale."

My mother laughed. "There's been no fire. They probably just realized that their stuff is so overpriced that no one is buying it."

"Maybe too much for us to afford on an ice cream shop salary, but she's got a New York income."

"I remember what you made," my mother said. "And unless she's robbed a bank or killed a rich uncle, Rory won't be going home with anything from that gallery."

chapter

SEVENTEEN

O h my goodness! Oh my goodness!" Maisie came barreling in through the front door of the ice cream shop. Late but excited. "Did you guys hear?" She stood on the customer side of the display case, bracing her hands on top of it—I think it was the only way she could stay still.

"What is going on with you?" I said. My mother came over and stood next to me. Rory and my PopPop were seated at his bench. He'd talked her into playing a game of backgammon with him before she headed over to Black Market Paper.

"Oh my goodness! They found a pair of bloody shoes."

"A pair of—"

"In a dumpster. In the alley." She didn't let me finish, talking over me. "What a clue!" She was out of breath, her cheeks flushed, you would have thought she'd found a million dollars. "Now we know it had to be a woman that killed Zeke Reynolds."

"You don't know that."

"And you don't know that I don't know that," she said.

I switched gears. "Are you the one who found them?" I asked. I knew it hadn't sounded like that was what she meant. But I knew that she'd been talking about solving Zeke Reynolds's murder, and I wouldn't have put it past her to go dumpster diving.

"You found shoes?" Rory got up from the bench, leaving in the middle of a game.

"No," Maisie said. "I didn't find them."

"Then how do you know?" I asked.

She ducked her head and cringed, pulling her shoulders together and crunching up her face. "I was kind of lurking around."

"Lurking around?" Rory said. She seemed concerned. "Where?"

"I went to see the crime scene and there were people there."

"People?" I said.

"You know," she said, "the forensic team."

"Oh my," Rory said, licking her lips. "Like on *CSI*?"

"I don't think Chagrin Falls has a forensic team," I said.

"I have to go," Rory said, her voice shaky. She swiped a hand across her forehead and I could see it trembling.

"What's wrong?" I said.

Rory shook her head, but no words came out.

"Are you okay?" my mother said to her and started around the counter to see about her, but Rory was already headed out the door.

"And she takes off again," Maisie said, like she was announcing a horse race.

"Rory!" I called after her. "Rory!"

"She's gone," Maisie said.

"Look what you've done," my mother said to Maisie.

"I didn't do anything!" she protested.

"Maybe not to Rory," I said. "But you're going to get into trouble with the things you do."

"With who?" she asked.

"Me, if you keep being late to work, especially if it's because you're snooping around in things that don't involve you." I hated sounding like the grown-up, but I did have to manage the shop.

And to be honest, with Aunt Jack snooping around, it made me even more aware of my duties in running the place.

"Detective Beverly—" Maisie began.

"Oh, here we go again!" I had to chuckle. She was still convinced that Detective Beverly had asked us to help him investigate. I just couldn't seem to make her understand that the police would not recruit amateurs to solve a crime. Yes, he accepted our help on the first murder, but not in the way she was trying to get involved. We'd given him information we had, but this time, like I'd told the detective, we didn't know anything. And it seemed what Maisie had found out, she had found from sneaking around following the investigators. I jerked a finger toward the back. "Get an apron and come help me out. I'm swamped."

Maisie looked around. "There's no one here." She glanced over at my grandfather on the bench. "Except PopPop."

"It's my shop," PopPop said.

"Customers will start coming in soon. I'm expecting a line out the door." I said that so my mind could overcome Aunt Jack's earlier statement about no one coming in. "And," I continued, "if you're not back here helping me, Aunt Jack will try to."

Maisie took to whispering. "Oh, is she here?"

"She was," I whispered back. "She hates my ice cream."

"Why?" Maisie asked.

"I don't know," I said, shaking my head. "She hasn't tasted any of it."

"She hated the window in the back, too," Maisie said.

"I know," I said, disgust in my voice. "She hates everything."

"Everything except the idea of her taking back the management of the shop," Maisie said.

"Yeah, I know," I said. "Like her ideas and skills are so much better than mine. She even said we should go back to selling lottery tickets and candy."

"Oh no," Maisie said, scrunching up her nose. "Did you tell her you put candy in your ice cream sometimes?"

"I know. That makes no difference to her," I said. "But this time I had buttermilk and tea. And per her that was terrible."

"She doesn't like that?"

"Oh no," I said. "She says no one likes that. Brought in a bunch of catalogs so 'we'"—I did the air quotes—"could pick out the stuff we needed to order to set it up."

"Ugh!"

"Exactly," I said.

"Where is she now?" Maisie asked.

"She went to get breakfast." I rolled my eyes. "She hadn't been here ten minutes, long enough to irritate me, before she left."

Maisie looked up at the clock. "How long has she been gone?"

"Two hours!" I shook my head. "Where did she go to get breakfast? Pittsburgh?"

Maisie chuckled. "I'll get my apron."

I heard the jingle of the door as soon as Maisie came back out from the back. "Welcome to Crewse Creamery" was out of my mouth before I realized who it was.

"Morning, O!" Maisie said.

Morrison "O" Kaye was a law professor over at Wycliffe University and the first person to come in and buy ice cream after we'd opened in the midst of a snowstorm. He'd told us he'd gotten his nickname as a child because he was always saying "okay." After I'd gotten to know him, I realized he still had that habit.

And after his first visit, he'd been in the shop almost every day since.

Like my grandfather, O came by the ice cream shop just to hang out. I didn't mind too much, it was good business for customers to see people inside sitting down. My grandfather enjoyed his company, but of course, my mother and Maisie teased that it wasn't the ice cream he liked.

"Morning, you two," he said.

"Hi," I said.

He glanced over at the seat usually occupied by PopPop and nodded a hello to him. O had quickly made friends with my family and friends, but if he was hanging around fishing for something more from me, he was going to be disappointed. I had a business to run. Added to that, commissioning and overseeing my new food truck, I didn't have time for anything else.

He stood in front of the display case and, lowering his eyes, he studied what was inside like he did every time he came. I didn't change ice cream that often, but like my father, he was thoughtful before making decisions.

I liked that he was like my father.

O wasn't bad looking. Dark with skin as smooth as the chocolate I melted in my double boiler. He wore his curly black hair cut low. He was tall—nearly six feet—with deep-set brown eyes and teeth that were white and straight.

He wore a bright smile always on display from the moment he walked in our door. But I wasn't going to let that wear me down.

"So, Maisie, you keeping up with the Zeke Reynolds murder?" O asked.

"Of course," she said. "Detective Beverly asked me to help him."

I rolled my eyes. I was tired of arguing with Maisie about whether the detective wanted her help or not. Cable television shows with everyday kinds of people solving complicated crimes had already taken over and devoured any common sense or reasoning she had. Plus, O was good friends with Liam Beverly and an advocate of the rule of law. He wouldn't believe that a legitimate law enforcement officer would recruit two girls from the local ice cream parlor to solve a gruesome crime.

"You got your favorite sidekick working it with you?" O asked Maisie.

"No," I said, answering as the sidekick. "And I'm not her sidekick." I heard a jingle at the door. "Welcome to Crewse Creamery," I said and left Maisie and O to their conversation. While I waited on the steady stream of customers, she gave O a double scoop of the mint mojito coffee with a squirt of chocolate syrup over it and talked about the shoes that had been found in the dumpster and how Veronica and Zeke had argued.

Oh, I thought, not wanting to confirm by getting into the conversation. But now thinking Maisie must have been the one who told my mother about the fight at her grandmother's restaurant.

I shook my head. If gossip could solve a crime, my mother and Maisie would win a place in the Guinness Book of World Records for solving the most crimes ever.

chapter

EIGHTEEN

I was sitting at my little makeshift desk in the kitchen, arms folded across my torso, and one leg on top of the other. I was supposed to be working on QuickBooks—doing invoices and expenses, busy backroom kind of work, but necessary if our little business was going to have a good standing in the business community.

But my laptop's screensaver had popped up at least a full thirty minutes ago. Hand perched on mouse, I stared at the bubbles bouncing around and tried to wrap my head around my friend's erratic behavior.

Rory.

Something was definitely going on with her. She wasn't her usual self. I had thought maybe it was because she'd gotten a demotion at her job. Or what she called a demotion because she couldn't work with art anymore. When you're unhappy with your job, it can affect so many other areas of your life. And someone would have to be very unhappy to travel over four hundred miles to try to woo someone back that had quit. That someone being me. She must be really desperate and maybe all those things were affecting her.

She was acting so strange. She'd left in what seemed like a panic and, it seemed, for no apparent reason. All that was said was that shoes were found. But now mulling it over, I had noticed a pattern with Rory. And with Maisie's news about those shoes being found in a dumpster, things were starting to come together. And not in a good way.

"What are you doing?" It was Maisie. "Thought you were doing some office kind of work." She pointed at my computer screen. "You're not doing anything."

"I know," I said. "I can't concentrate." I turned on my stool. "How's business out there?"

"Good," she said. "Busy. Line out the door just like you predicted. First break I had; otherwise, I would have been back here long before now to check on you."

I frowned. "I don't need checking on."

"Okay," she said, thoroughly unconvinced.

"Did Aunt Jack see the crowd?" I asked.

"Oh, that crowd tuckered her out a long time ago," Maisie said and waved a hand.

"Good," I said and let out a huff.

"So you want to tell me what's wrong with you?"

"No," I said, knowing better than to let Maisie in on what I'd been thinking.

"Does this have anything to do with your friend rushing out?"

I let my eyes drift off past Maisie. It had everything to do with that. But I thought it better to keep my lips tight.

"You can tell me," Maisie said. "I am one of your best friends."

"You are," I said and gave her a warm smile.

Riya, Maisie and I had known each other since kindergarten and didn't miss a day seeing each other until we left for college. But we didn't miss a beat once I got home. I could count on her through thick and thin. Riya, too. Our friendship had transcended those bounds long ago—now they were family.

I eyed Maisie. She was going to run with what I'd been contemplating. Fuel for her fire. But she was right, I could share anything with her.

"I hate saying this," I said. "And you have to promise that you are not going to freak out and jump to all kinds of conclusions. Okay?"

She frowned and sucked her tongue. "You know I can't promise that," she said and grabbed my arms, giving me a shake. "Anybody who knows me would know I can't promise that."

"That's true," I said.

"But I will try," she said and pulled up a stool.

I blew out a breath. "I think Rory knows something about the murder."

"I knew it!" Maisie said and jumped up.

"Oh my, Maisie, I'm just getting started."

"Oh, right. Sorry." She sat back down. "Continue." She made a rolling motion with her hand, prompting me.

"When we went to eat at Molta's last night," I said, ready to spill all I'd been thinking about, "Ari acted as if he'd seen her the night before we saw her at the coffee shop."

"I thought you told me she didn't get in until just before we saw her?"

"That's what she told me," I said. "And even Mr. Mason said he saw a red ball bouncing the night before."

She nodded, her face seemingly not registering that observation.

"Rory is the red ball," I said, helping her get what I meant.

"Oh," she said, nodding her understanding. Her hands went up to her head. "Her hair." She pretended to pat the bushy red mane that was Rory's hair.

"Yes," I said. "And there's another thing."

"What?" Maisie said, scooting to the edge of her seat.

"Rory, for as long as I've known her, has worn Louboutins. She bought a pair once and didn't pay her light bill because she couldn't afford to do both."

"Red-bottomed shoes?" Maisie questioned.

"Red-bottomed shoes," I confirmed. "Although I looked it up and the news report didn't say anything about them having a red bottom." I squinted my eyes at her, silently questioning if she was sure that was what she saw.

Maisie nodded her head, telling me that was what they were. "I saw them, Win. They had red bottoms to them."

I sucked my teeth. "I believe you," I said. I really hadn't doubted what she saw, I was just hoping that maybe there was a chance . . .

"What?" Maisie prompted me to continue.

"It's those red-bottomed shoes." I inhaled a breath. "They just really have me worried."

"Why?"

"Rory loves Louboutin shoes. She has this one favorite pair

that I know she would have brought to Cleveland, and I haven't seen her in them yet." I bit my bottom lip. "Not to say she doesn't have them with her."

"Those are her shoes." It didn't sound like Maisie was asking a question. I gave her a snarly look, so she said it again, this time forming a question. "The shoes found in that dumpster. You think they're hers?"

"Oh, Maisie, I don't know." I slumped down in my chair. "I hope not. I hope those weren't Rory's shoes."

"So you were right," Maisie said, appearing to be proud of me for some reason. A broad smile emerging across her face and her eyes brightening.

"I was right about what?" I asked.

"That it might not be a shop owner who killed Zeke Reynolds."

I had to think about that comment for a moment to get what she meant. "Maisie!" I shrieked. "I am not saying that."

"That what?" she said, egging me on to say what she meant out loud.

"What you're saying," I said. "You know what."

"That Rory is the killer!"

"Oh!" My head fell to the desk with a *thud*. It hurt, but I didn't care. I wished I could knock such a thought out of my head.

"If those were her red-bottomed shoes that they found in the trash . . ." Maisie stood up and walked in circles as she laid out her theory. She sounded like she was telling a scary story. "Red-bottomed shoes, and red blood all over the top of them, then . . ." She stopped and looked at me, eyes wide. "Your friend Rory Hunter would be the murderer."

I bounced out of my seat. "Don't say that!" I said. "Don't say it." I turned around in a circle and wiped the sweat I could feel beading up on my head with my hand. My heart was racing and my mouth was dry.

Had I shared my house with a murderer? Did I really consider a *friend* someone who was capable of murder?

Oh my goodness!

"You know she did it, don't you?" Maisie said.

I turned and stared at her. "No. No, I don't know she did it." Something was telling me she hadn't done it. "And neither do you."

"A lot of evidence is pointing toward her."

I held up a hand to stop her from her further speculations. "There was a lot of evidence pointing to my father when Stephen Bayard was killed. A family nemesis injected with succinylcholine, a drug that only surgeons should have access to. And my father," I said, talking fast, my words spewing out, "with no witnesses other than my dead grandmother to corroborate his whereabouts."

"Yeah, but everyone knew your father couldn't do something like that." Maisie wasn't going to be easily persuaded from the decision she'd come to.

I knew I shouldn't have shared my thoughts with her.

"I know Rory couldn't do something like that," I said.

"Do you?" Maisie asked.

"I do," I said. "You don't know her like I do and she wouldn't kill anyone." I had lowered my voice and was talking fast. I had pointed a finger at Maisie but pulled it back. I was getting upset with her. "And, Miss Agatha Raisin from Acorn TV, why would

Rory kill Zeke Reynolds?" Maisie was standing looking at me wide-eyed. "How in the world would she come all the way to Chagrin Falls, just happen to run into someone she hates enough to kill and then have the opportunity to do it?"

"I don't know," Maisie said. "But that sure looks like what happened."

chapter

NINETEEN

I hadn't the faintest idea of where Rory had gone when she left, and I worried about her the entire time I waited on customers alongside my mother and Maisie. Wilhelmina had called in sick. I hoped it didn't have anything to do with the old-lady-you-can't-have-my-man face-off she'd had with Rivkah. She was a good employee. I'd hate to lose her.

I wanted to talk to Rory. To find out why she kept running when things about the murder or her whereabouts the night it happened were brought up. I could have kicked myself for not having that conversation when I first started thinking that something was wrong with her. Now she may have gotten away, and I'd never be able to talk to her about it.

It bothered me so much that I told my mother I needed to leave.

"Leave?" she said.

"I need to find Rory."

"Where is she?" my mother asked, lowering her voice and looking over her shoulder at the customers lined up.

"I don't know," I said. "But I need to find her. Check on her. See if she's okay."

"Oh," she said, nodding thoughtfully. "You think she went back home?"

I raised my eyebrows and gave her a look that said I hoped not, but she may have.

"Yes, then go," she said. "You think something's wrong?"

"I don't know that either," I said, pulling off my apron. "That's what I want to find out."

This was one of the days I wished I'd driven to work, I realized as I left through the front door of the ice cream shop. My little car was tucked on the side of the house where I rented space. I needed a quick way to search a lot of places because I didn't have the foggiest idea where she'd go. A coffee shop down Chagrin Boulevard. The art gallery. Home.

I wasn't chasing her if that was where she went. But I had to admit that it was a possibility that she hopped on the highway and headed back to New York.

Especially if she had something like murder to hide.

I shook that thought out of my head. Like I told Maisie, I knew my friend.

And then I saw that red mop of hair and I released a breath I didn't know I was holding.

"I thought you had left," I said.

Rory was sitting on the steps in front of the Victorian where I lived. Technically, those steps belong to my landlord and she was trespassing, but I didn't care. I was happy to see her, and I know it was easy to see the relief on my face. Her face, however, wasn't easy to read at all.

Her eyes were puffy and her cheeks tear stained. Her usually fully gloss-covered lips were bare and she sat motionless, arms wrapped around her like she was cold.

"Your door was locked," she said. "I couldn't get my bag."

"You were going to leave?"

"I can't convince you to come back, so why not?" She shrugged.

I sat down next to her and put my hand on her knee. "Were you just going to sit here until I closed the shop and came home?"

"I really hadn't decided," she said. "I was thinking I could leave without my bag. Let you send me my things later."

"You were going to leave that Dooney and Bourke here with me? I can't believe it." I tried to make light of the conversation to see if I couldn't get her to feel better.

She tried to chuckle at my comment, but it got caught in her throat. And the hiccup that came out of it seemed to bring tears, too.

"I really don't know what I was going to do," she said. Talking to me, she couldn't seem to let her eyes meet mine.

"Then it's a good thing I came home early, huh?" I said. "Maybe I can help you figure out what to do."

"I don't know how you could," she said.

"Why don't you let me try?"

She straightened out her arms and rested them on her knees. "I don't even know where to start." The words bubbled out with a sob. A sob that took control of her entire body. She folded her arms so that her hands rested on either side of her head. "How cliché, huh?" she said through tears. "I don't want to be cliché."

"Aww. Don't cry." I leaned forward to make my head even with hers. "You have been acting too crazy to be cliché," I said. I wanted so much to make her feel better. For her to tell me what was wrong. To tell me that how she'd been acting had nothing to do with Zeke Reynolds's murder and that Maisie was crazy.

Actually, I didn't need her to tell me the last part. I already knew about Maisie.

"Why don't you just tell me what it is that has you so up in arms? Why do you keep running out on me?"

I waited for her to answer. Getting dizzy from my head hanging to meet her face, I gazed into her eyes. Hoping to see something there. She just stared back. I took my knee and bumped her with it. "Well?"

"I don't know," she said. She drew out her words like a petulant child. "What do you want me to say?"

"Oh, I don't know," I said and bumped my knee against hers again. "Maybe you could start by telling me why you lied about when you got to Ohio."

She looked at me with what seemed like fear in her eyes. "You know about that?"

"Wasn't hard to figure out," I said. "Ari saw you. Mr. Mason saw you. Right?"

"Yeah, they did," she said.

I raised my brow, letting her know she hadn't been as surreptitious as she thought. "And I'm thinking you lost your room at Dell's bed-and-breakfast because you showed up a day late, not hours late."

I finally got out a chuckle. "You are some kind of detective, aren't you?"

"I don't know about that because I still haven't been able to figure you out yet. What is wrong with you?"

She hung her head, and I could see her eyes filling up with tears again.

"Tell me what is giving you so much grief." I rubbed her back. "Please. Let me try to help."

That opened the floodgates, and those tears just kept coming. She buried her head in her lap and sobbed. I was worried she was going to be dehydrated she cried so much and so hard. I didn't have a tissue or any calming words to offer—I had no idea what to say. I didn't know what was wrong with her, and my trying to get her to tell me just seemed to upset her even more.

After a few minutes, I thought I needed to say something. I opened my mouth a few times to speak, but words didn't come out. I just took a deep breath and tried again to get her to tell me what could make her so upset.

"Rory," I said, lowering my voice and trying to exude some compassion. "You have to tell me what's wrong. I might could help." She mumbled something and shook her head. I took that to mean she didn't think I could help. "Is it about your job? You hate your job now that you're not able to do the artwork?"

I felt like one of those mothers talking to their wailing infant. A child who had no understanding of the language, yet Mom still asking, "What's wrong?" and expecting an answer.

"Because you can always get a new job," I said. "I can help you, if you want." I nodded my head to reassure her although she wasn't looking at me. "If you want to draw or paint or whatever it is that you want to do then do it. Don't be sad about it."

I put my arm across her shoulders and leaned into her. "Rory," I said. "I want to help you. Please let me help you." Then I tried the line that Maisie threw at me. "I'm your friend. You can tell me anything."

That seemed to make the crying slow down.

Rory lifted her head and, sniffing, she swiped the tears from her face with her hands.

"Those were my shoes," she said. She said it with such a calmness after all that sobbing that it took me aback.

"What shoes?" I asked, knowing full well which shoes she meant.

"The bloody shoes," she sputtered out. "The ones Maisie was talking about they found in the dumpster."

"Oh my goodness," I said. Then the words tumbled out of my mouth. Words I didn't believe. Words that couldn't be true. Words I *hoped* weren't true. "You killed Zeke Reynolds?"

"No! No!" She sat up and grabbed my hands in hers. I wasn't sure if they were just clammy or filled with her tears.

"It's okay. If you did, it's okay," I said, knowing good and well that if she had killed him it wasn't okay. That nothing was ever going to be okay for her again. It couldn't be if she killed a man. And nothing was going to be the same for me if my friend did turn out to be a murderer.

"No, Bronwyn!" She stomped her foot. "I didn't kill him! I could never kill anyone!"

"Your shoes were there. You were there. How are those your shoes, then, if you didn't kill him?"

"He was already dead when I saw him."

"Already dead?"

"Yes." She hissed out the word. "When I found him." She

hung her head and shook it. "When I found him. He was already dead." She lowered her voice and said the words again. I didn't know if she was trying to convince me of it, or convince herself. "He was already dead!"

I repeated almost the same thing I'd been saying since I found her on the steps of my house. "Tell me what is going on. Because I don't understand."

She sniffed and swiped at her eyes again with both hands. "I came in the night before, you were right. I had a reservation at that bed-and-breakfast on American Street, but I was hungry and didn't want to turn in on an empty stomach. I didn't know that there wouldn't be some kind of fast-food restaurant or all-night diner or something in Chagrin Falls. But when I couldn't find anything, I thought I'd at least get a cup of coffee at a gas station if I had to. So, I decided to drive around the block but I got turned around and ended up in the alley behind the shops."

"That's where they found his body," I said.

"That's where *I* found his body," she said.

"You saw him when you drove around there."

"Not at first," she said. "But then . . . then I turned on my bright lights. So I could see better." With her arms wrapped around herself, she bent forward like she was in pain. "And that's when . . . That's when . . ."

"When you saw his body?"

She sniffed and nodded.

"How did your shoes get there?"

"I got out of the car. I don't know why." She stared blankly. "It was dark in that alley and I just wanted to . . . I don't know . . . make sure I was seeing what I thought I was seeing."

"You got close?"

"Too close," she said. "It's really been bothering me ever since."

"Yeah, I can tell."

"My shoes had all that blood on them and I didn't want to get it in my car. So I pulled them off and threw them away."

"But they were found two blocks away."

"I didn't want them to be associated with the body." She closed her eyes and pulled in air through her nose. "I walked the two blocks. No one was out. No one saw me and I figured no one would look that far away for any evidence. They'd just go out with the trash."

"Why didn't you just call the police?"

"Because who is going to believe me?" She looked at me, her eyes wild. "I'm not from here and I was standing right in the alley with him."

"I believe you," I said. Then I remembered how she had asked me how I felt when I stumbled over a dead body. That had worried her.

"You're not the police," she was saying. "And . . ." Her words were hesitant. "I didn't know if I'd be able to talk about it."

That I believed. It took me forever to get her to tell me about it. She had to understand it was the right thing to do, though, but before I could impress that on her she said something that stopped me.

"This isn't the first time this has happened to me, Bronwyn."

"What do you mean?"

"I found a body before."

"Oh no," I said.

"When I was sixteen." She blew out a breath trying to keep

the tears at bay. "I had to go through all kinds of therapy. Feelings of guilt and depression."

"Why? Did they accuse you of something? Is that why you didn't think the police would be unbiased?"

"No." She shook her head. "No one ever accused me. It was just so traumatizing. I was in that police station for hours. In a room all by myself. I just wanted to go home. To forget everything I'd seen. I didn't think I'd ever get past it." She looked at me with pleading eyes. "I just don't want to go there again. Can't you understand that?"

"Again," I repeated softly, thinking how hard it must be. Rory wasn't anything like Maisie. Maisie found it intriguing to keep stumbling across murder victims.

"Yeah, again," she said. "I just can't believe it happened to me again." She turned, her eyes sad. "I'm sorry, Bronwyn. I just panicked." She threw up her hands. "I panicked and I was ready to run." She started crying again. No sniffling back the tears.

"Don't worry, I'm here with you," I said. "You don't have to do this by yourself this time."

"Thank you, Bronwyn," she said.

I stood up and brushed off my pants. "C'mon," I said and stuck out my hand to help her up. "We're going to the police and get this all straightened out."

"No!" she shouted and smacked my hand away. "We can't!" She shook her head so hard I thought she'd rattle her brains loose. "I can't."

"Yes, you can. You have to."

"I don't have to."

"Yes, you do," I said. "Because if you don't they will think that you killed him."

"I didn't kill him!" she shouted.

"I know. I know, Rory. But you were here. In town. People saw you and you lied about it."

"I only lied to you."

"And my family," I said, then I cocked my head to the side. "And you have his blood on your shoes."

"No one will ever know those are my shoes."

"Why wouldn't they know?" I questioned. "Didn't you take them off?"

"Yes. I just told you I took them off and I threw them away."

"And I'm guessing you're thinking that your shoes won't have your fingerprints on them."

She bounced up like a jack-in-the-box. Realization lighting up in her eyes. "I hadn't thought about that," she said.

"And didn't you have to get a background check and finger-printed before going to work at Hawken Spencer? I know I did."

"Yeah." She nodded.

"So, they *will* find you," I said. "With the wrong idea in mind."

"I need to go and talk to the police, don't I?"

"Yeah, you do." I wrapped my arm around her shoulder and gave it a tug. "It'll be okay, Rory," I said. "I'll go with you and stick by you. I won't leave your side."

chapter

TWENTY

I had been inside the Chagrin Falls police station only one other time. And, like Rory, it was to talk to Detective Liam Beverly. I knew how scary it had been for me, but I couldn't imagine how she felt.

When I came to talk to him, I was trying to plead with him to understand how my father could not have murdered anyone. I remembered him saying to me that everyone said they were innocent, and it didn't mean they were.

Still I tried to convince him that my father was a skilled surgeon and a distinguished doctor. He had an answer for that, too. He said wherever the evidence led him that was where he would go.

That was what had made me decide to figure out who had killed the man I'd found at the bottom of the falls because after that visit, I knew the detective didn't care anything about my father.

Just like I was sure he didn't care anything about Rory.

I did find, though, by the end of that investigation, that Liam Beverly was open-minded and took pride in doing the right thing.

I hoped that worked in Rory's favor.

After we got to the police station, amid my loud protests, Detective Beverly took Rory to a back room without letting me go with her. She looked back at me when they led her away, her eyes wide with fear, her bottom lip trembling, tears that wouldn't stop falling. I felt so bad for her and I felt like I had let her down. I had told her I'd be right there by her side. She wouldn't have to face another police interrogation about murder alone. And now she was in there. All alone. Just like she said she had been after she found that first body.

I just hoped Rory was faring in there by herself better than I was out in the lobby by myself because I was a nervous wreck. When I had come in to talk to Detective Beverly, I had been mad. I'd come in wanting to give him a piece of my mind, and the more I had talked to him, the angrier and more determined I'd gotten. But today, like Rory, filled with fear and uncertainty, I was scared and I needed somebody to hold my hand.

I fished my cell phone out of my jeans pocket and put out an SOS. I called my mother first, then I called PopPop. I repeated the same story on each call and they both said the same thing when I finished—"I'm on my way." PopPop even wanted to know should he bring a thermos filled with coffee.

Rory had made friends with my family, and when my family welcomed a person in, they were always willing to come and help out.

I paced the floor, wringing my hands, clicking my nails, worrying about what the police were saying to her. My mind was in a whirl. I didn't know whether they were going to arrest her or whether they believed that she'd only found the body, and that she wasn't responsible for it being there.

It wasn't long before both my parents arrived and my grandfather. I was so happy to see them.

"Daddy," I said and buried my face in his chest. "I'm glad you're here."

"Of course I was coming to see about you, Pumpkin." He held me tight. "I don't have to go to the hospital until later," he said. "To check on a couple of patients. Your mom told me what happened."

Even though she'd told my father, my mother made me explain everything to her all over again, rubbing my arms the whole time, trying to comfort me. Her alarm was escalating with each word I uttered, even though it was the second time she was hearing it.

After I'd gone through the story—twice—I went back to pacing. My mother paced with me. I could see that she was just as upset as I was. My father and grandfather had this innate calmness to them that I definitely didn't inherit.

PopPop stood against one wall and my father against the other, both with their hands in their pockets. Both of them telling us, at different times, we should sit down before we wore a hole in the linoleum.

But I knew if I stood still I was going to explode.

Then after what seemed like an eternity, Rory emerged. Her eyes were as red as her hair. Her shoulders slumped. And her head was down. I don't know if it was from shame, from disgust or because she was tired. I rushed over to her.

"What did they say?" I asked.

"They told me not to leave town," she said.

"They couldn't think you did it," my mother said, putting her arm around Rory. "You couldn't ever do anything like that."

My mother didn't know what kind of girl Rory was, what she was capable of. She'd only just met her. But when she said it, she looked at me, and I knew that she knew if Rory was a friend of mine, she was okay.

I wondered why I had let thoughts contrary to those seep into my head.

"No. I couldn't," she said. "I only hope they believe me." She turned around and looked back at the door she'd appeared from. "I don't know." She shook her head. "They said that I could get into trouble just for not reporting the body." Her face tuned up for another bout of crying. "I didn't know that. I didn't mean to do anything wrong. I just wanted to get away."

My mother looked at my father. "Can she get in trouble for that?" she asked.

My father raised his eyebrows and shook his head. "That's something I don't know, but we sure can ask a lawyer about it."

"I don't have a lawyer," Rory said, sniffing.

"I do," my father said.

My father had gotten a criminal lawyer, a superlawyer, as they're called, after Detective Beverly put him at the top of his suspect list for no other reason but that my father was a surgeon. The detective had questioned him once at the house, then asked him to come down to the station. My father knew better than to go in without representation.

I wished I had thought about that before I sent Rory in alone. I wasn't well versed in all things murder. And I hoped I wouldn't ever have to be.

My father must have read my thoughts. "Don't worry, Rory. I'll give him a call. You won't have to talk to that detective without one from here on out."

WE WALKED OUT of the police station and the rush of warmth from the sun felt good after spending an hour wrapped up in turmoil and fear for my friend.

As soon as I got outside, my cell phone rang. To my surprise, it read *Morrison Kaye, Ohio Call*. I put up a finger to tell my family to wait a second.

"Hi," I said, almost like a question. "How did you get my number?" I didn't ever remember giving it to him.

"Your grandfather gave it to me."

"He did?" I swung around and glanced over at him. He was talking to Rory, looking like he was completely innocent of anything.

I swung back. "No matter." I shook my head to clear thoughts of what my grandfather's intentions were in sharing my phone number. "I'm glad you called."

"You are?" He sounded just as surprised as I'd been seeing his number pop up on my phone. I could hear the smile in his voice.

"I need your help."

"With what?"

"It's confidential," I said.

"Okay. You know I do confidential."

"I have a friend—Rory Hunter—who found a body and didn't report it."

"*The* body?"

"Yes," I said, letting the "s" linger. "*The* body." That was a good way to put it. "Zeke Reynolds."

"How did you find out she found the body?"

"She seemed to be hiding something. The time she said she got in was off, people saw her and every time someone said something about the murder, her face went pale."

"So she kind of gave herself away? No poker face?"

"Exactly. Plus, she's the owner of the shoes Maisie told you about this morning."

"Ohhh." He let the word drag out. "How unfortunate."

"To put it mildly."

"Okay, and is this the girl you told me about earlier from out of town?"

"Yes." He remembered. "I talked her into going to the police."

"Liam," he said.

"Yeah, and he told her don't leave town."

"Okay."

"That upset her, and I just want to try and help Rory feel better."

"I can try and help you do that," he said. "She needs a lawyer."

"My dad is getting her one. But I'm not sure when he'll be available to talk to her." I shrugged. "I don't know, can you just answer some questions maybe?"

"Sure," he said. "Whatever you need."

"Thank you."

"I understand," he said. "She came down to visit and gets tangled up with this kind of stuff. She probably won't want to come back again."

"Rory actually came down to get me to come back to New York and to my old job," I said.

He didn't say anything, so I kept talking.

"And then my aunt Jack came to town."

"The one that used to run Crewse Creamery?" he asked.

"Yes. And I'm sure she wants to take back over the store. She doesn't like anything I've done and grumbles and complains about it every time she's there." I huffed. "Rory thinks that it's a sign that she came at the same time as Aunt Jack."

"A sign of what?"

"That I'm supposed to go back. My boss, old boss, authorized her to tell me about a big raise they're willing to give me along with my own office instead of a cubicle."

I finished my sentence and waited for O to answer. There was silence over the phone.

"Hello?" I said, then looked at the phone to see if I had dropped the call.

"No. I'm here," he said.

"Anyway, I don't want to talk about me, I want to talk about Rory."

"You want me to come back to the ice cream shop?"

"No," I said. "Don't you have a class?"

"I do," he said. "In about an hour. You want to come out here to the university?"

"I'd have to go home and get a car," I said.

"How about you just ask me now, then? Ask me your questions."

"I wanted to include her." I felt like I was making this hard and that was definitely something I didn't want to do.

"Okay," he said. "How about we just do a three-way call?"

"Or I just put you on speaker."

"That'll work," he said.

"Now I just gotta figure out where me and Rory can go that's private and talk to you." I chewed on my bottom lip. I was more or less me thinking out loud, not expecting an answer.

"Go in the alley between your building and the Flower Pot," he said. "No one ventures that way."

I smiled. "Perfect."

Even though it was where we kept the garbage cans, it probably was the only place nearby where there wasn't foot traffic and a lot of listening ears.

"I'll call you back," I said. "Is this a good number?" I glanced at my phone. "The one that popped up on my screen?"

"Yep, that's my cell phone. Call it anytime."

"Okay. Bye," I said breathlessly and clicked on the "End" icon.

"You going back to work?" my mother asked when I rejoined the group. My mother had her arm around Rory and she had put her head on my mother's shoulder.

"I was thinking I'd talk to Rory for a minute, Mom," I said. I looked at Rory, she looked deflated and I knew she wanted to talk to someone now. I didn't know how long the lawyer my dad was getting would take to sit and talk with Rory, but I didn't want my parents to think I was wasn't grateful for their help. "I want to find out everything that happened."

Rory lifted her eyes to look at me. They looked like they were too heavy for her to keep opened.

"Everything is going to be okay," my mother said and rubbed Rory's arm. "But you take your time. I've got the store covered."

"Rory and I will walk back that way with you," I said.

"Okay," my mother said.

My father left to call his lawyer and get over to the hospital to see his afternoon patients. He promised Rory that he'd make sure the lawyer got over to talk to her as soon as possible.

The four of us, PopPop, my mother, Rory and me, walked back over to the ice cream shop in silence. Rory and I took our aforementioned detour—after we passed the Planted Pot, we ducked between the two buildings.

"Don't worry," I said as I pulled out my phone. "Everything is going to be okay, I promise."

chapter

TWENTY-ONE

How I was going to keep my promise to Rory, I wasn't exactly sure, but I was going to try.

I trusted that my father would get Rory a lawyer. And he would be a good one, but I knew O would help us right now and make everything we needed to know easy to understand.

I hadn't ever seen O handle a case, and as far as I knew, I don't think he even practiced law, he taught it.

Former police officer and current law professor at Wycliffe University, O was a wealth of information. He didn't actually tell me things, he mostly told me where I could find them. I was hoping this time to get more specific information.

As for us having a personal life, that was only in the hopes and dreams of my mother and Maisie. O was handsome, I couldn't deny that, and if I opened my mind (and heart) to him, I was sure feelings for him would spread like wildfire. He was so agreeable and helpful. Always seemed to show up just at the right time. But, right now, I wasn't open to that. Didn't know if

I'd ever be. I hadn't had a boyfriend since high school, and there was way too much on my plate right now—building a business, readying a food truck and dealing with the murders that kept popping up in Chagrin Falls—to deal with matters of the heart.

"I'm putting you on speaker," I said to O after I called him back. First, though, I had to explain to Rory what we were doing. Rory and I stood facing each other and I held the phone between us.

"I'm still going to talk to the lawyer your father is getting for me?" she asked.

"Yes, but O will help you understand."

She nodded to let me know she was okay with that.

"Hi, Rory," he said. "Sorry you have to go through all of this."

"Thanks," she said. I saw a weak smile cross her lips.

"So, O, Detective Beverly said that she could go to jail for not reporting the crime. Can she?"

"No," he said. He didn't even think about the answer. "Not for not reporting."

"Why did they say that?"

"It was a scare tactic," he said. "Not many things he could have charged her with. Maybe obstruction of justice. Evidence tampering. Abuse of corpse."

"What are those things?" Rory asked. Her eyes filled with confusion and panic.

"I don't think they are anything you have to worry about. But let me ask you a couple of questions," he said. "Is that alright?"

"Yes," Rory said. "That's fine."

"What do you know about the actual murder?"

"Nothing," she said.

"Did you see the murder happen?"

"No."

"Think about what you saw that night," he said, and he paused in speaking as if he was giving her time to do that. "Do you think you saw the person who did it?"

"No, I definitely did not," she said. "I didn't see anyone."

I was concerned with that answer because I knew she'd seen Ari and Myles Mason, but I didn't say anything. I'd talk to her about it later and if necessary talk to O about it, too. I didn't think either one of them had been the killer, but it might just be important.

"Did you want to or try to hide something or someone from the police so they wouldn't find out about the murder?"

"No," she said. "I would never do that."

"Why did you throw your shoes away?" he asked.

"Because they had blood on them."

"O," I said and leaned into the phone. "This isn't the first time she's found a dead body."

"No?" he said. That seemed to catch his interest. "Were you charged with anything that time?"

"No," she said adamantly.

"Did you touch Zeke when you saw him?"

"Oh my goodness no," she said. "I got close because it was dark and I wanted to be sure I was seeing what I thought. That's how I got the blood on my shoes. It was all over the ground."

"Well, to me, it doesn't sound like you did anything illegal," he said.

"You know that from those few questions?" I asked. "Because

she was back there talking to Detective Beverly for an hour or more."

"He asked way more questions," Rory agreed, nodding her head.

"Every crime has elements—components—more than one—and for the crime to be able to be proven, every single one of the components has to be completed. You understand?" he asked.

"Yes," we both said.

"I just asked you a couple questions. Each of them was one element of things I thought Detective Beverly might have been talking about when he said he could arrest you."

"And she didn't do any of those things," I said.

"Right," he said.

"And if I didn't do any part—any one of the elements—of whatever he was saying he could charge me with, then I couldn't have done the crime?"

"Exactly," he said. "Liam kept you so long and asked so many questions because he has to be thorough. He needs any and all information he can get to solve the murder. But he can't charge you with anything, Rory."

"That's a relief," she said.

"Yeah. You'll be fine. If all the things you told me are true, you did nothing wrong."

She blew out a breath. "It's all true." She sniffed back tears. I rubbed her shoulder. I didn't want her to do any more crying.

"Okay," he said.

"Can he really stop me from leaving town?"

"Not really," he said. "Not unless he was going to charge you with something and he's not. But you should stick around. You need to get yourself untangled from this whole affair. Okay?"

"Okay," she said.

"And don't be afraid of my friend Liam, he is just trying to do his job."

"I wouldn't want his job," Rory said, "if I had to scare people to get it done."

"There are plenty of days he doesn't want his job either," O said. "Especially after all these murders started happening in his usually crime-free city.

"But," he continued, "with you having blood on your shoes and the police finding them, people, including the killer, are going to know you'd been around where the murder took place and they won't know what you saw. Or rather didn't see."

"Small town, Rory. Gossip fuels enough flames to keep fires burning all winter long."

"I told you," Rory said, "I don't know anything. I didn't see anything—other than the body."

"No one will know that for sure, and the killer might not want to take any chances."

"What are you saying?" Rory asked.

"I'm saying that you have to be careful," he said. "And to you, Win . . ."

"Yes?" I said, surprised that it sounded like he had a warning for me.

"I was kidding this morning when I asked about you and Maisie looking into it."

"I didn't say anything like that this morning."

"I know," he said, "but you can't go around trying to solve this crime. Rory might not be safe after word gets around that she was there that night."

I didn't say anything.

"Win, you hear me?" he said. "You guys should leave this one alone."

"YOU KNOW WHAT we have to do." Maisie assaulted me as we walked through the door. She came around the counter to the door in a frenzied rush, grabbing my arms and dragging me into the back. I was sure my mother had told her everything that had happened. Rory followed behind us.

"Investigate," I said. "We have to find out who did this."

"Wait. Really?" she said, seemingly deflated that I had agreed so easily. "I thought I was going to have to talk you into it."

"No, we have to help Rory, I see that now. And I don't know anybody better to help me to help her than you."

A smile beamed across Maisie's face.

"Didn't your friend just tell you not to investigate?" Rory said.

"What friend?" Maisie asked.

"O," I said. "We just talked to him so he could help explain what kind of trouble Rory could be in with the police for throwing away those shoes and not reporting seeing the body."

"Can she get in trouble?" Maisie asked.

"O says no," I said. "But that doesn't mean that Liam Beverly won't give Rory grief as he follows his clues."

"So what was O saying about not investigating?" Maisie asked.

"He thinks that it may be dangerous for Rory if we did. But I'm thinking the dangerous part is already out."

"What do you mean?" Rory asked.

"People will find out that you were the owner of those shoes whether we investigate or not," I said.

"People like the killer," Rory said pointedly.

"Right," I said.

"Don't you think that the police can solve this without our help?" Rory asked.

All I could think about while I was pacing the floor waiting for Rory to finish talking to Detective Beverly and while we were on the phone with O was that I wanted to find out who really killed Zeke Reynolds. I wanted my friend, who had come to Chagrin Falls because someone sent her to talk to me, to be able to go back home and paint or draw or whatever it was that she wanted to do that would make her happy. And I prayed that never again in her life would she find another dead body. I was sorry that she saw one because of me, and it seemed to me that it was my responsibility to see to it that she got back to New York safe and happy.

Yeah, yeah, that meant trying to solve another murder. I didn't like the thought of it, or what had happened the last time I did it. I pushed out a breath. I was going to have to shove my brush with death to the nether reaches of my mind.

"Yes." I nodded. "I know that he can solve it," I said to Rory. "But sometimes it takes a long time to solve a crime—a murder."

I looked at Maisie for confirmation. She knew more about this stuff than I did. She nodded. "You want to wait around for that?"

Rory looked like she wanted to say something, but instead a sorrowful look filled her eyes. She rubbed her temples with her fingertips and shook her head.

"We were at that meeting when everyone got mad at Zeke Reynolds," I said. "And while Detective Beverly didn't ask us to solve the murder when he stopped by the morning after"—I looked at Maisie—"he did make a good point. We might have been there with the murderer that night. I think that's where we should start."

"I don't think the murderer was at the meeting." Maisie raised her eyebrows. "But if you're willing to do this, I'll go along with your theory. One way or another we'll figure this out," Maisie said.

"You think you can?" Rory asked.

"I hope we can," I said. "I think it had to be someone here in Chagrin Falls. It was just like the last murder. The person was from out of town and came here and was murdered. We didn't have a roomful of potential suspects that time and we solved it."

"Yeah, we did!" Maisie said, dipping her shoulders and rocking them back and forth like she was some gangland East Coast rapper.

"I think we can do it this time. But we need to stay under the radar. Not get in the way of the real investigation. But if we do find out anything, we can take that information to Detective Beverly."

Maisie beamed with happiness and satisfaction. I thought she might explode.

"And I know just where we should get started," I said.

"Where?" Rory and Maisie said in unison.

"The Village Dragon Chinese Restaurant."

"What is that?" Rory asked.

"Maisie's grandmother's restaurant," my mother said. I was surprised to see her—she must have popped in the back while we had our heads together on what to do.

"I don't know why you think you should go there, Win," my mother said.

It was understandable she felt like that. She'd been quite distraught about me being caught up with a knife-wielding murderer in a stairwell. Talk about my family being overprotective. For months after that, I thought my parents were going to make me move back into my childhood home.

"You know the people that were there at that meeting. Most of them," she said. "Known them all your life. And the ones you don't know are neighbors. I feel safe with you talking to them."

"Unless the person they're trying to get information from *is* the killer," Rory said. "Then Bronwyn wouldn't be safe."

"Oh my," my mother said. She placed a hand on her cheek and looked at me like something bad had already happened.

"Hey, can I get some help out here!"

It was Aunt Jack.

I looked at my mother and I could see her trying not to laugh. "I don't think she's used to having this many people in here," she said. "Bet it surprises her that people will buy ice cream."

I walked out front and Aunt Jack was running around like a jackrabbit. She had sweat running down her face and beading over her top lip. Her lipstick was smeared and her wig was lop-sided.

"I can't do this all by myself," she huffed when she saw the four of us.

"Thank goodness she was around to help even though I knew you wouldn't be so happy with her being here." My mother leaned into me and lowered her voice. "PopPop suggested we call her in to help Maisie when we came up to the police station."

"I was happy you guys could get to the police station," I said.

But watching Aunt Jack trying to dip up ice cream out of the display case and make milkshakes with the machine, I had to chuckle. I guess I should be grateful she had been available. But I was definitely going to talk to my grandfather about her. I needed to find out what she was up to.

"We need to go," Maisie said, coming up behind me. "We have to get this investigation rolling."

"I can't leave," I said.

"Your mom's back," Maisie said.

"My mother has Zumba or yoga or something," I said. I knew she could only take so much drama, even though she seemed to seek it out, before she had a meltdown.

"It was my jitterbug class but don't worry about it," my mother said. "I'm going to stay here, even with your aunt Jack underfoot. And PopPop is here."

"Okay, good," Maisie said, "because we need to strategize and to do that we need food."

"Is that why we're going over to her grandmother's restaurant? To eat because I couldn't—"

Maisie looked over at Rory. "You have to eat." She looked at me. "She needs food so that she'll feel better."

Maisie was so much like her grandmother, she thought food would help solve everything. I've never known her to sit shiva or go to synagogue, but there was a little old Jewish woman nestled somewhere deep inside of her trying to wiggle her way out.

chapter

TWENTY-TWO

The Village Dragon Chinese Restaurant was on the opposite leg of the town triangle from the area where Zeke Reynolds's company wanted to build a mall.

A *paifang* graced the front entrance, and inside the entryway was a beige carpet with cherry blossoms that butted against wood floors in the dining area. There were golden dragons everywhere and mural landscapes on the walls and red lanterns hanging from the ceiling.

Everything was Chinese including the cook, everything except for the owner.

"What's the plan?" Rory said.

"First thing is that we eat," Maisie said. "Can't think on an empty stomach."

We were sitting in our favorite seats. The ones that Maisie, Riya and I occupied whenever we came to the restaurant since we'd been in the second grade. I slid in on one side, Rory sat beside me and Maisie took her place across from us.

Rory held up her hands like she was defeated. I assumed she was thinking we were her only hope, so she figured she would have to go along with our cockamamie plan, though her eyes told a different story. I understood how she felt. She wanted to hurry and get out of this whole mess. But what she didn't understand was that there was no getting around eating, not when it came to Maisie or her grandmother.

"Fine," Rory said. "I need a menu."

"No," I said. "No menus. When Savta sees us she'll just get us food." I shrugged. "She seems to think she knows what we want better than we do."

"Bronwyn," Rory said, leaning over to me and lowering her voice. "I don't know if I can do this."

I rubbed her arm and nodded and tried to sound reassuring. "It'll be okay," I said. "We'll eat and figure this all out."

I couldn't believe I was saying "eat" and everything was going to be okay. I was turning into Rivkah and Maisie.

Rory blew out a breath and sat back up. "Okay," she said. "I'm not sure how much I can eat, and I don't like a lot of things."

"Don't worry," I said. "She'll bring us enough food that you'll find something that you like."

"I brought you coffee," Savta said. She came over to our table after we got settled in with a bowl of boiled eggs and a pot of the dark, steamy hot drink. "I heard you can't live without it."

Rory looked at me.

"Information travels fast around here," I said, and figured I may as well make Rory's introduction to Savta formal. "Rory, this is Maisie's grandmother, Rivkah Solomon. Savta, this is my friend from New York, Rory Hunter."

"I know who she is," Rivkah said as she poured the coffee in Rory's cup. "It's good to meet you. You are in good company." Rivkah nodded. "And I'm Win's grandmother, too."

"Yes, she is," I said and smiled.

"But not that Riya's," Rivkah said. "She's a bad egg." Then she pointed to the bowl she'd set on the table. "Eat," she ordered. "I'll be back with more food."

"Do you have Szechuan chicken?" Rory asked, catching her before she left the table.

"I know just what you need," Rivkah said. "Lin, my cook, is the best cook anywhere around. You'll be okay, once you eat." She patted Rory on the arm and leaned down toward her. "My granddaughters will make this all okay for you. You'll see." She smiled at Rory.

I gave Maisie the eye. I didn't want it being spread around what we were doing. That we were going to investigate the murder.

Savta, like my mother, was big on gossip. I suspected it had probably been my grandfather who had informed Rivkah what we were up to. First giving O my phone number, now telling Rivkah what we were doing. I'm sure PopPop was trying to make up about the Wilhelmina thing, not that I was sure that he and Rivkah had a thing. Now our operation would be all over town. Me and Maisie trying to be Sherlock Holmes and Watson. I'd rather people we questioned funneled us information instead of us giving it to them.

"We're not helping in any way, Savta," Maisie said. I think she understood. "We're just trying to figure out what happened to help Rory feel better."

"Sure." She winked. "I'll get you two something to drink," she said before walking away.

Rory stared down into her coffee cup, took the spoon and stirred, before putting it up to her nose and setting it back down.

"Who is Riya?" she asked.

"Our other best friend," Maisie said. "She's a doctor and our bodyguard."

Rory frowned.

"Long story," I said.

Rory reached across me and grabbed the condiment stand. She dumped four packs of sugar in and three of the little tubs of cream.

I raised my eyebrows. "You haven't even tasted it yet."

"I'm afraid to," she said. "Coffee is my comfort, and as stressed as I am right now, if I get a bad cup it might just shove me over the edge."

"Don't worry," Maisie said. "We'll get you a gallon of it to keep you calm. We can go over to the Juniper Tree."

"Oh no!" Rory said. "I cannot get a cup of coffee from that place."

"Why?" Maisie said. "It's pretty good."

"Not if you're a coffee connoisseur like Rory is," I said. I looked at Rory. "But you might have to suck it up and drink it, Rory, because it's the only coffeehouse around." I pursed my lips. "I don't know if 'not leaving town' means the Village of Chagrin Falls or not. Because technically, we're a part of Cleveland, so would it count if we drove one suburb over? Not sure."

"They have decent coffee one suburb over?" Rory asked.

"Java Joe's are practically on every block," Maisie said.

Rory acted as if she was swooning. We laughed. First one for Rory. I was happy to see it.

Rivkah came back with a Pepsi for me and a ginger ale for Maisie. We ripped the paper off the straws and took huge gulps.

Rory, on the other hand, picked up her coffee cup and took a sip and set it back on the table. "I'd rather have your grandfather's coffee."

"So," Maisie said, "what now?" She picked up an egg and cracked it on the edge of the table and started peeling it.

"Well, like I said back at the shop, I think it may be true that we might have had eyes on the murderer when we were at that SOOCFA meeting. That gives us a place to start."

"Well, you know, like I said back at the shop, I think it was someone who wasn't there, but you're in charge," Maisie said. I raised an eyebrow. It was not like her to give in so easily.

"Oookaay," I said, not knowing what Maisie was up to.

"What?" Maisie said. "I just want to get this investigation going. So who do we talk to first?"

Now I could see why she'd agreed.

"Well, after I said it to you guys about looking into the people at the meeting, I started trying to think who was there and I realized I don't know if I remember."

Maisie tilted her head thinking. "I remember the guy who sat in front of us and turned and said they were taking everyone's livelihood. And I remember the guy who was standing by the manikin."

"I do, too," I said. "But who are they?"

Maisie let out a laugh. "I don't know," she said. "Your mother said that you knew most of them."

"I know the people that have owned their shops for a long time," I said. "I do know people like Mrs. Cro, who was there, and I remember Amelia Hargrove."

"Yeah," Maisie said. "She came in with Zeke Reynolds."

"Debbie Devereaux," I said.

"And who else?" Maisie asked.

"You know, now I remember looking around at the faces that night and not knowing a lot of them."

"So how will you know who to question," Rory said. "Or who the killer is?"

"I have someone in mind," Maisie said. "And they were there that night."

"Who?" I asked.

"With the fight that Zeke and Veronica had," Maisie said, "and coupled with the high-heeled shoes found in the dumpster"—she looked at Rory and smiled a "sorry"—"I had decided Veronica was our number one suspect."

"You don't think that now?" Rory said, remorse over her actions with her shoes written all over her face.

"No," Maisie said and handed Rory an egg. "She is still a good suspect." She took a bite of her egg. Rory laid hers on the saucer in front of her untouched. "The number one suspect in my mind, or at least a good place to start, especially since right now we can't identify a lot of the SOOCFA members that were present."

"You originally thought it was Ari," I reminded her.

"Ari is a shop owner, so to speak," Maisie said.

"Ari is the guy who owns Molta's, right?" Rory said.

"Right," I said.

"Yeah. He saw me when I got out of the car and tried to go into the Juniper Tree for a cup of coffee."

"And it was closed," I said, finally finding out when it was she saw him.

"Right. Which now I know was a good thing," Rory said.

"You've never tasted that coffee!"

"All I know is that I wish I had some of Ari's coffee right now," Rory said. "That is, if he's not the killer."

"He's not," I said.

"He's still on my list," Maisie said. She looked at Rory. "Did he have any blood on him, or look like he was hiding a gun in his pocket, or something?"

"No," she said.

"And about what time was it that you saw him?" Maisie asked. I could tell the clue had just come to her as it did me. For me, it helped set a timeline. I knew Maisie was still trying to find out if Ari was indeed a killer.

She shrugged. "I don't know. Maybe around nine, nine thirty?" Her eyes drifted off as she thought about it. "I remember my directions said my arrival time was nine, but after I got here I drove around for a bit."

"I have food for you!" It was Lin. Speaking low, he had a sparkle in his eyes. He knew about the gossip swirling around Rory and what we were doing, I was sure, but he, without even knowing her, was trying to put her at ease.

He had two trays full of it, balancing on his arms, but he still was able to bow. Without even teetering the plates, he placed platters on the table and announced what each one was. "Spicy kung pao. It's really spicy." He nodded, scrunching up his nose. "Made with peanuts swimming in soy-sesame sauce and hot chili paste. These are crispy golden-fried egg rolls. Hot." He shook his hands as if the rolls were burning his fingers. "They're filled with shredded cabbage and juuui-cy shrimp." He brought his shoulders together and puckered his lips. "Sweet and salty browned curls of thinly sliced twice-cooked pork stir-fried with leeks, fried rice, steamed rice, fresh broccoli and chunks of white-meat chicken. Really good. I stirred in brown sugar and ginger sauce. And . . ." Lin placed the last dish on the table in front of Rory. "Szechuan chicken. Just for you."

Lin Hou Xie came to the United States from China when he was seven years old. He attended grade school and high school in Newark, New Jersey. He graduated from Rutgers with a degree in English and food science then went to the Culinary Institute of New Jersey before moving abroad to study French cuisine in Paris.

Now, on his own initiative, he was working as the head (only) cook in a Chinese restaurant owned by a Jewish woman in the Village of Chagrin Falls, Ohio.

I had always believed, from the time I was a little girl, that Lin was actually only in our small town because he was hiding out from the law. Why else, with his training, would he be in such an out-of-the-way place with the skills he had.

Savta, of course, swore her cook hadn't ever done anything even close to illegal, although the two of them tended to whisper a lot. And, of the two murders we'd had in Chagrin Falls, Maisie had never once thought of suspecting Lin. I guess she would know, with her penchant for sleuthing, if he was some sort of fugitive from justice.

But he was a really good cook, and I'd eat anything he made.

"I thought I wasn't going to be able to eat," Rory said. "But this smells so good."

"I made it just for you," Lin said again, a big grin on his face. "I knew you'd like it."

"He doesn't always come out and talk," I said, surprised.

"I don't serve customers, but today is special." He turned to Rory. "I like to see my customers smile. You smile. Okay?" he said, then backed away before turning around and walking briskly into the back.

"Does everyone around here know about me?" Rory asked.

"Probably," Maisie and I said together.

"So, back to the investigation," Maisie said, heaping a big helping of the twice-fried pork onto her plate.

But before we could start talking, we heard a commotion from the kitchen area. Lin had made a U-turn and was coming back out of the swinging door he had just disappeared behind. Rivkah was following him.

"I don't have a gun. Okay?" Lin's voice went up three octaves. "The gun's not here." Lin stopped abruptly, held out empty hands and shook his head as if he was at a loss.

"Don't act innocent with me," Rivkah said. "It was here. Right there in the kitchen."

"And now it's not!" He scratched his salt-and-pepper hair. "Okay! I know nothing!" He waved both his hands back and forth. "Nothing!" he said. "You look for it!"

"I did," Rivkah said. She seemed sure he knew where it was. "I've looked everywhere."

"Did you look here?" he said and pointed to the counter. He walked over and, without actually looking for anything, said, "No. Not here!" Then he walked to one of the dragon statues and looked into its open mouth. "No. Not here, either!" He went back to Rivkah. "You know why?" But before she could answer, he said, "Because it's not here!" With that, he marched off and disappeared through the swinging kitchen doors.

"Did you hear that?" Maisie said, her voice straining. I was sure she wanted to scream what she'd just learned. I didn't let her know I knew what she meant, but she had to know that little show was too contrived and coincidental for her to think it just *happened* in front of us.

"What?" I asked.

"The missing gun."

"A missing gun?" Rory said, almost losing the green peppers and chicken she was stuffing into her mouth. She took her fingers and stuffed them back in.

"Thought you couldn't eat," I said.

She hunched her shoulders while she was chewing on the steamed rice that followed, then she took her napkin and wiped her fingers. She'd been so engrossed in the food, she hadn't heard us. "I just realized, I haven't eaten in forever and with all the crying I've been doing..." She took a big bite of the egg roll she'd doused in Lin's homemade duck sauce. "I guess I'm just drained. Gotta fill back up."

"You guys. There's a missing gun," Maisie said, getting us back on track.

"What?" Rory said, blinking her eyes, tuning back in. "Now what did you say?" She swiped the napkin across her mouth.

"The missing gun," Maisie said. "There's a missing gun."

"Missing gun?" Rory frowned. "Oh," she said, nodding. "The cook." She chewed and swallowed whatever leftovers she had. "Does that mean Lin had it and killed Zeke?"

"What? No!" Maisie said, her forehead filled with creases. "Someone else took it." She raised an eyebrow. "And I know who."

"Veronica?" I said flatly.

"Yes!" Maisie nearly leapt out of her seat. She acted as if she'd just discovered the smoking gun. Literally.

"And how did you come to that conclusion?" Rory said, then she looked at me, leaning over her plate ready for another mouthful. "And how did you know that's what she meant?"

"We've been friends a long time," I said. "I know how that brain of hers turns."

"It works the same way as everyone else's," Maisie said.

"I knew she'd come up with that because Zeke and Veronica were in here arguing," I said. "And according to my mother, or whoever she heard it from"—I eyed Maisie—"Veronica left via the kitchen in tears."

Rory stopped, fork midway to mouth. "She put all that together from those two different events?"

"Yes," I said. "It's what she does. How she works through to find the true criminal."

"Oh," Rory said, pushing the food to a corner of her mouth. "Does it work?"

"No," I said.

"It doesn't hurt," Maisie said. She took a sip of her pop. "But I know a way to find out."

"Uh-oh," I said. No telling what Maisie was going to say.

"Savta." Maisie wiped her mouth and turned to her grandmother. Rivkah was searching behind the counter. "Savta!" Maisie called.

"What?" Rivkah stood up. "You need more food?"

"No. We have plenty. I want to ask you something."

"I am in a crisis right now."

"I know. That's what I want to talk to you about."

"Do you know where the gun is?" she asked, her eyes narrowed. She seemingly had no concern for what she was saying and how it would affect her other customers.

"Savta!" Maisie said. "You can't say that out loud."

"You don't think they heard Lin yelling about it? Everyone knows about the missing gun now."

Maisie shook her head and hopped out of her seat. She grabbed her grandmother's wrist and pulled her to the table. "When did the gun come up missing?" she asked.

"How am I supposed to know that?"

"When do you think it was?" Maisie plopped back down in her seat.

"I don't know," she said, putting her hand on her cheek, "how"—her voice got louder—"am I supposed to guess when it went missing when I don't know!"

"I was thinking, Savta, that when Veronica ran through the kitchen, she may have taken it."

"Who is Veronica?" Rivkah asked.

"Remember you told me about that couple who were arguing in here?" Maisie reminded her.

"Oh yes," she said. "And the one who turned up dead?"

"Yes, well, Veronica . . ." Maisie looked at me. "What's her last name?"

"Russell."

"Veronica Russell is Zeke's girlfriend." Maisie turned her attention back to her grandmother. "That was the woman's name who went out crying after the argument."

"Oh!" Savta's entire face lit up. "You think she took my gun and shot him with it?"

Everyone in the restaurant was looking at us now.

"Maybe, Savta," Maisie said, lowering her voice, hoping, I'm sure, that her grandmother would do the same.

"And she ran through the kitchen on her way out?" Rory asked as she crunched her way through a piece of broccoli. "Why would she do that?"

"If I knew that, I would know why the stars don't fall out of the sky," Savta said.

"Because they aren't under Earth's gravity," Rory said. She pushed her plate aside, leaned back and rubbed her stomach. "I wish solving all of this was as easy as answering that question."

"Tell us what happened, Savta," Maisie said. "Tell us every detail."

Rivkah waved for Maisie to scoot over then sat down in the booth next to her. "I can't stay long because I have a gun to find. Unless you're right"—she nodded at Maisie—"and the girl took it. Otherwise, I need to find it before someone else does."

"Zeke and Veronica were arguing," Maisie said, moving her grandmother along.

"I know that," Rivkah said, not getting the hint. "I told you."

"Then what happened?" Maisie asked. "Tell Win and Rory."

"Okay." Rivkah turned to us. "They were arguing. First, whispering across the table, but it was easy to see it was heated. Then she started screaming and crying. Poor thing." Rivkah waved toward a booth across the room, probably the one they'd sat at that night. "She said, 'I wish you were dead,' or something like that, and—"

"Wait, Savta!" Maisie grabbed ahold of her wrist. "You didn't tell me that part."

"What part?" she said.

"The part about her saying she wished he was dead." We all said some iteration of that line all at once.

"How could you just be telling someone that part now?" I added.

"Is it important?" she said. "Because now she got her wish." She shrugged.

"Oh my, Savta," Maisie scolded. "You should have told us."

"Well, now I have," she said. "You want to let me finish the story?"

"Yes," I said. "Go ahead, please."

"Such good manners. She says please. Her grandmother taught—"

"Savta!" Maisie said.

Rivkah shrugged. "See what I mean?"

"Savta, please," Maisie said.

"That's better." She smiled at Maisie. "So then she, the girl or girlfriend, so you say, tried to go that way"—she pointed to the front of the store—"but there were a lot of people standing waiting to come in. I think she was embarrassed. So she ran toward the bathroom."

"And?" I said.

"That's the last I saw of her," Rivkah said.

I frowned. So did Rory.

"So you don't know if she went out the back door or not?" I asked. "Through the kitchen?"

"I never said she did," Rivkah said. "I agree with Maisie that if she did go out that way, she might have taken that gun." Her voice trailed off. "I could have sworn that was where I put it." She got up without saying anything else and disappeared behind the swinging black door.

"That didn't sound promising," Rory said.

"Especially since she didn't say that she'd gone through the kitchen."

"Right," she said, biting her bottom lip.

"It's what you said, Maisie, and I'm almost sure it's what my mother said," I said accusingly.

"It gives us someplace to start," Maisie said, oblivious to the fact that her grandmother's story was like a kaleidoscope, full of different colors and ever changing.

"Someplace to start?" Rory asked.

"A lovers' quarrel, you mean?" I said.

"Yes. Because a lovers' quarrel has always been a motive for murder," Maisie said, answering Rory's inquiry with a definitive statement.

chapter

TWENTY-THREE

This already was turning out to be an übermessy investigation. In the course of one meal (albeit a very big meal), Maisie had come up with *two* definite killers.

The only good thing that came out of our powwow session was that Rory was doing better. She ate seconds and I think thirds, and even washed it down with two cups of Savta's coffee. Seeing how well I knew her aversion to any weak cup of joe, after those two cups with no complaints, I figured she was coming around or she was more traumatized than I'd thought.

"Where are we going to find Veronica Russell?" I said when we stepped back outside. I had to pull out a pair of sunglasses to cover my eyes—coming out from the low-lit restaurant to the bright sunlight made them hurt.

"I don't know," Maisie said. "She and Zeke were staying at Dell's bed-and-breakfast, but after what happened, Veronica probably left."

"I wouldn't want to stay so close to where it happened," I said.

"If they were dating, she has to be feeling pretty sad right about now."

"If they are big-time businesspeople, or in Zeke's case *was* big-time businesspeople, she probably didn't stay in Chagrin Falls," Rory said.

"Why not?" Maisie said.

"Because this place is . . ." Rory looked at me and smiled. "Quaint," she said. "And they are in the big league and like to live like that."

"Then how will we find her?" Maisie said.

"Maybe we should start somewhere else," I said. "The crime took place here, right behind Ms. Devereaux's place. The evidence has to be here, too, don't you think?"

"Do you think she did it?" Rory asked.

"Who?" I said, Maisie saying the same thing right after me.

"The lady you just mentioned. Ms. Devereaux."

"Oh no," I said. "She don't take no mess, and didn't seem to like him the night he spoke at the meeting. But she wouldn't kill a complete stranger. Or leave him at her back door."

"I don't think she did it either," Maisie said. "Her store isn't one of the ones that would need to be cleared out for the mall."

"She didn't do it," I said. "But she is the person we need to talk to." I remembered what my grandfather had told me when I had decided to investigate the last murder. He said she was the first person I should have gone to.

"Who is she?" Rory asked.

"She has the inside scoop on everything." I nodded. "I'm sure she would have found out something with everything happening right in and around her shop."

Debbie Devereaux owned the Exquisite Designs clothing boutique. And she was the epitome of that name. She was always dressed sharp, always ready with a quip and like I had said to Rory, knew what was going on in town. But unlike my mother and Rivkah, she didn't dispense the information she had willy-nilly. You had to go to her, and like she was the Queen of Chagrin Falls, petition her to get her to tell you whatever she knew.

We walked into her shop in a clump, sticking together. We wended around the racks of clothes and waited for her to appear. I don't think any of us, although for different reasons, were as ready as we thought for starting our own investigation.

"Hi," Ms. Devereaux said, coming out from the back. "What are you girls doing here?"

"We came to see you," I said.

She was dressed in a white sheath dress with glittery rhinestones dancing around the neckline that fit nicely over her still-present curves.

"What did you want to see me about?" she said, her eyebrows rising over her brown Wayfarer glasses.

"This is my friend Rory Hunter," I said, backtracking some. Ms. Devereaux wouldn't want to say much if she didn't know who she was saying it to. "She came down to visit me and—"

"Got caught up in all of that murder mess?"

Rory looked at me. She shouldn't be surprised anymore how fast word got around in our little neighborhood.

"Yes," I said.

"Don't tell me you two"—she wiggled her finger from me to Maisie—"are trying to solve this thing."

I opened my mouth to deny it, but didn't want to lie to Ms. Devereaux. I respected her too much for that.

"We're just trying to help our friend," Maisie said.

Looking at Maisie, I smiled. I liked that she said Rory was *our* friend.

"By investigating?" Ms. Devereaux said.

"By helping the police have suspects other than my family and friends in their crosshairs," I said.

"Good for the two of you," Ms. Devereaux said. "But you better be careful." Pointing a finger at us, she continued as she went behind the counter. "Because whoever killed that man, and I'm sure it could have been anyone in my back room that night, is still out there. They haven't come forward and confessed, so my guess is they don't want to be caught." She started writing on something on her counter and, without looking up, said, "He or she just might be willing to kill again. And this time it might be one of you."

"Do you know who he or she is?" Maisie asked.

"If I knew, I would have told the police," she said. "They would be in custody and the three of you wouldn't have to be running around here like the Keystone Kops."

"We wanted to get a list of the people that were at the meeting the other night," I said. "Do you have one?"

"No. People just came," she said. I figured she'd ask me why I needed it, but she didn't.

"I didn't recognize a lot of those faces," I said. "I hadn't realized there were so many shop owners I didn't know."

"Most of those people weren't shop owners," Ms. Devereaux said. "I was surprised they were there—it was like a town hall meeting. Then after that man started talking, I realized that must've been why they were there."

I looked at Maisie, wanting her to see that my idea to check shop owners was a good idea.

"How did they know about him? And how did they know what he was going to talk about?" I asked.

"I don't know," she said. "To both questions. I had no idea. I thought we were there for your announcement, Maisie. Took me completely by surprise."

I looked at Maisie. The fact that people who were there were not shop owners meant, to me, that it wasn't necessarily a disgruntled shop owner. It could just be a disgruntled citizen of Chagrin Falls.

"We were also wondering if you knew where we could find Veronica Russell," Maisie asked.

"And who is that?" Ms. Devereaux asked. I knew she knew exactly who that was. They both had been in her back room and had, before the murder, stayed at her sister's bed-and-breakfast.

"Zeke Reynolds's, uhm, partner," Maisie said, seemingly unsure of what to call her.

"Oh, the woman with the easel?"

I didn't know why Ms. Devereaux was playing like she didn't know. She had just freely given us information—now she wanted to be coy. But we needed to push forward if we wanted to get answers and help Rory.

"Yes." I spoke up. "We were thinking if we could talk to her . . ."

"You don't think the police have done that?" she asked.

"Do they know that the two of them argued?" Maisie asked.

"I know," Ms. Devereaux said. "Stands to reason they would know, too."

We lowered our heads, me trying to rethink the situation. I don't know what Rory and Maisie were thinking.

I guess we hadn't thought about what the police already knew and that we were probably retracing their steps, and that took the wind from our sails. The whole idea of being an amateur sleuth was to come up with something the police hadn't thought of.

But now, thinking about that, the police would have had to be the ones who were the Keystone Kops if we were able to outsmart them that easily. And Detective Beverly was anything but.

"We wanted to ask Veronica, Zeke's assistant, about something we just found out," Maisie said. "Something the police probably don't know about yet."

Ms. Devereaux looked up from whatever she'd been doing and stared at us for a moment. It looked as if she was trying to figure out if we were trying to bluff her. Something I was sure she wouldn't stand.

We didn't say anything. I thought it smart of Maisie to come up with the idea of us chasing the gun and that being the reason, and even smarter that she didn't say what it was. The police couldn't have known about the gun found to be missing. It had only just happened.

"Veronica Russell and Zeke Reynolds booked one room, and later two, at Dell's bed-and-breakfast. And after the murder, Veronica didn't check out of her room. For whatever reason," Ms. Devereaux finally said. She nodded her head toward Rory. "Curly Top over there would know that if she had checked into her room when she got in instead of trolling around the city in the middle of the night."

"It was nine—"

I grabbed Rory's wrist, gesturing for her not to say anything. She didn't know Ms. Devereaux like I did. "Is she still there?" I asked.

"Best way to find out," Ms. Devereaux said, "is for you to go and see."

"Thank you," I said.

"Mm-hm," she murmured. She'd gone back to writing whatever she was working on.

Once we got outside, Rory asked, "Who are the Keystone Kops?"

"Who *were* the Keystone Kops," Maisie said.

"Bumbling, inept cops," I said. "Who ran into and over each other trying to solve a crime."

TWENTY-FOUR

We left with a renewed mission, and it even seemed that we had Ms. Devereaux's blessing. She hadn't said we were on the wrong track, she'd just told us to be careful. I think that helped each of us to feel more confident in what we were doing.

"Are we walking up to American?" Rory asked.

"We walk everywhere around here," I said.

"I know," she said, "and I don't mind, but what if we have to make a quick getaway?"

Maisie and I stopped walking. We hadn't thought of that.

We hadn't considered what would happen if we were confronted by the killer, who may very well be Veronica. And perhaps it may turn out she was the killer and still had the gun.

"Good point," Maisie said. "Whose car should we take?"

"Mine is at Win's house," Rory said.

"That's where mine is, too," I said. "At home."

"We could take mine," Maisie said.

"You have a fast car?" Rory asked. "One that can outrun bullets?"

We chuckled. "Maisie has a VW Bug," I said. "A lime-green one."

"To outrun bullets, we need Riya's car," Maisie said.

"This Riya must be one bad girl," Rory said. "I can't wait to meet her."

"It's best to wait," Maisie said. "She's kind of dangerous."

Rory looked at me and I nodded.

"Let's get your car, Rory," Maisie continued. "It's a rental, right?"

"Yeah," Rory said. "How did you know?"

"Because Win said people in New York don't own cars." We turned the corner and headed up the hill to my house. "And, that way, if it does get shot up, you can just turn it in and let the rental company worry about covering up the bullet holes."

"Maisie is the one who sounds dangerous," Rory said.

I laughed. Maisie smiled, she seemed to like that designation.

"So. This place might be quaint, Bronwyn," Rory said, "but there is definitely something criminal about this one." She meant Maisie. If she thought Maisie was bad, Maisie was right, it probably was a good thing to keep her away from Riya.

As we walked, we tried to strategize about how to approach Veronica.

"We can't just ask her right out if she killed the guy," Rory said. "We need to figure out how to get her to confess to us."

"Why not ask her right out?" Maisie asked, seeming genuinely not to understand why we couldn't. "We catch her off guard and she may spill the beans."

"We can't just ask her that because she might not like it and, like Ms. Devereaux said, might shoot us," I said, figuring that would make her see why being direct wasn't a good plan.

"We've already discussed a getaway plan," Maisie said. "That's why we're going to get the car."

I rolled my eyes and Rory giggled. "I probably should change shoes," Rory said, looking down at her heels. "Looks like we might have to do some running this afternoon."

"Probably is a good idea," I said. "And maybe grab a bullet-proof vest."

"I can't believe we're making light of this," Rory said. "Or that we are going to question someone who might have killed a man."

"I know." I sighed. "You're going to owe me big-time after this," I told Rory.

"I'll be forever in your debt if you help me with this. For the rest of my life," Rory said. "That is, if your friend doesn't get us shot."

WE TOOK RORY'S car, but I drove. I figured if we did have to make a hasty getaway, I'd know the fastest way out. But after we circumvented running into Dell, Ms. Devereaux's sister and the proprietor of the Rose Cottage Inn, and knocked on four of the five doors that were guest rooms, I thought maybe we'd worried for nothing. Veronica didn't look like she'd hurt anyone.

Today her hair was loose and tousled, her eyes behind her dark-rimmed glasses puffy and her face, devoid of makeup, pasty. She had on yoga pants, a sleeveless tank top and no shoes.

"Can I help you?" she said.

"Hi," I said, pasting on a smile. With all our talk about coming to speak with her, here I was, standing in front of her, at a loss for what to say. But I knew I needed to say something before Maisie decided to take over the conversation. "We were at the shop owners' meeting the other night—"

"They're sending someone else down," she said. "You'll have to talk to whomever that is when they arrive."

"Oh no," I said. "We wanted you ... uhm, because we wanted ..." I looked at Rory, then Maisie. I was stuck.

"To look at those drawings that you had the other night," Maisie said.

"Yes," I said. I followed Maisie's direction. "To get a better idea of how things are going to be. How, you know, it will affect our shops."

She stared at us and drew in a breath. "You own shops?" It didn't seem as if she believed us.

"My family owns Crewse Creamery," I said.

"My family owns the Village Dragon Chinese Restaurant."

"I don't think it will affect you," she said, not even flinching when we mentioned Rivkah's Chinese restaurant. "Our proposed strip runs on the adjacent leg of the triangle."

"Any change affects us," I said. "And while we're not averse to the change, it's good to get a handle on it so we're prepared to speak to other shop owners about it."

She gave us another once-over. "They did tell me to hold things down after . . ." She turned her head away and I saw her swallow hard. I surmised she might've been trying to hold back tears. "Until someone from the office got here."

"So you think it would be okay?" I asked. "Might make it easier to get the support of the village if we talked to them." I indicated the three of us.

Maisie had a stern look on her face. I don't think she liked talking about selling our land even if it was a ruse to get in the door and question the woman about Zeke Reynolds's murder. But she kept quiet and let me do the talking.

Veronica shrugged. "I guess it'll be okay. It might even help."

"It might," I said.

We walked in single file. Rory the last one in the door.

"What shop do you own?" Veronica said to Rory.

"She's representing the coffee shop," I said, answering for Rory.

Rory frowned.

"Oh, the Dixby sisters," Veronica said. Her face showed the same distaste for them as did Rory's.

This time, once inside, we didn't stay clumped together. We spread out and formed a triangle in three areas of the small room.

Each guest room in the inn had a small seating area off to one side and a queen-sized bed in the middle. Veronica had a corner room so there were windows on two of the walls, which let a lot of light in.

She had a suitcase flung open and things were haphazardly tossed about inside. I could see they were expensive clothes and shoes, and the way she had them in a disheveled mess, I could tell she probably had a lot more at home. Lined up against the wall were a pair of red-bottomed shoes. I glanced at Rory to see if she'd noticed them. She did—as soon as our eyes met, she came over to me and whispered, "That pair," she pointed to the suitcase, "are Pradas."

Veronica's bed wasn't made, and from the appearance of it and the way she looked, I guess she'd been in it when we knocked.

It was easy to see that she was down about something.

Was she feeling bad because Zeke Reynolds was dead, or was it because she was the one that had killed him?

"We're sorry to hear about your coworker," I said as she pulled out the same artist case she'd brought to the meeting two nights prior.

"Thank you," she said, and with that she seemed to soften somewhat to our intrusion. "Here they are." She had pulled out the renderings and placed them on the bed. We all converged to look at them under the guise of genuine interest.

But before we even got a good look, or at least pretended to, Maisie jumped in.

"So where were you when it happened?"

"When what happened?" Veronica asked. Maisie's words had jarred her.

"The murder."

With those words, Veronica's back straightened up and she jutted out her chin. Just that quickly she had become defensive. "What kind of question is that?" Veronica asked. Her voice had changed, as had, it seemed, her attitude toward us.

"I'm sure the police asked you the same question," Maisie said, like she was making some point. I kept my head down pretending I was looking at the drawings on the bed, but I was keeping an eye on Veronica and any sudden moves she'd make.

"And are you the police?" Veronica asked. She was livid now. I don't know if she had been questioned or accused of something, because she became distrustful of us once we posed the one question after she'd just welcomed us into her room.

"No," Maisie said, "but this is our town and because of all of this"—she waved her hands over the drawings—"everything has really gone sour. Did you have anything to do with it?"

"Do with what?" she said. She came over, took the pictures and stuffed them back into the portfolio. She was finished showing us anything.

Not that we really cared anything about them.

"This whole thing?"

Veronica turned around and narrowed her eyes at Maisie. "I know who you are. Are you the one that threw the shoe?"

"What shoe?" Rory whispered to me. "Threw a shoe at what?"

"It was a *whom* and I'll tell you later," I said.

"Maybe I should ask where you were," Veronica said.

We weren't getting anywhere with Veronica. She responded to everything Maisie asked her with another question. And she was getting angrier by the second. She slammed the portfolio against the wall and I thought maybe I should reassess what I initially thought about her when we first came in.

From the conversation, I wouldn't think Veronica was the type of woman who cried and cowed. But she did an about-face really quickly. Exhibiting a temper.

Detective Beverly said that might have been what happened. Zeke Reynolds was killed because someone couldn't control their temper.

"We apologize, Veronica, we aren't assuming anything here, and we're not trying to throw blame around," I said, trying to calm her down. "We just wondered and, you know, were concerned about what the drawings depicted and, of course, being residents here, about what happened to . . . uhm . . . Zeke."

"Weren't you two dating?" Maisie asked, not giving me the chance to repair the damage she'd done. "What were you crying about at the restaurant? Was he breaking up with you?"

"What does that have to do with you?"

I was getting nervous. I knew we'd never find out anything from her at the rate we were going, if in fact she knew anything.

Veronica hadn't answered one of Maisie's questions.

"They found my shoes in a dumpster. I had found him that night. They were all bloody," Rory said. It was the first time she'd spoken to Veronica. She pointed at the ones lined up on the wall. "They were Louboutins. I hated to throw them away."

"What a waste," Veronica said with disgust. It was the first time since Maisie had started questioning her that she made a statement in response to the conversation at hand. "How much did you pay for them?"

"Two thousand," Rory said. "It took me a while to save up enough out of my paychecks to afford them."

"Zeke wanted to quit Rhys Enterprises," Veronica said, like that had been the question we asked her. Her kinship with another wearer of designer products seemed to open her up and calm her down. "Go back home to Florida. Leave Dallas. And I'm guessing, he wanted to quit me, too."

Ah, there was the answer to Maisie's question.

"I was lost in that alley," Rory said. The two talking but each one telling a story not part of the same conversation. But Rory was getting answers, even if it was in a roundabout way. "Couldn't find coffee," she continued. "What place doesn't have a Java Joe's?"

Veronica let out a chuckle.

"Saw his body and I wanted to help."

"I wanted to help get him to stay," Veronica said. "Rhys Enterprises wanted him to stay. He was good at what he did."

"I wish I understood their language so I could get some questions in," Maisie, who'd walked over to me, leaned in to whisper.

"I got in late," Rory said. "I live in New York."

"So did Zeke." She glanced at Rory. "Get in late, I mean." Veronica puffed out some air through her nostrils. "At least that's what I thought." She sucked in enough air to finish vocalizing her thought. "Guess he never really made it back at all. He'd gone to check on the owners of the buildings we were purchasing. And he wanted to stop by the art gallery. He was real excited about that place. Went over there two or three times since we've been here. He had said since they were selling, he'd probably get a good deal on some artwork. He knew exactly what he wanted to get."

"They were selling," I whispered to Maisie. "Black Market Paper."

"We can cross them off the list," she said.

"Bet wherever he is, he sure is sorry he missed that." Veronica glanced up and out the window as if she assumed it was the way Zeke had gone. Not up. Not down. Somewhere horizontal. Just like the mall they were trying to put up.

"He liked art?" Rory asked.

"He did," she said. "He loved art."

"Rory's an artist," Maisie said. "Aren't you, Rory?"

Veronica ignored Maisie.

"What time did he go to check on the stores? The bookstore and the art gallery," I asked, hoping I'd have better luck getting an answer to my question.

Veronica shrugged. "It had to be after dinner because I never saw him again. And then he had the one holdout, he needed to talk to that owner, too. That's why I thought he was gone for so long."

"Had he bought the building next to the lot where my community garden is?" Maisie asked. That was the building she wanted.

"Those were going to be purchased as one lot. You'd have to speak to the owner about that," Veronica said, answering one of Maisie's questions for the first time.

"There's a gun missing from the Chinese restaurant where you ate," Maisie said. Guess she figured if she was getting something out of Veronica, she should keep going. "I was wondering, did you see it?"

"Are you insinuating I took the gun?" Veronica said, again asking Maisie a question instead of answering the one that Maisie posed, her mood changed all over again. "I think you should go." She marched over, swung the door open and stood glaring at us.

Well, at Maisie.

But that didn't deter Maisie, she was bound and determined to get another question in. "Did you say you wished he was dead?" Maisie got the question in before she got out the door.

If looks could kill, Maisie would have been as dead as Zeke.

When Rory passed by her, Veronica said, with what seemed like sincerity, "Sorry about your shoes."

chapter

ೲ

TWENTY-FIVE

We sat in the car and waited in quiet reflection.

We'd parked down the street from the Rose Cottage Inn. We hadn't learned a thing inside of Veronica's room, except that she felt a certain kinship with people who had had some misfortune with designer wear.

"What do we do now?" Rory asked after we'd been waiting for a while. "Do we have any other leads?"

"We could start questioning shop owners?" Maisie said. Her inflection at the end made it sound more like a question. Even the self-professed amateur sleuth, Maisie, didn't quite know what to do.

"Or," I said, sitting up in my seat, "we could follow her."

"Who?" Maisie asked.

I pointed out of the window. "Where is she going with that envelope?" I said. Veronica had a big brown envelope cradled in her arms. She had pulled her hair back in a ponytail, thrown on a pair of flats and walked out of the inn with a determined look on her face.

"To the post office?" Rory guessed.

"Or maybe it has the gun," Maisie said, getting excited. "That's what happens when you tell people you know about evidence—they try to hide it."

"I didn't see that envelope when I was in her room," I said.

"I didn't either," Maisie said.

"That does not mean she didn't have it," Rory said. "Maybe it was at the bottom of that messy pile of clothes hanging out of her suitcase, or under the covers on her bed."

"And after we left, then she remembered she needed to take it somewhere?" Maisie asked.

"Maybe her office called and needed her to send it to them," Rory offered. "Maybe they said they needed to have it—whatever 'it' is—right away."

"Through regular mail?" Maisie said.

"Companies big enough to buy a whole city block, Rory, don't use the post office when they need a document," I said. "She could have scanned it."

"Maybe she didn't have a scanner," Rory said.

"There's an app for that," I said. "Tiny Scanner. There is an app for everything."

"Is there really an app called Tiny Scanner?" Maisie asked.

"Yep," I said. "Just for things like when your office needs something right away and you're nowhere near one."

"What about if she needed one of the owners of a shop to sign it?" Rory suggested.

"Why didn't Zeke get it signed?" Maisie asked.

"Maybe because he's dead," Rory said.

"I think no one would be signing papers in the wake of the

murder, especially if they're sending someone else down to take over."

"Okay. Okay." Rory relented. "I just don't like to jump to conclusions as big as 'she has an envelope with the murder weapon in it' when we don't even know why she has it or what's in it." Rory looked at me. "We shouldn't wrongly accuse people."

I understood that. It was exactly what had happened to my father in the last case.

"Just because the two of you had that designer-love thing going on," I said, "doesn't mean we should cross her off our list of suspects. And that's why we should follow her."

"I think she did it," Maisie said. "I think she took my grandmother's gun after their fight in the restaurant and shot him with it for wanting to break up with her."

"Does she always jump to conclusions like that?" Rory asked.

"Don't worry," I said, "she'll work through it. Before this is over she'll have lots of suspects for a variety of reasons."

"I already do," Maisie said, patting her book bag. "It's all in my little notebook." Her grin turned to a frown soon after it had formed. "Look! She's getting away." Maisie was pointing at Veronica, who had turned the corner off of American onto Bell Street.

I started the car and jerked the gear into drive.

"Wait!" Rory said, holding up her hand. "We can't follow her in a car if she's walking. We'd have to drive, like, two miles an hour."

"True," I said.

"So let's go catch up with her on foot," Maisie said and started to open the car door.

This time it was me who said it. "Wait!" I held on to Maisie so she wouldn't bolt. "The three of us can't go following down the street after her, she'll see us. Everyone will see us." I shook my head no. "It's too obvious."

"What are we going to do?" Maisie asked. She was bouncing around in her seat.

"We could just park at the corner of each street she turns onto and watch where she goes," I offered. "Then go to the next corner, you know, and do the same thing."

"What if she sees us?" Rory asked.

"Who cares," Maisie said. "We're not breaking any laws, we can do what we want."

"Stalking," Rory said. "We're breaking the law against stalking."

"We're trying to apprehend a murderer," Maisie said. "I think if we get caught they'll be lenient with us."

Rory looked at me. "When you're hanging out with her, do you ever feel like you might end up in jail?"

I made a U-turn and headed in the direction we'd last seen Veronica. Maisie was pushing down on my knee trying to make me go faster, as if it were connected directly to my foot. I swatted her hand away.

We found Veronica before she rounded the next corner onto North Main Street.

"Hurry!" Maisie said. "She'll lose us on North Main, it's a busy street."

"Isn't North Main the street your ice cream shop is on?" Rory asked.

"Yep," I said.

Rory chuckled. "Maisie should see the streets in New York if she thinks that's a busy street." Rory patted Maisie's shoulder. "Don't worry," she said. "I think we'll be able to find her."

I drove down to North Main and parked. "C'mon," I said. "We walk down this street all the time. Following her won't be obvious."

We piled out of the car and kept pace with Veronica at a safe distance as she walked down North Main for another block and a half and then turned the corner onto West Washington.

As we turned the corner, I could feel it as Rory fell back, then she stopped walking altogether when Veronica turned into the two-story redbrick building.

It was the city's administrative office building. Attached to it was the police station where Rory had made her confession.

"I don't want to go in there," Rory said.

"We need to go in to find out what she's doing in there," Maisie said. "Maybe she's going in to kill more people."

"Maisie. If she killed Zeke, it was a crime of passion. She doesn't have any reason to kill anyone else."

"Unless she figured out we were on to her."

"Then maybe *we* shouldn't follow her," I said.

Maisie's look of determination showed me she was going to find out whether I went with her or not, and whether Veronica had gone in dead set on a killing spree or not.

"Maisie, you go ahead, then," I said. "Keep up with her." Then I turned to Rory. "You don't have to come in, but you shouldn't stand here either, just milling around." I bit my lip trying to think. "I know." I smiled at the idea. "Go to the art gallery. Black Market Paper Fine Art." I rubbed her arms up and down

like my mother always did when she was trying to calm someone. "You didn't get to go this morning after you did all your
research. Right?"

She nodded.

"Okay, good. Art will make you feel good—you might even
decide which Florida Highwaymen painting you want to buy. Keep
your mind off of all this stuff for a little while. Then that'll give us
time to see what Veronica is up to and where she's headed next."

Rory took in a deep breath and let it out. "Sounds good," she
said. "I did want to get back to that art gallery." She gave a reso-
lute nod and turned to leave. "I only hope," she called over her
shoulder, "Baraniece and Ivan haven't heard about my shoes and
the dumpster. I'd be so embarrassed."

"I hope so, too," I mumbled and hustled off to find Maisie.

When I got inside the administration offices, Maisie was nowhere in sight. I walked up and down the halls until I found her
on the second floor outside the mayor's office.

"What are you doing here?" I asked.

"Veronica went in there." She pointed to the mayor's door.

There was an outside door that said *Mayor's Office*. But just
inside the doors was a reception area and the mayor's administrative assistant. His personal office was just beyond that. I remembered I'd visited the mayor once with my grandfather. He'd
given a resolution for my grandmother for her funeral.

"Did she go all the way into the mayor's office, or is she in
there waiting?"

Maisie hunched her shoulders. "I don't know. I didn't want to
look, but I know she can only get out through these doors."

"Oh," I said and stared at the door. "Maybe she's here on business. I'm guessing the mayor is probably part of the mall deal."

"Maybe she's here to kill the mayor," Maisie suggested.

"That would be very bold on her part," I said. "She has no reason to kill him, Maisie. Do you really think she's capable of killing in cold blood?"

"I don't know," she said. "I don't know her, other than she seems to have mood swings. But if you hear gunshots, you've got your answer."

I shook my head, having to stop myself from rolling my eyes. "So, what's the plan? We can't wait here—when she comes out, she'll see us."

"Where is Rory?" Maisie asked.

"I sent her to Black Market Paper," I said.

"Why? To interrogate them again?"

"No," I said. "And we've never interrogated them. I sent her to take her mind off of this. She didn't want to come inside and she loves art. She's an artist."

"And a coffee aficionado?" Maisie asked.

"Yes," I said.

Maisie nodded her understanding. "I don't blame her for going. I'd be freaking out, too, if they were going to arrest me for murder."

"No one is going to arrest her for murder," I said, not believing Maisie would say such a thing.

"Okay, if you say so. So, since she's not here, we can wait downstairs. There's a bench in the annex to the police station that faces the door that goes out. We'll see Veronica when she leaves and we can tail her and see what else she's up to."

"How will we know what was in the envelope?"

"We could sneak back into the mayor's office and see."

"No, we couldn't!" I tried not to shriek. "That would be breaking and entering, and probably a whole bunch of other things that are illegal."

"Then how will we find out?"

"Maybe we could just ask her when she comes out?"

"Yeah, and how do you think that'll go," Maisie asked, her hand going to her hip. "She didn't answer any of my questions when we went to her room at the inn."

"Okay. You're right." I eyed Maisie. "And we don't have the 'Designer Wear Whisperer' with us."

"Rory?"

"Rory. So then what?" I asked.

"We follow her," Maisie said. "That's the only thing we can do until we figure out something else."

Hadn't I just said that?

"Okay—" But before I could finish my sentence the door to the outer office swung open. It made Maisie and me nearly jump out of our skins. We bumped into each other and both had to muffle screams. The mayor smiled at us as if it was a usual occurrence for him to scare people lurking outside his office.

Mayor Greer had been in office for three terms. He was always smiling, but I never took it as him being happy, only being a politician. He was in his midforties with all-white hair, another product of the job, I assumed. He had soft blue eyes, always behind rimless glasses, and an athletic build. Most times he was seen riding his bike to work. But it was well known around the village that his eating habits were anything but healthy.

At least five foot ten and 160 pounds, he always looked good in the blue or tan suits he liked to wear. Today's suit was blue, and he wore a baby blue tie to match.

"Win!" he said. "I've been meaning to stop by your family's ice cream shop. I need an ice cream cake." He pulled the office door shut. "It's for Cecelia." He used his thumb to point back to where he'd just been, indicating his administrative assistant. "Her birthday is coming up." He patted me on my shoulder. "I have someone in my office now, but if you could just wait a minute, I want to talk to you about it."

"Sure," I said. I tried to avoid eye contact with Maisie. I knew she'd be ecstatic about the opportunity to get into the mayor's office.

"You can wait just inside there." He pointed to the reception area of his office. "I'll be right with you."

"Okay," I said, because I couldn't think of anything else to say. Surely I didn't want to sit there and let Veronica see me.

Veronica already knew we suspected her, and with us having to wait for the mayor in the reception area right outside his door, she'd probably figure out we had followed her. Too big of a coincidence for us to just happen to be going to the same place. I swallowed hard.

If Veronica was the killer, Maisie and I were in hot water now.

chapter

TWENTY-SIX

I watched as Mayor Greer made his way down the hallway. I peeked inside the doorway into the reception area and found, but for Cecelia, it was empty.

I backed into Maisie, stepping on her toe. She let out a yelp, which made Cecelia look up.

"May I help you?" she said.

"No," I said, waving a hello. I put on a smile. "I mean, yes, we're waiting to talk to the mayor, but we'll be right back."

"What are we going to do now?" Maisie whispered, her voice strained as we stepped back into the hallway and I eased the door shut.

"I don't know," I said, the strain in my voice matching hers. "Can you believe he wants to talk to me?"

"No. I can't believe it," Maisie said, "but it is providence."

I rolled my eyes. "One good thing, at least we know Veronica didn't come to shoot him."

"At least not yet," she countered.

"It must be Rhys Enterprises business," I suggested. "She did say someone else was coming from the company to take care of the project, remember?"

"I remember." She nodded. "You know this means we can't follow her now to see what else she's up to. Not if you have to talk to the mayor."

"I can talk to the mayor by myself," I said, "then you can still follow her."

"I'm not leaving," Maisie said, like what I had suggested was unthinkable. "Not with the possibility of that envelope being in the office. I want to know what's in it."

"It may not be anything. And how are we supposed to find out anyway? We can't take it."

"You could distract him."

"No!" Maisie was definitely a fan of "by any means necessary." "Plus, I don't think she'd bring the murder weapon and give it to the mayor."

"Unless they were in it together."

I hadn't thought about that.

"Well, either way," I said after I'd let that comment sink in, "we can't wait in the reception area until she comes out. That might not be good for us."

"Where did the mayor go?" Maisie asked. She leaned to the side to see around me.

"I don't know," I said and turned to look the way he disappeared. "To the restroom, maybe?"

"Oh," she said.

I snapped my finger. "What a good idea."

"What?" she asked.

"We can go, too," I said.

"Go to the restroom with the mayor?" she asked.

"No. Just go to the restroom. We can wait there until Veronica leaves."

"How will we know when she leaves?"

"I don't know," I said. "But c'mon." I grabbed her arm. "Let's check it out. We can't stay here, that's for sure."

"What about if she comes into the restroom on her way out?" Maisie asked.

"Cross your fingers she doesn't." I channeled the Dixby sisters' mentality. "Or we might just have to take her out."

MAISIE AND I managed to make it into the mayor's office without being seen by Veronica Russell. Although I think that Maisie secretly wished she had stopped by to use a stall. She'd come up with a dozen scenarios of how we'd overtake her and force her to confess.

"Have some chocolate," the mayor said as we sat down in two leather nailhead chairs that were in front of his desk. He pointed to a crystal bowl that sat atop it.

"No, thank you," I said.

"I'll have some," Maisie said and grabbed a handful.

"So, Mayor Greer, you could have just called. We could've taken your order for the cake over the phone."

"Oh, no problem," he said and grabbed one of the chocolates and popped it into his mouth. "You were here and . . ." He cocked his head to the side and licked his finger. "Why were you here standing outside of my office?"

"Oh," I said. Maisie and I exchanged glances. "Uhm, we just came as concerned citizens," I said. Thinking I'd use the same story as I had with Veronica.

"Yes," Maisie chimed in. "We were wondering why you decided to side with being in favor of a mall coming to Chagrin Falls."

His smile left and he sat up in his seat. "I don't know what you mean," he huffed. "I'm not for any mall."

"We saw you bringing Zeke into the SOOCFA meeting," I said.

"He was a visitor to our fair city. God rest his soul."

"Didn't he ask you to come to support him?"

"No," the mayor sputtered. "He came to the village, and I just wanted to show some hospitality." He hung his head, it seemed to me insincerely. "Shame what happened to him. Especially with the fact he was our guest."

"You came in with Amelia Hargrove," I said.

"No." He shook his head and started stroking his tie. "I didn't."

I decided not to argue with him. I knew what I'd seen and didn't know why he'd deny it other than that she was probably one of the ones who had sold her store to make way for the mall. I couldn't corroborate with Maisie that they'd entered together— she was too wrapped up in Zeke and his message to have noticed anything else.

"Do you know if she sold her building?" Maisie asked. That was her method of weeding shop owners out. It was also typical of her to jump from suspect to suspect. I was guessing that Amelia may as well be next on her list.

"I wouldn't know anything about that," he said. "How would I know?" He shrugged. "But I can say unequivocally, you have never heard me suggest or speak out in favor of a mall coming to Chagrin Falls. We'd just turn into Woodmere Village." Lips pursed, he shook his head like he had a bad taste in his mouth. "Traffic jams and with nearly a two-to-one ratio of residents to businesses."

"You don't know whether Amelia Hargrove sold her business and is closing shop, or you don't know whether you came into the meeting with her?" Maisie asked.

"Amelia . . . uh . . . Ms. Hargrove is a fine, upstanding citizen and longtime resident and business owner in the village. Her store has been here for more than thirty years."

That was politician doublespeak. His response had nothing to do with the question we'd asked.

"If there is some big Texas company coming in buying parts of Chagrin Village, don't you think you should know about that?"

He raised an eyebrow at Maisie's questions. "Who says I don't know anything about it?" He cocked his head to the other side. "What are you ladies trying to do? I find you lurking outside my office, and when I tell *you*, Win, that I have business for you, you come into my office and don't mention one word about it."

"I am trying to extend my community garden." Maisie spoke in my place.

"Is that why you're here?" he asked, his eyes traveling from one of us to the other. "To see about expanding your garden. Have you run that idea past my office?"

"I might not need to if someone has already bought up all the land and the buildings surrounding it." Maisie tilted her head to the side to match his angle. "Something, I'm thinking, you may have had a hand in, since you were just meeting with Veronica Russell of Rhys Enterprises."

Maisie had spilled the beans. There went the idea of being discreet out the window. I could only hope she wouldn't mention the envelope.

"What did she bring you in that envelope?" Maisie asked and let her eyes roam across the top of his desk.

Geesh! I hung my head. I was going to make Maisie write the meaning of "tact" on the menu chalkboard in my ice cream shop one hundred times.

The mayor's eyes followed Maisie's. There was no envelope like the one Veronica had been carrying on his desk, and when he locked eyes with Maisie again, he smiled.

"When and if the time comes for me to speak to the village about the existence of a mini mall here, I will make a public announcement." He turned and looked at me. "Win, I'll see if Davis Bakery can't supply me with a cake." He stood up and walked to his door. "You ladies have a good day."

It was the second time in the course of an hour that we had been thrown out of somewhere without finding out one single thing about Zeke Reynolds's murder. I'd say our investigation was going downhill quicker than hot fudge could melt soft-serve ice cream.

TWENTY-SEVEN

Maisie and I made our way out of the administration building by way of the steps in record time. Walking back into the heat made me frown—the air inside had felt good. Once back outside, I shielded my eyes from the bright sun with a cupped hand and looked up and down the street. I wasn't sure if Rory had left or not, when I told her maybe she should wait for us elsewhere.

"What now?" Maisie came up behind me. "Wanna try and find Veronica?"

"I think we should try and find Rory," I said. "We can head back toward the car. See if we see her."

We walked down West Washington not speaking about what had happened in the mayor's office. I was sure Maisie wasn't ever going to vote for him again, and I was also sure he was going to have a word or two about me with my grandfather. Maisie's concerns were legitimate, but he acted as if we were the kids who kept throwing balls into his yard, breaking windows.

As we rounded the corner onto North Main, I saw the car but no Rory.

"I wonder where Rory went," I said. "I hope she did go to the gallery." I was feeling protective of my friend. I didn't want her going over the edge again.

"She probably went back to the ice cream shop," Maisie said. "And if not, we can walk over to the gallery. I'm sure she's okay."

"Yeah, you're right," I said. Looking over toward the ice cream shop I spied Riya coming our way. She spotted us at the same time and started waving.

She was dressed in white short shorts and a red belly shirt. Riya had the right idea on how to dress for the weather.

"Hey," she said. "Where've you guys been?"

"The police station."

"No!" Riya said. "To see that cute detective?" She fell in step with us, turning as we headed back down the way she'd come. "Why didn't you take me?"

"We didn't know where you were," Maisie said. "And why would you want to see that bumbling idiot detective?"

"He is not a bumbling idiot detective, and he is not cute either," I said.

"I was at the ice cream shop." Riya looked back toward where the police station was located. "I had the afternoon off, and I knew I hadn't been around. Thought I'd come to help."

"Your hospital work, saving lives and all, isn't as rewarding as dipping up scoops of ice cream?" I asked.

She chuckled. "It is. But get this. Imagine my surprise when I got there and your Aunt Jack is behind the counter." She widened her eyes as if letting me know she knew that was a bad thing. "Waiting on customers! What is that about?"

"I know," I said and huffed. "She was there and I needed to leave to help a friend. Wilhelmina's not coming in tonight because I needed them both to work tomorrow night. It's Family Chef Night."

"Who's gonna do the cooking?" Riya asked, her face lighting up in anticipation.

"My dad," I said.

"Oh, I'm coming," Riya said.

"Me, too," Maisie said, clapping her hands.

"Was Aunt Jack doing okay?" I wiped the sweat off my forehead. It was warm out, but just thinking about Aunt Jack at the ice cream shop made my temperature rise. "She is not happy with what I did to our family's novelty shop. No telling what she'd do while I'm gone."

"You mean your family's ice cream shop," Riya said, correcting me like I didn't know.

"Not if Aunt Jack has her way," I said. "I mean, what's so bad about an ice cream shop selling ice cream?"

Riya and Maisie chuckled. "That is a little crazy," Maisie said.

"Was everything alright?" I asked.

"Yeah, but I could tell she wasn't happy about it." Riya waved her hand in front of her face. "She was sweating and grumbling.

Huffing and puffing. Barking at the customers like she was the big bad wolf."

"I don't even know why she's back in Chagrin Falls," I said.

"I was going to ask you the same thing," Riya said. "But it looks like you've got something way juicier going on. Spill."

"What are you ladies doing?" A man's voice came up behind us and interrupted before I could answer Riya. "Riya, you know these girls?"

I turned around to meet a face that sported a wide smile, too big to be genuine seeing I didn't know who he was. He was dark skinned, with short, silky black hair and a heavy Indian accent. He wore a light brown linen suit, a blue button-down shirt and a polka-dot tie.

"Uncle Garud," Riya said. "Where did you come from?"

"Are you going to introduce me to your friends?" he asked, a greasy grin on his face.

"My friends?" she questioned, then turned to look at us before resting her gaze on him. "Why?"

"I've been keeping an eye on them," he said, and he struck the side of his nose with a finger before stuffing his hands down in his pockets. He rocked back on the heels of his shoes, like he'd just discovered the answer to a pressing question and was awaiting his reward. "Following them. I am surprised that you have such friends."

"That's creepy," Maisie said under her breath.

"Stalking is illegal, Uncle Garud," Riya said flatly. She didn't seem to have much patience for the man, but she was polite just the same. "You should mind your own business."

"*Hmph,*" he said. "I watched them follow the young lady that came out from Rose Cottage," he said. "That's what's illegal. I am an upstanding citizen of the community."

"That's questionable," Maisie mumbled.

"What business do they have with her?" Riya's uncle Garud wiggled his fingers at us.

"How do you know we did that?" I asked, narrowing my eyes at him. He may be Riya's uncle, but he was sounding more like Big Brother. How could he know we'd followed Veronica, unless he was following her, too?

"Be gone with you," Riya said, leaning in to him. "I will tell Auntie Neera I saw you leering after women." She gave him a once-over and stood waiting for him to leave.

He kept his smile and nodded, not one bit flustered by Riya's threat. "I'll see you ladies again."

"What is your uncle, some kind of detective or something?" I asked.

"No," Riya said. "And he is not really my uncle."

"Who is he, then?" Maisie asked.

"Didn't you hear? He's Neera's husband," Riya said, as if she knew them.

"And . . . ?" I drew out the word, showing my confusion.

"She's a friend of my mother's." Riya shook her head. "Indians claim lots of random people as auntie and uncle."

"What does he do—why was he watching us?" I asked.

"I don't know," Riya said. "What were you two doing?"

"Trying to investigate the murder of that guy that was at the SOOCFA meeting."

"Zeke Reynolds?" Riya said.

"You remembered," I said.

"Of course I do." Riya pressed her lips together. "I try to keep track of the people I throw shoes at."

Maisie shook her head. "What? Was there more than the one?"

chapter

TWENTY-EIGHT

When we walked into the ice cream store, before I could comment that Rory hadn't gotten back, my mother came from around the counter and grabbed my arm. I glanced over at PopPop sitting calmly on his bench and Candy, my other official employee, was sitting across from him. Young, lots of energy and dependability, she must've come in early for her shift. Probably a good thing, because Aunt Jack was nowhere in sight.

My mother pulled me to the back and into a corner. First thing I saw was Aunt Jack. She'd dragged one of the ice cream parlor chairs in the back and was slumped down, legs spread-eagled. Her head limp and resting on the back of the chair. Her wig sat precariously, appearing as if it might fall off at any minute. She looked like she'd gone through ten rounds with Floyd Mayweather.

"Mom," I said before she could talk. "What's wrong with Aunt Jack?"

She turned and took a gander at Aunt Jack, and waved a hand in dismissal. "I don't think she's ever worked this hard in the store before. At least not since your Grandma Kay and PopPop ran it." She leaned in and whispered conspiratorially, "She never had as much business as you. We had a steady stream of customers come in from the time you left."

"Candy's here and we're back." I glanced at Aunt Jack. "So she can go home now."

"She's just taking a breather." My mother glanced over at her. "Let her keep working," she said. "Make her too tired to come to Family Chef Night tomorrow night."

"Mom!" I said.

She waved a hand. "You want to deal with her all night?" I kept a straight face. "Now back to you," she said. "Don't try to change the subject."

"I'm not."

"I sent Riya to find you." She bumped her body into mine showing me she was concerned. "You were gone so long."

"You did?" I glanced toward the front where Riya was waiting on a customer. She hadn't mentioned that. I shrugged. "She found us, I guess. What's wrong?"

"You tell me," my mother said.

"Uhm . . ." I made my eyes wide. I wasn't sure what she meant. "I don't know?" It came out a question.

"I can see you don't," she said. "I also see that you don't have Rory with you. Why is that?"

"Because we ended up at the police station—"

"The police station!" my mother squawked before I could finish explaining. "Oh my God. What has happened now? Is everything okay?"

"Everything is fine. We just went there to—"

"You went there!" She stomped her foot and let her head roll back on her neck. "Why would you take Rory there? Do you want to traumatize her more?"

"No, Mom. And I didn't *take* her there. I knew that wouldn't be a good idea."

"No, it wouldn't."

"And I knew she wouldn't want to be there either. So I told her to wait for me."

"Why were *you* there?" she asked, hand on hip.

"We were following Veronica Russell and that's where we ended up. Well, where she ended up."

"Zeke's girlfriend?" Confusion threaded through her face.

"Alleged girlfriend," I said, remembering that you couldn't always take what Maisie said at face value.

"I can start early, if you need me." It was Candy. She appeared next to us, pushed her glasses up on her nose and had a look on her face that said she didn't mean to interrupt. "Your aunt looks tired."

I swung a look at Aunt Jack, it seemed she was out cold. I heard a soft snoring coming from her. "Is it getting crowded out?" I asked, peeking out toward the front.

"It usually gets busy around now." Candy looked at the watch on her wrist. "Just thought I'd go ahead and clock in if it was okay with you."

I didn't actually have a time clock. I scheduled Wilhelmina and Candy, and they signed a sheet I'd made on Excel. But they both had turned out to be such good employees, I didn't need to monitor much. Even like now, Candy volunteering to get started early.

I smiled. "Thank you, Candy. No problem. Go ahead and sign in."

My mother watched as Candy put on an apron and tied it around her waist. I knew her. She was biding her time. She wanted to get more information out of me, and she wouldn't rest until she did.

Without missing a beat. "So you've been looking for a murderer. What did you find out?" she asked after Candy ambled back to the front.

"We didn't find out much," I confessed. "We found out that Rivkah has a missing gun."

"Oh?"

"Yeah, so we thought maybe Veronica took it to kill Zeke."

"Why would you think that?" Then she nodded. She got it. "Oh. Because Zeke and Veronica had been in the restaurant that night?"

"Yes, and she may—and I emphasize the word *may.*—have left by way of the kitchen."

"Is that where Rivkah kept her gun, in the kitchen?"

"That's how it sounded when she and Lin were discussing its whereabouts." I tilted my head and looked at my mother. "Why did you say it like that?"

"Like what?"

"'Is that where she keeps her gun,' like everyone has one and you wondered where hers was."

"Because everyone does," my mother said.

"We don't," I said.

"We do," my mother said. "We kept it in the shop. Your grandfather took it out when you remodeled." She looked around. "He may have brought it back by now, though."

"Why didn't I know that?"

"Why would you want to know that?"

"Because if we did have one, I'm guessing it would be for me to use." I thought about that and put my hand on my forehead. "Why do we have a gun? And why does everyone, so you say, have one?"

"To protect ourselves." She thought about it, and she sounded like she wasn't sure why. "So you probably should know if it's here." She looked around. "I'll have to ask your grandfather about that," she said absently.

The thought of a gun in all the establishments down North Main nearly bowled me over. Chagrin was one of the safest cities in North America, at least according to Wikipedia. At least until we started having a murder every six months.

"I don't know if everyone has a gun now, though." My mother was still talking. "Probably not the newer businesses around. We all got ours when the Dixby sisters sponsored a gun show."

"They sponsored a gun show?" I almost wanted to laugh, picturing them, two old ladies, with gnarled fingers, handling a six-shooter. Then I remembered what they said earlier about how they had no qualms about "taking out" their competition.

"Yes," my mother said. "You know they are gun collectors, right?"

"The Dixby sisters? No. I didn't know." I couldn't believe what I was hearing.

"Yes. Delilah and Daubie," my mother said. "They have a whole room full of guns. Fascinating." She wiggled like a shiver had gone down her spine. "Scary."

"Why didn't you tell me this before?"

My mother frowned up at me. "Why would I tell you? What does it have to do with anything?"

"Zeke Reynolds was shot with a gun," I said. I couldn't understand how she didn't see the connection.

"You really do need help with this snooping—"

"Sleuthing," I corrected.

"Sleuthing stuff," she finished. "Just because someone gets shot, it doesn't mean that everyone with a gun is a suspect. Especially when *everyone* has a gun."

"Yeah, I see that. I guess that's true."

"But Veronica with a gun would be different." My mother went back to talking low. "She was angry with him and there was no reason for her to have a gun."

Just like there is no reason for anyone along Main Street to have a gun either.

"Truth be told, Mommy," I said, skipping over that tidbit of information, "we really didn't come up with anything on Veronica."

"You didn't talk to her, did you?" She grabbed my arm and shook it. "She's the murderer. Oh my God." She put her hand over her chest. "If you got yourself in another predicament like the last time."

"Calm down, Mommy. She was fine. Sad. But fine. We just 'questioned' her." I used air quotes. "But we got nothing."

"And she didn't try to go for the gun or anything?"

"No."

"Did you see one?"

"No. She was kind of moody, but didn't say or act like she was guilty of anything."

"They never do."

Now she was a killer profiler . . .

"Then we followed her—"

"You followed her?"

"Yes."

"Why? Where?"

"We followed her to the police station. And nothing happened."

"It could have, unless she was there turning herself in," my mother ventured.

"She didn't. And we're safe." I patted myself all over. "I'm fine."

She sighed and seemed to relax some. "You did find out that she'd gone through Rivkah's kitchen and took the gun, though, right?"

"We aren't sure if that's how it went," I said. "Savta said she couldn't be sure Veronica left by way of the kitchen."

"Uh-huh," my mother said, nodding her head. "That's what Maisie told me Rivkah said."

"She changed her story when we talked to her," I said.

My mother sucked her tongue. "Back to square one?"

"It looks that way. Maisie did think the real killer was probably one of the owners whose shop was on the land Rhys Enterprises wanted and who didn't want to sell."

"I don't think it could be one of the shop owners," my mother said.

"I used to agree with that," I said. "And that's what I told Maisie, too. But now we know they all have guns."

"Who all has guns?" Maisie came in back and went to the storage.

"It seems all of Chagrin Falls," I said.

"Oh," she said. Eyebrows raised, she left her mouth in the shape of the word.

"Maisie," my mother said. "I don't think that any of the shop owners would kill that Zeke guy."

"Oh! Are we talking about the case?" Her voice conspiratorial, she came over with a package of napkins in her hands.

"Mrs. Crewse, the man was in Chagrin Falls for the sole purpose of buying up our shops and land. Who else would be upset with him?"

"Right," I said. "And now that I know everyone around here has a gun."

"Just *anybody* wouldn't do something like that," my mother said. "At least not the citizens of Chagrin Falls.

"And," she continued, "if one of the shop owners did kill him, that wouldn't stop Zeke's company. They'd just send someone else to do his work."

"Veronica said that was what was happening," I said, impressed with my mother's reasoning. "She said she was waiting for Zeke's replacement to come from Dallas."

"See," she said in her motherly I-know-everything way. "It wouldn't work. They'd have to shoot everyone that came up here from that company to stop that mall from being built."

That sent a shiver through my spine. "Don't say things like that, Mommy."

"People will treat their business like it's their baby," she said. "They nurture it, want it to grow healthy and strong, and will do just about anything to keep it that way, even defending it from harm that others try to inflict on it. But not many will resort to murder. Especially not here." Then in an afterthought: "Who owns the buildings and land that that company was trying to buy?"

Maisie looked at me. It was what she'd been saying earlier. I hunched my shoulders. "We don't know."

"We could find out," Maisie said.

"That's a good idea," my mother said. "And a safe idea. Find out. But remember, don't go talking to people who are potential murderers with guns."

"So let's plan on doing that," Maisie said, then she held up the package of napkins. "These are needed up front. Gotta go."

"We all should get back to work." My mother glanced down at her watch. "Don't you have a meeting about the ice cream truck today?"

Every time my mother referred to my refrigerated truck like that, I had visions of the slow-moving, painted-advertisement-splattered, "Turkey in the Straw"–playing vans of my childhood.

That wasn't what my truck was going to be.

"It's a food truck that sells ice cream." I tried to say it without too much defiance in my voice. "And no, that's tomorrow," I said and looked at my watch. "I have to approve the final design. And he found the cutest mini blast freezer." Excitement from that made my mother's misnomer sink to the back of my mind. "That would mean I could make ice cream on the truck and bring it back to sell in the store if there's some left."

"Sounds good. You taking Rory with you?"

"Rory," I said wistfully.

"Where is she?"

I remembered O had warned us that she might be in danger if the killer thought she'd seen something. And now I hadn't seen her in a while. Certainly she had had enough time to look at a painting and come find me. Panic set in. "I don't know," I said.

"You should go and find her."

"I know," I said. I didn't want her tripping over any more dead bodies. Or for that matter, anyone tripping over hers.

chapter

TWENTY-NINE

I left my mother in the back trying to resuscitate Aunt Jack. Her snoring had gotten louder by the time my mother and I had finished our conversation, and I was afraid she was going to swallow her tonsils.

"I need to go find Rory." I spoke to no one in particular, still they all turned and looked at me.

"Why?" Riya spoke first. "Isn't that her right there?" She pointed to the window seat.

Rory was sitting in the window, holding Felice, stroking her fur. Rory's face was puffy, her eyes slack and her shoulders slumped. You could just see the stress balled up in her. It seemed even that snobby cat knew that she needed comfort. And I was sure Her Royal Highness was enjoying all the attention she was getting, too.

"Oh." I let out a relieved chuckle. "Yeah. I didn't know she'd gotten back."

"She's been back," Maisie said as she passed us on the way to the cash register. "When do you want to talk? We have to get a plan of action together."

"Tonight. After we close up," I said.

"What about Veronica?" Maisie asked.

"I don't know," I said. "But I think you're right about pursuing other avenues."

"She stays on the list."

"Yes." I nodded in agreement. "She stays on the list. But now we check out shop owners," I said. "The other people on your list."

"I want in," Riya said, as she came over to us. "I've been missing out on everything. Again."

"Is that why you've been hanging around here?" Maisie asked. "I wondered why a doctor wanted to moonlight as an ice cream server."

"I hang around because I like this place and my best friends are here."

"Aww," I said. "We love you, too."

"And," Riya said, pointing a finger, "if I'd been included in you two's shenanigans in the first place last time, you might not have gotten yourself in that pickle."

"What pickle?" Maisie asked.

"She means the Althea Quigley pickle," I said. Although, I wouldn't call being locked in a corridor with a knife-wielding killer a pickle, but I knew what she meant.

"Just fill me in and include me, will you?" Riya said.

I smiled. "Just as long as you don't get too *supportive*." I pictured shoes flying everywhere.

"Funny," Riya said.

"Okay," I said. "You staying, Riya?"

"You bet I am."

"You know Maisie and I aren't very good at sleuthing and nothing usually happens," I warned. "It was just that one instance."

"It's okay," she said. "I'm still sticking around."

"Hey, Rory." I ended my conversation with Maisie and Riya, and went over to Rory, relieved she was back safe and sound. I figured I should keep the conversation light.

I hoped her little side excursion had gone well. At least more productive than ours.

"So did you find anything you wanted to buy?"

"They were closed," she said, adjusting herself on the seat. "In preparation for the sidewalk fire sale."

"Really?"

"Yep." She nodded in affirmation, her lips tight. "Why do they need two days to get ready for it?"

"I don't know." I turned to look out of the window and at the row of shops across the street. "And with them being so expensive, what are they going to sell cheap enough to put on the sidewalk?"

"Exactly," Rory said. "Then I went over to the visitors' center."

"You did?"

"Yeah, I remembered you said they were having an art show."

"They are. I thought you might like that one."

"It's been canceled."

"What?"

"Something happened at the last minute, I don't know what.

The lady there said something about the paintings having to be authenticated."

I frowned. "You getting your art fix was a bust, huh?"

"Yes, it was," she said, exhaling deeply. "But one good thing, the lady from the Florida DeLouise Foundation called back."

"The woman who has the catalog for the Florida Highwaymen artwork?"

"Yep." She nodded. "She said she would overnight it to me. But since it's late, she won't send it until tomorrow. So I'll have it for the sidewalk fire sale."

"That's a good thing," I said.

"Yeah, it is." She patted my hand. "Still, I'm beginning to think that Chagrin Falls isn't the cultural haven you think it is."

I chuckled. "We'll see what you think after you get your artwork. You'll be singing our praises."

"I doubt that. Plus, it wouldn't be good PR for me to tell you how good this place is when I'm trying to get you to move away from it."

"Yeah." I pressed my lips together and shook my head. "Don't think that'll ever happen."

WHEN WE LOCKED the door at eleven, there were still about five customers in the store. We'd been so busy that no one had time to even think about Zeke Reynolds and the trouble he stirred for us all when he was alive and after he died.

"So what are we going to do? How are we going to solve this?" Riya said after I'd told her what had happened and what we'd done so far. We'd served the last customer and she was wiping down the round tables out front.

"We're going to question shop owners," I said.

"You think one of them did it?" Riya asked.

"I don't," my mother said.

"Maisie was thinking that Veronica was the killer," Rory said.

"And is she the killer?" Riya asked.

"We don't know," I said. "That's why we're still looking at other people."

"We did find out they had a lovers' quarrel," Rory said. "And maybe Veronica, right when she was angry with Zeke, gained access to a gun." It seemed to make Rory feel better to help around the shop and with our attempts to solve the murder. "We also found out that Zeke wasn't too happy with his company. He wanted to quit, remember?" she continued. "Although, I'm not sure how that would fit in as a motive for his murder by Veronica, unless she was being supportive of her company."

"Oh yeah," I said. "We did find that out."

"Better for me to be supportive with a shoe than with a gun," Riya said.

"You don't need either to take down the bad guys," Maisie said, stopping over to sweep Riya's trash into a dustpan.

"I have tomorrow off, too." She stood up and stretched. "After my morning run, I'm free." She shook her head and sighed. "I miss one afternoon and all this has happened. What happened to this being the quiet, nothing-ever-happens village?"

"What kind of work do you do?" Rory asked Riya. Rory was

sitting in the window seat. She and Felice had become good friends. She was holding the fluffy white cat in her arms, and they were rubbing cheeks.

"She's a doctor, remember?" Maisie answered for her.

"And a shoe supporter," I said.

"A shoe supporter?" Rory said, her face squished up. "Oh, wait." She chuckled. "You're the one that threw the shoe at the meeting?"

"I *was* being supportive," Riya said. "I don't know why that's so hard for people to understand."

"See," I said. "A shoe supporter. She shows support by way of the shoe."

"So why does Maisie think Riya wouldn't need a shoe or a gun to take down bad guys?" Rory asked. "You a superhero?"

"No, I'm not," Riya said.

"Maisie seems to think Riya's invincible," I said.

Rory looked at Maisie with her eyebrows arched.

"She has a black belt in *everything*," Maisie said. "And when she's angry, there is no stopping her."

As we talked, I was running a report from the cash register on the sales for the day, and my mother was cleaning out the display case and putting up the ice cream. At least what was left of it. Tomorrow was going to be a busy day, we were going to need more ice cream. I'd have to come in early.

"I don't have a black belt in everything," Riya said. "I like to be prepared." She eyed Maisie. "In whatever kind of situation I encounter. I like to help people. Take care of them. That's why I became a doctor."

Riya didn't mention that all the black belts came out of a

need to control that temper of hers. I didn't say anything about it either.

"And now I want to help in other ways, too. That's all," Riya said. She looked at Rory. "Even though I just met you, any of Win's friends are also friends of mine."

"Thank you," Rory said. "Because it seems like I'm going to need all the help I can get."

chapter

ॐ

THIRTY

W e didn't go to the Chagrin Falls Public Library, the place where we'd first learned to use the internet to parse out clues. O had told Maisie and me, when we were trying to solve the first case we worked on, that we could find a wealth of information about people. Even if we just checked out their social media pages. This time, he had directed us to the county auditor's site to find out property owners. We decided to do it at Riya's house. The library, our usual spot to do our internet searches, was long closed.

Riya lived in a big house, and for the most part, it was void of any furniture or anything that would make it seem like a home. Our voices and footsteps echoed through the house as we walked through empty rooms, across bare wooden floors, and headed into the kitchen. There, Riya had put some effort forth. And knowing Riya's family, it was easy to understand.

Riya, on her mother's side, was Italian, and on her father's side Indian, both sides boasting they were the best cooks. Her family was large and spent lots of time in the kitchen feeding their brood. It was the family gathering place.

"I can whip us up something to eat while we think this thing through," Riya said.

"Sounds good," Rory said and rubbed her tummy like it needed tending to.

"We ate earlier at the Village Dragon," I said, directing my comment to Rory. "Lin cooked us a spread. You ate like it was your last meal."

"I'm hungry now, though," Rory said and eyed me. "But you know, just something light."

I shook my head.

"I could eat something, too," Maisie said.

"I'm good," I said.

"Okay," Riya said. She opened the refrigerator and pulled out a carton of eggs. "How about a Riya omelet?"

"What is that?" Maisie asked.

"Oh no," I said. "Don't tell me my father told you about that." I laughed at her suggestion.

"Yep. Gave me the recipe, too. I was honored for him to name a dish after me."

"What is it?" Maisie asked.

"My father named it after Riya because it has, like, a little basil, some sweet Italian sausage . . ."

"Turmeric"—Riya took over naming the ingredients—"garam marsala and red chili pepper."

"Oh," Maisie said. "I see. A little Italian. A little Indian."

"And a little hot, just like me," Riya said, putting her hand on her hip and a grin on her face.

"Sounds good to me," Rory said.

"You have all that stuff?" I asked.

"Food, I have," she said. "Let's just hope I have enough dishes. I'm the only one eating here."

"How about bottled water?" I said. "You have any of that?"

"Yes," Riya said and went back to the refrigerator and pulled four bottles of water out of it. "I hope you like your H_2O chilled."

"That's fine," Rory said.

Riya passed out the bottles to us. "Okay, before I start cooking, let me go get you guys a couple of laptops."

"You have more than one?" Rory said.

"Yes, I got one from each of my grandmothers," Riya said over her shoulder as she headed out. "They are always competing with each other."

Riya left and Rory turned to me. "She seems very nice."

"She is," I said, wondering why she'd think otherwise.

"But Maisie said . . ."

"Oh," I said, remembering Maisie's consistent warnings about Riya. "It's her temper." I lowered my voice.

"She has a bad temper?" Rory asked.

"Yep. My father didn't add that hot chili pepper to his recipe because she's good-looking," I said.

"We met in kindergarten when she was beating up a little boy for being on the swing she wanted," Maisie added.

"I heard that," Riya said, coming back into the kitchen lugging two laptops. "And, Rory, you should know, I'm working on keeping my temper under control. I didn't hit that guy with my shoe. And I could have, you know. I missed on purpose."

I laughed. "I'm rooting for you, Riya," I said. "I know you can do it."

"I don't have as much confidence," Maisie said.

"Why don't you guys fire up the laptops and I'll start on the omelets," Riya said, ignoring Maisie's comment.

"Come put in your password," I said after I got the computer booted up.

While Riya cooked, we looked up who owned what. It took a minute to figure out how the website worked and then the range of addresses we wanted to look up, but once we did, we found our answers fairly quickly.

Maisie, Rory and Riya ate eggs and took notes, and I recited the information from the website. We discovered that Rhys Enterprises had already bought up Amelia Hargrove's Around the Corner Bookshop and Baraniece Black and Ivan Rynok's Black Market Paper Fine Art gallery, which we already knew thanks to our little talk with Veronica. Also the Blue Moon, and the Sassy Kitten, the souvenir shop. We hadn't known who owned the Blue Moon, but checking the records we saw that it was transferred to Rhys from one Reginald Ingomar. I had always thought a woman owned it because they sold women's clothing, but I guess I was wrong. The Sassy Kitten was owned by Rosabelle Pfeiffer. I knew her. She was old, probably too old to kill Zeke Reynolds, plus she'd been sick and the store had sat dormant for at least the last few months.

The building that housed Juniper Tree was owned by Delilah and Daubie Dixby. And the building that Maisie wanted to buy and two of the vacant lots were owned by Kvest LLC. The land where Maisie already had a community garden was owned by the Village of Chagrin Falls.

We finally knew for sure which properties Zeke Reynolds still needed to get in order for his company to erect that mall.

"Did you know that?" I asked, looking up at Maisie when I read that name off. "Did you know who owned the land where you garden?"

"No. I didn't know the village owned the land," Maisie said. "I inherited that garden, remember?"

"Oh yeah, Mrs. Newman used to keep that lot up," I said. "Those other lots, the ones owned by, what was it?" I looked back at the computer.

"Kvest," Rory said. "Kvest Limited Liability Company."

"That's what LLC stands for?" Maisie asked.

"Yep," she said.

"Those other lots used to have gardens, too, I remember," I said. "When we were little. I wondered why it was only the space you have now, Maisie."

"So that leaves us with the Darling Dixbys as a suspect and Kvest LLC, whoever that is," Maisie said, scribbling in her notebook. "They were holding out for more money, or resisting selling all together."

"Remember," I said, "if they held out because they didn't want to sell, killing Zeke Reynolds would not have stopped Rhys Enterprises from pursuing it with a different representative."

"And remember," Rory added, "that if Rhys wasn't able to purchase all the land, they couldn't proceed with their plans."

"Seems like they'd be the ones killing someone, then," Riya said.

We looked at Riya.

"What?" she said, throwing up a hand. "It's true. They'd want to get rid of the holdout. Especially if they were going to lose money. Big money." She made her eyes large. "And remember Veronica said that Zeke had only one holdout?"

"So maybe he confronted them," Maisie said. I could see the wheels turning in her head. "Zeke, that is. Maybe he confronted them. They had a standoff."

She stood up from her chair. "He threatened the shop owner, trying to bully them into selling. Then he pulled a gun on them"— she acted as if she was pulling one from her pocket—"ready to get rid of the obstacle in his way. In the way of Rhys Enterprises taking over Chagrin Falls. The shop owner ran outside." Maisie stepped aside of her chair. "Zeke followed. They wrestled for the gun." She started jerking her body back and forth. "The shop owner got the gun. *Bam!*" she said and made all of us, except Riya, jump. "They shot him dead!" She dropped, her body slack, back down in her chair.

"Oh brother," I said.

"Maisie, you need help," Riya said. "Believe me, I know when people have mental issues they need to deal with. And darling, that would be you."

"I think it could have happened just like that," Maisie said, sitting upright in her seat. She seemed quite pleased with her deduction and performance.

"It's not a totally outlandish theory," Rory said. "It would make sense if Zeke were some kind of loose-tempered, egotistical, maniacal, ruthless businessman."

"Veronica made it sound like he was excited about going to see the shop owners," I reminded Rory and Maisie.

"She said the bookstore and the art gallery," Maisie said. "They had already sold their places. He wasn't mad at them."

"True, Maisie," Rory said.

"So who is this Kvest?" I said. "How are we going to find that person to question?"

"Uhm," Rory said. "I think you can look up who owns a business with the secretary of state's office."

"You're right," I said, snapping my finger. "I remember that now from my business organization class from college. How did I forget that?"

I typed *Kvest LLC* into the business search box on Ohio's secretary of state's website. It gave me a link to the organizational articles. "Okay," I said, reading it, "looks like the incorporator listed himself as president and his name is—Garud Khatri."

"Oh geesh," Riya said.

"You know him?" I asked hopefully.

"You do, too," she said. "You met him after he was following you guys today."

"Your uncle?" I asked.

"My auntie Neera's husband. There's a difference."

I thought about him and remembered that I thought he looked familiar.

Then it hit me.

"And I saw him before today, too," I said.

"Where?" Riya asked.

"At the SOOCFA meeting," I said. "Sitting right next to Amelia Hargrove.

"Oh man," I said. "She came into the shop the other day." I

smacked myself on the forehead. "That's why they're having a 'fire sale.'" I couldn't believe I missed it. "Those are all the stores that already sold to Rhys Enterprises. They are getting rid of their inventory because they're moving out."

"That clinches it," Maisie said. "Everyone else is happy to go. Getting rid of all their stuff." She tapped her notebook. "It's got to be either Garud Khatri, Delilah and Daubie Dixby or Veronica Russell."

"That is?" Riya said.

"The killer," Maisie said. "Sorry, Riya. I know one of them is your uncle."

Riya shrugged. "Not my real uncle and I don't like him."

"And," Maisie said, scribbling in her book, "I guess we should add the mayor since he represents the village." She jotted something on the page and sat back in her seat satisfied with what she'd concluded.

"Why the mayor?"

"Because he was a holdout. My garden is owned by the village."

"Yeah, I'd probably agree my shady uncle might have done something, but I don't know about the mayor," Riya said. "That's not a big chunk of land the city owns." She got up from the table and started collecting the plates. "Would the mayor kill over that little thing?"

"Like I said, Rhys couldn't build a mall if they were missing even one piece of real estate," Rory said. "Especially if that parcel is in the middle of the land they need. It could have been the mayor that was the shop owner in Maisie's story."

"Did you guys ask Mayor Greer where he was when you interrogated him today?" Riya asked.

"No, we didn't," I said.

"We can go back and ask him tomorrow," Maisie said. "When we question the Darling Dixbys and Garud Khatri."

"Why do you call them the Darling Dixbys?" Rory asked.

"I don't know," I said.

"We can ask tomorrow," Maisie said.

"They're called the Darling Dixbys because they used to be in a traveling carnival act," Riya said.

"What kind of act?" Rory asked.

"They were sharpshooters."

That made Maisie so happy that it set off an uncontrollable fit of giggles. I was sure she'd end up on the floor.

chapter

⤜ ⤛

THIRTY-ONE

Garud Khatri shot to #2 on Maisie's list of suspects as soon as we found out who he was. The Darling Dixbys were, of course, #1. Maisie had wanted to talk to them from day one, even before she knew about the love affair they had with guns—hosting gun shows, keeping their very own armory—and especially after I told her what they'd said the day they visited the shop.

We had to figure out a way to get to them and get some information out of them—useful information.

"I knew something was up with that Khatri guy," Maisie said. "Him and that bow tie just made him seem like a criminal to me."

I laughed. "Maisie, you're just suspicious by nature."

"Didn't you think so, too?" she said. "You had to think he was up to something if he was following Veronica around," she reasoned.

"True," I said. "But that doesn't mean he could kill someone."

"He's a shady guy," Riya offered. "I never liked him, I wouldn't put it past him."

"Then why is your aunt married to him?" Rory asked.

"Again, not my real aunt. But probably because he has a lot of money. Guess my auntie liked that about him. Won over her heart with it."

"He'd have even more with the property he owned if he sold it," Rory offered. "Don't see why he'd stand in the way of progress."

"You know," I said, "I never thought about who owned the land or the buildings that those shops sat on. Never gave a second thought to whether they were renters or not."

But glancing up at the clock, we knew it wasn't going to be tonight.

It had been a long day.

We decided to reconvene in the morning. I had to get up early to get to the shop to make ice cream. After the busy day, we'd nearly run out. I wasn't sure what I was going to be able to make—I didn't know offhand what was in the refrigerator at the ice cream shop. I probably would have gone shopping by now if a murder investigation hadn't come up.

We had all piled into Rory's rental car when we had decided to go to Riya's house. So I took Maisie home, and Rory and I went back to my Victorian upstairs apartment.

Rory had spent half of the day crying, the other half we had spent chasing clues to keep Detective Beverly's paws off of her. I don't know that anything we'd found so far had any value to them or were viable as clues. But we had tried our best and right now it was the only thing we had. We just needed to keep pushing forward.

I wondered what the Dixby sisters would have to say for

themselves and their gun-wielding tendencies. I wondered what Riya's uncle would have as the reason he was following Veronica. And why did he decide to approach us? Did he think we had found out some information about the deal that we'd be willing to share with him? Or maybe he thought we'd found out something about the murder. Or the murderer . . .

That sent a chill down my spine.

We'd been warned on several occasions that the killer, if confronted or backed into a corner, might kill again. And this time it might be one of us.

"Tell me again why you have all of these stars hanging from your ceiling." Rory's voice intruded on my thoughts. We were sitting on opposite sides of the bed. She was doing her night hair routine, and I was looking inside my commercial refrigerator on the virtual app that came with it. I needed to see what I had, to figure out what I was going to make the next morning. "You told me this morning, but I was still half-asleep," she said.

"You should be half-asleep now," I said. "We've had an exhausting day."

"I won't be able to sleep if I don't find out why I have to wake up with glitter all over me and in my hair from your stars."

I giggled. "They were in my room at my parents' house," I said. "My Grandma Kay helped me make them when I was seven. She told me to always reach for the stars."

"You were really close with your grandmother, huh?"

"Yep," I said. "I've told you that before, I'm sure. I tell everyone that'll listen about her."

"That's why the glitter is falling off of them. They're old."

"But full of memories. And hope."

"Cute," Rory said. "I guess me and my hair can suffer through."

"I doubt if anyone could even tell that there was anything in that nest of a hairdo you have," I said.

"It says I am stylish and creative."

"Oh, it talks, too?"

"Funny."

I got up and turned off the light and climbed into bed. Lying on my back, I yawned and my last thought before drifting off was whether we were really going to find the answers we needed.

"So, Bronwyn, what do you think our chances are on solving this thing?" Rory's voice cut through my sleep.

"I think that we are in way over our heads," I said, sleepily. I let out a chuckle. "We don't have the faintest idea what we're doing, we're probably chasing down the wrong clues and people, and if the detective finds out what we're doing, he'll probably throw us all in jail."

"I thought your friend O said the detective couldn't charge us with anything."

"Sometimes they arrest people and convict them when they haven't done anything."

"Is that why you're helping me?" Rory asked.

"Yes," I said. "That's why I'm helping you."

"Then, hopefully," she said, "Detective Beverly won't find out what we're doing."

"I hope so, too." Mumbling the words, I yawned. "You know, on the TV shows Maisie watches, the people that do the stuff we're doing never get into trouble."

"All of this I'm going through doesn't seem real," Rory said.

"Feels like I'm on television or in some kind of dream. Huh! Some kind of nightmare!"

"Don't worry," I said. "You'll wake up soon. And you'll see everything is okay."

"Thanks, Bronwyn."

"You're welcome, Rory." I plumped up my pillow and snuggled in. "Anytime."

THIRTY-TWO

I woke up two hours later at four thirty and tried to be as quiet as I could as I dressed and got ready for work. I didn't want to wake Rory up that early. She'd had a hard day the day before and needed her rest.

I needed to get to the shop to make ice cream. The virtual tour of my fridge didn't give me much inspiration. I still didn't know what I was going to make.

I checked the weather, found it was going to be another scorcher, threw on some jeans and a T-shirt, and headed out. I stopped by PopPop's house just like I did every morning. Bypassing my parents' house entrance, I walked around the back and knocked on his door.

PopPop was already up and dressed as usual. He opened the door for me without saying a word. As I stepped over the threshold I could smell the coffee brewing.

"Good morning, PopPop," I said.

"Good morning, little girl." It was the nickname he had for me, no matter how big or old I got. I was still his little girl.

I followed him into the kitchen and pulled out one of the chairs around the table and sat down. He grabbed a cup out of the cabinet and poured himself a cup of coffee.

"You want a cup?" he said as he pulled out the chair next to mine.

"No, thank you," I said.

"You want to take Rory a cup?" he asked. "You didn't bring her with you."

"No," I said. "I left her sleeping." He nodded and stirred in milk and sugar. "Thank you for offering, though. She doesn't seem to like anyone's coffee but yours. Oh. And Ari Terrain's."

"Over at Molta's?"

"Yep." I nodded. "But I wouldn't be surprised if she stopped by here after she wakes up this morning. Molta's doesn't open until four. Hope that's okay with you."

"I wouldn't mind at all," he said. "I enjoy her company."

"Good," I said.

"I'll make sure I keep some hot for her."

"I wanted to ask you about Mayor Greer," I said.

"I heard that you upset him yesterday."

"How do you know that?" I asked.

He lifted up his cup and looked at me over the rim. "He told me."

"I bet he didn't tell you what he was upset about."

"Didn't have to," PopPop said. "I knew it must have been about the murder."

"The village owns some of that land that Rhys Enterprises wants to buy."

"And?"

"And do you think that Mayor Greer might have killed Zeke to keep him from getting it?"

"Zeke didn't want that land personally."

"You know what I mean, PopPop."

"Kevin is a good politician. An okay mayor, but not a killer. I don't think he would have done it."

"He didn't seem to be too honest about the mall," I said.

"Like I said, he's a good politician. Did you see how those town folk reacted to the news that a mall was coming? Wouldn't help his reelection none if they thought he was a part of that."

"He owns the land and according to Zeke they were going to get it."

"He said they were working on getting it. But the mayor doesn't control the land because the village owns it. It would have to go through city council."

"City council," I repeated. "I never thought about that."

"Oh no, you're not adding all the council members to your list of suspects, are you?"

I turned, surprise on my face. "How do you know I have a list of suspects?"

"You don't live as long as I have and not know things," he said. "But before you start suspecting people, you have to look at their motives. Kevin doesn't have any motives."

"I've been wondering about motives lately, too." I looked at PopPop. "You have lived a long time and know stuff . . ." I hesitated, but I needed to know. "What do you know about Aunt Jack?"

"I know she's my daughter."

I chuckled. "Okay. I didn't mean it like that. I meant her *motives*."

He took another sip of his coffee, not giving me an answer.

I decided to push a little more. "Is she back to stay?" I asked.

"You'd have to ask her that," he said.

"What about the ice cream shop?" I said

"What *about* the ice cream shop?" he asked.

"Is she back to take over the shop?"

"Why would you think that?" he asked, his voice never changing, not even to reassure me. Maybe because he couldn't. Maybe because she was there to take it back.

"Well," I started. I had to lick my lips and clear my throat—it had gotten dry. "Because she brought in all those catalogs. And because she's there every day." The pacing of my words picked up. "She doesn't like anything I make. I was just wondering what it is she's doing."

"Like I said, you'd have to ask Aunt Jack what her plans are," he said and took another sip of coffee. The sip took forever and I wanted to say something while he was quiet, but I couldn't think of anything. "But"—he started talking again—"as long as I'm around, I'll decide who's running the ice cream shop." He looked at me as he stood up. He walked over to his coffeemaker and poured another cup, again not finishing what he was saying until he'd finished what he was doing and came and sat back down. "I've chosen you to run the ice cream shop, and I haven't changed my mind."

I let out my breath. Then a thought popped into my head. "Does that mean I can tell her what to do?" I asked.

He chuckled. "She's still your elder, you know. Probably best to remember that, little girl," he said. "Don't be disrespectful."

"I know. I won't," I said. "I wouldn't ever do that."

"But you can certainly tell her to stop bringing in those darn catalogs," PopPop said.

I grinned. "Thank you, PopPop," I said. I stood up and kissed him on the cheek. "I have to get to the shop and make ice cream."

"What kind of ice cream you making today, Win?" he said, getting up so he could walk me to the door.

"I don't know," I said and winked. "Maybe with Aunt Jack and her candy obsession, I'll make something candy-like—maybe some licorice-flavored ice cream."

He thought that was hilarious.

I left PopPop laughing at his door and headed down the hill. The sun had made it out and it cast orange tones across the sky. I cautiously turned the corner off of Carriage Hill onto North Main, worried that I'd see Aunt Jack standing out in front of the shop with her arms filled with catalogs and maybe even a lottery machine slung across her back. But thank goodness she wasn't there.

The soft glow from the lanterns that hung on either side of the new door, the one Aunt Jack didn't have a key to, made the blue and yellow Crewse Creamery awning shimmer. It was like a beacon calling me. Telling me that it was all mine.

Well, at least the management of it.

I loved our family's ice cream shop. I loved how well it was doing, how sales had ramped up exponentially since that first day we'd reopened. And I loved my PopPop for putting me in charge and sticking by me.

I had started to worry that if Aunt Jack was going to take over the ice cream shop, I might have had to take Rory up on her offer and go back with her to New York City.

Just the thought of that made me sad.

The morning was busy. I got started on the ice cream before any of my help showed up. I had to get my ingredients from the windowsill garden that Maisie had started in the kitchen. I went with the ice cream flavor of tart lemon basil—bright lime-green colored, it was tangy and tart and tasted licorice-like (take that, Aunt Jack!). Next I crumbled up pieces of bright red peppermint and swirled them into a creamy French vanilla base, a cool winter flavor made into a sweet summer treat. Another nod to Aunt Jack—it was the candy she was always eating.

I had a whole crate of juicy blood oranges stuffed in the back of my commercial fridge, so I decided to do something with them. I made an orange lavender sorbet, made with the succulent, beautifully colored fruit that naturally had a hint of raspberry, it was that aromatic and citrusy.

And while I was pulling out the oranges, I spotted a couple of mangoes. Mmmm. I loved mango sorbet. What the heck, I plucked them out as well.

I knew my unusual choices would send Aunt Jack for a loop.

Then I thought about how I had promised PopPop I'd be nice. So, I made a batch of Neapolitan. I'd fill the layers with chunks of milk chocolate and morsels of fresh strawberries, and I'd make black walnut. I had a bag of them in the pantry. Those had been two of her and Grandma Kay's favorites.

Time flew by, and before I knew it, my mother, Rory and Riya came in. Maisie was late as usual, but we wouldn't have had the black walnut made in time for opening if it hadn't been for her.

"We've got an appointment with Uncle Garud at four o'clock," Riya announced after the first wave of customers left.

"Four?" I said and glanced up to the clock on the wall. My appointment with the food truck guy was at one. I'd be cutting it close.

"Yep. At his office."

"What are we going to do when we get there?" I asked.

"Ask him why he killed Zeke Reynolds."

chapter

THIRTY-THREE

I'd met the food truck guy the night Maisie and I had figured out who the murderer was in our last "investigation." If it could be called that.

He'd seen us sell our wares off of a frozen food cart and had offered his business card. His name (Charles Randolph Manuto), company name (Manuto Systems) and contact info were written on the one side. I flipped it over per his instruction and the other side was embossed with *We Make Food Trucks*. "I can get you a good deal," he had told me and sure enough he had.

I'd been skeptical about investing in one. I'd just spent a boat-load on remodeling the store, upgrading our commercial appliances, paying our two new employees a living wage. But soon after people got wind of our delicious ice cream flavors and me solving a murder, it didn't take long, even with the snow we were having at the time, for a steady stream of customers to start rolling in. And when the weather broke and just a sliver of warm sun shined through, we were generating enough profit to justify me making another investment. I'd hoped a solid investment.

Manuto Systems was located on the west side of Cleveland in North Olmsted. A good forty-minute drive from Chagrin Falls. I took Rory with me and tried to keep the conversation light. No murder or jail talk.

"This is a tiny office for such a big operation," Rory said.

And she was right. It was almost a storefront, although it was located in one of those industrial parkways. "He doesn't outfit the food trucks here, I'm guessing."

I pulled open the door and we met his receptionist, Pam, as she was coming back from getting coffee. The mug in hand, steam wafting from it.

"Hi, Win," Pam said.

"Hi. Is Mr. Manuto around?"

"Sure is," she said. "Hold on, I'll buzz him."

Charles Manuto and his assistant were an odd pair, but they were perfectly matched. They both reminded me of beach bums that were now trying to break into Hollywood as agent and starlet. Pam's hair was straggly, a dirty blond with dark highlights. She wore tight clothes and high heels. Cheap high heels.

"Where did she get those vinyl shoes from? Payless?" Rory nudged me. Her nose was turned up like she'd smelled a dead mouse.

"Everyone can't wear designer shoes," I whispered back.

Rory winced. "They should at least try."

"Bronwyn Crewse!" He came out to the lobby. His arms outstretched. "My favorite customer."

"Hi, Mr. Manuto."

"Call me Chuck." He'd said it every time I'd seen him, but for some reason I just couldn't do it.

"And who do you have here?"

"This is my friend Rory," I said. "She's visiting from out of town."

"Nice shoes," Pam said from behind her desk.

"Thank you," Rory said. Her smile was an I-told-you-so. "Nice to meet you, Mr. Manuto."

"Chuck!" he said. "Everyone calls me Chuck." He gestured with his hand. "Come on in, have a sit-down and let's talk." He stepped back into his office, waiting for us, then closed the door after we went through. "Sit. Sit."

Mr. Manuto. Chuck. Was tall and lanky. His shoulders were in a constant state of hunched as if he wanted to keep his full height a secret. He had a brownish-orangey tan, so evenly colored that even with our streak of hot weather, I was thoroughly convinced it had to be done at a tanning salon. His hair was brown, combed back and hung right below his ears. He'd been in a suit every time I'd seen him, never one that seemed tailor-made.

He sat at his desk across from us. "It won't be long now." He waved his hand over his head like my name was going up in lights. "The Crewse Creamery Food Truck," he announced. "*Bom, bom bah bah!* Will make its maiden voyage right to your front door in less than thirty days."

I couldn't help but to beam. "I really can't wait."

"Don't worry, you won't have to wait much longer." He ran his hand over the stubble on his face. "I was just in your neck of the woods and saw a line coming out your door."

I beamed some more.

"This truck is really gonna be the icing on the cake for you," he said. "Or should I say, the sprinkles on the ice cream." He laughed at his joke.

I was still smiling about getting the food truck, so that worked—he thought I thought he was funny, too.

"You've got a good thing going on over there." He smacked his lips. "A real good thing."

"She makes delicious ice cream," Rory said.

"Thank you," I said and bowed my head. "Thank you both."

"I was meeting another client when I passed your establishment," he said. "Otherwise, I would have stopped in."

"Another client?" I asked. *Guess I won't be the only shop owner on North Main with a food truck.*

"Yes," he said and looked off thoughtfully. "New concept for me—a mobile bookstore."

"Oh really?" I asked.

"Yes, spoke with the mayor," Mr. Manuto said. "His idea is sort of like a bookmobile only it's not the lending of books, but the selling of them. He told me the only bookshop in the village was going out of business and he still wanted to be able to serve his residents."

"Around the Corner Bookshop." I nodded not because I knew, thanks to our search, they were going out of business, but to confirm the name. Although it was just the answer Maisie and I were going to try and find.

"The mayor owns the bookstore?" Rory asked.

"No," I said, just then realizing that part of what Mr. Manuto said. "The food truck—uh, book truck—is for him?"

"No. It's for the owner of the bookshop."

"Oh," I said, remembering Amelia Hargrove coming into the store to hang flyers. I guess she would need to reduce inventory. She couldn't fit all those books in a truck.

"Prime retail space." Mr. Manuto was stroking his stubble again. "I tried to get office space over that way, always had a dream of opening my business in Chagrin Falls. But they told me nothing was available"—he focused his eyes on me—"although I knew there was."

"Who told you that?" I asked. There were a couple of empty storefronts for rent or sale available most of the time.

He let out a chuckle. "The same guy who wants my help now." He nodded. "He knew I'd know just how to get him what he needed."

"Oh," I said and sat up a little straighter in my seat.

That was interesting.

"But what he doesn't know," Mr. Manuto said with a smirk, "is that I'm going to make up for my lost cost in opportunity in the price I'm giving him."

THIRTY-FOUR

I couldn't wait to get back to the ice cream shop and tell Maisie about the mayor buying Amelia a book truck, and the fact that he was telling prospective shop owners there wasn't any space available on North Main. Had he done that because he'd known the mall was coming? What was going on with him?

And if he had, what, if anything, did that have to do with Zeke Reynolds's murder?

When Rory and I walked into the store, there was a line that snaked around the lobby, people licking on cones and gobbling down big spoonfuls of scoops and whipped cream–covered sundaes. Riya was still there helping Maisie and Wilhelmina. My mother had already left. Candy was due in later. Everything seemed to be under control now. Afternoon crowd would be coming in soon, though.

I decided to walk around and talk to my customers. I liked to get feedback on my flavors and let the customers know that our place was filled with a family atmosphere.

Four o'clock rolled around in no time and it was hard to break away. Especially hard since all four of us were going—Rory, Maisie, Riya and me.

This was one time I was happy Aunt Jack was in town. I called her to come in. She hadn't showed up that morning. I think she had been worn out. She answered the phone grumbling and grumbled all the way through the conversation, but she agreed to come in and help. I had to promise her, though, that she wouldn't have to stay all the way to closing.

I didn't know how long we'd be gone. Especially since this little outing had nothing to do with the family's business.

"How are you going to get him to talk to us?" I asked Riya as we set out.

"I'm going to use my auntie Neera as a weapon against him," she said.

"Are we going to go talk to her first?" Rory asked.

"No," Riya said. "We don't have to. I'll just tell him I'm going to tell her what I know, and he'll tell us whatever we want to know."

"How do you figure that?" Maisie asked.

"Because everyone is afraid of my auntie Neera."

Garud Khatri had an office on the second floor of an office building that sat between Davis Bakery and McGuire's Pharmacy. It took up almost the entire floor.

"Ah," he said when his assistant showed us in, his big phony smile spread across his face. At least he had nice teeth. He opened his arms like he was happy to see us, his too large suit jacket hanging off of him like he was a scarecrow. "I was surprised when my dear, sweet niece called and said you all wanted to speak to me."

"Thank you for taking time to see us," I said.

Riya cut an eye at me. I think she felt like since she didn't like him, I shouldn't be nice to him.

"And to what do I owe the pleasure of this visit?" he asked, gesturing for us to sit. There were only two chairs in front of the desk. But there was a gold-colored couch on one wall where Rory sat down. Riya stayed on her feet.

"I was wondering, Uncle Garud," Riya said. "Does Auntie Neera know about you and that woman?"

Lowering his voice, he talked out of the side of his mouth. "What woman?" His smile dimming a watt or two.

I laughed to myself and wondered how many women there were because he didn't deny Riya's accusation, it seemed he just wanted to clarify it.

"The woman I saw you with at the meeting for the shop owners," she said.

"You were there?" He narrowed his eyes, apparently trying to think about what he'd done there that night.

"I was there," Riya said, "and I saw you."

"I did nothing." He waved both his hands, dismissing the notion. "What did this woman look like?" His voice went down again.

"I think her name is Amelia Hargrove," Riya said.

"Oh, if that is the case"—his smile returning—"it wasn't anything. Amelia Hargrove is with the mayor," he said, smoothing down his bow tie.

"What do you mean she's with the mayor?" Maisie asked. She had sat down in the chair next to mine. "Isn't the mayor married?"

"Ah," Uncle Garud said. "I see I know something you don't. Did you come to me for information? Because I can tell you that being married does not always stop a man from going after a woman."

"It has never stopped you, has it?" Riya said. "Does my poor auntie Neera know that?"

He opened his mouth, closed it and let out a groan.

"I think she does, because she is the one who asked me to keep an eye on you at the meeting."

I didn't think Riya had even seen him at the shop owners' meeting. She was too busy being "supportive." At least she would have mentioned it—heck, she'd never even mentioned an Auntie Neera. But if she thought this was a way to get information from old Uncle Garud, I was all for it.

"I am not concerned," he said, "about your fantasy. I have done nothing wrong."

"But who will Auntie believe, Uncle Garud, you or me?"

"What is it that you want, Riya?" He balled up his hands into fists and placed them on his desk. Seemed as if he was trying not to show his anger with us. "You bring your friends here, you want to lie about me to the love of my life . . ." He placed one fist over his heart. "All I want to know," he said, now putting the palms of his hands together like he was praying, "is what it is I can help you with so that you and your little friends can leave."

"Why were you following my friends yesterday?" Riya asked.

"I wasn't following your friends," he said curtly.

"Then why did you say you were following them?"

"Did I say I was following them?" he asked. "I don't remember saying that."

"Don't play games with me, Uncle Garud," Riya said. "Auntie Neera is coming to see me at the hospital tomorrow. I have to check on her heart. Do you want me to have to break it by telling her about you and this woman I saw you with?"

He coughed into his hand and looked around the room at us. "As I said, I was not following these women. I was following Veronica Russell."

"Why were you following her?" Maisie asked.

"Why were *you* following her?" Uncle Garud asked.

"We're here to ask the questions," Riya said and put a hand on her hip. His shoulders fell and he lowered his eyes. She really knew how to handle this man. We should take her on all of our interrogations.

"I was following her because I wanted to see where she was going," he said and held up his hands, surrendering. "Isn't that why you follow people?"

"Why did you want to see where she was going?" I asked.

"Because I needed to see what she was up to," Uncle Garud said. "Rhys Enterprises is to buy my property and their representative is killed. It is in my best interest to keep track of what's going on."

"You are going to sell your property to Rhys Enterprises?" I asked.

"Of course!" he said enthusiastically. "I am a businessman. I am in the business of making money."

"Do you think because Zeke Reynolds was killed you're not going to be able to sell your property?"

"Of course not. What do they say? 'One monkey does not stop a show.' They will send another representative."

"Then why did you care where Veronica was going?" Maisie asked.

"Because she went to see the mayor. That couldn't be a good thing for me."

"How did you know that's where she was going?" Rory asked from the couch.

"What?"

"Good point," I said. "When she started out you didn't know where she was going."

"And why is her going to see the mayor a bad thing for you?" Riya asked.

"I just needed to keep an eye on her because the mayor and Amelia will get a kickback if they strike a deal. If he makes a deal with them before he can make a deal with me."

"Who?" all of us asked together.

"The new guy. The new representative that's coming from Rhys Enterprises, that's who. You girls know nothing about business." He shook his head. "I wanted to make sure that I was the first to see him when he got here."

"Were you afraid that Veronica was going to make a deal with the mayor and Amelia?"

"No." He thought about that. "Maybe. Zeke was a good friend of mine. He told me lots of things. I told him all about Chagrin Falls. How he could come and buy my buildings and put up his mall. How I would help him to get everyone to sign the deal. I am very influential, you know."

I wondered about that. I hadn't ever heard of him. Nor had I heard my grandfather or mother talk about him. He was more smoke and mirrors, I thought, than anything else.

"But when Zeke got here, he had a change of heart," Uncle Garud was saying.

"So you killed him?" Maisie asked the question that Riya had said we were coming to ask.

"No." Garud said it just as calmly as if Maisie had asked him would he like a piece of gum. "I did not kill him, but I did want to wring his neck." He pretended with his hands to grab an imaginary body by the neck and gave it a good shaking. "But I didn't." He dropped his hands. "He decided to quit. Go home to Florida. And not take any more property from people who didn't want to sell it."

"Like who?" I asked.

"Like those ancient twin spinsters," he said. "They would not give. Everything else was a done deal."

"You didn't want to sell yours?" Maisie asked.

Uncle Garud pointed at Maisie but looked at Riya. "Does she not understand English? Did I not say I wanted to sell my property? Sell. Sell. Sell." He stood up and leaned over the desk toward Maisie, spittle flying with his words. "Even that building you want to expand your little garden." He swiped the palms of his hands together. "Gone!"

"We get it, Uncle Garud," Riya said. "You wanted to sell."

"Yes," he said and sat back down. He gave his bow tie a tug on both sides. "I didn't like that Zeke wanted to leave. I needed him to work for Rhys until this deal went through. I needed him to make sure I got the good deal and not the mayor and Amelia."

"What kind of deal would they get?"

"Kickbacks." He said it like it was obvious. "The mayor could offer Rhys Enterprises many things I couldn't. And Amelia, *his* woman," he emphasized, looking at Riya, "would stand behind him and they would get rich together, and I would not get a thing, even though I was the one to bring Rhys Enterprises here.

"I couldn't kill him," he continued. Cupping his hands and holding them out, he shrugged. "Because then I would not make any money."

chapter THIRTY-FIVE

Family Chef Night. My mother's creation after us kids grew up and flew the nest. It was a way to make sure her children didn't stay away from the coop too long. One family member was designated head chef, the others acted as sous chefs. We'd cook, eat and spend the evening playing games, laughing and, per my mother, "creating lasting family moments."

My daddy, skilled surgeon and culinary master, was up tonight and we all knew that meant we'd be in for a treat.

Riya on her last day off for a while had been a big help. Letting us meet at her house, making an appointment with Garud Khatri for us and steering that conversation in the right direction. All without losing her temper.

That was practically a miracle. And an inspiration.

After talking to him, our little sleuthing squad was raring to go. We decided to talk to all the people who'd sold their shops and the one (even though there were two of them) who stood in the way—the Dixby sisters.

But first it was dinner at the Crewse house. Dr. James Graham Crewse, acting head chef, with sous chefs galore. Who said too many cooks spoil the pot. Not when the cooks were the Crewses.

Wilhelmina worked the late shift with Candy so the rest of us could leave early. Not that we'd been there all day. It was a good thing I'd come in and made ice cream that morning.

I scooped up enough of the shiny and creamy mango sorbet I'd made and added a touch of tart lime and the tangy lemon basil from trays in the walk-in freezer to fill up two gallon cartons. Didn't know what was on the menu for dinner, but fruit goes great for dessert with any entrée. Especially when the fruit is in ice cream.

Rory, Maisie, Riya and I walked up to my parents' house and found my mother pulling groceries out of bags when we got there.

"Can we help?" Rory asked when we walked inside.

"Sure can."

"What is Dad making?" I asked.

"It's a surprise." My mother winked, a big smile on her face. She was my dad's biggest cheerleader. "Now come on, help me set the table."

The table was a twelve-foot hand-carved, live edge one that had been specially made when my parents remodeled after they became empty nesters. The dining area was right aside of the open concept kitchen and attached family room. Too much space for them, as was the rest of the five-bedroom home, but I'd never heard them say they needed or wanted to downsize.

We were laughing and giggling when I heard the first of family trickle in.

"Hey!" came the voice from up front and a few seconds later Bobby appeared at the doorway to the kitchen. He was standing there grinning. He had a knapsack over his shoulder and across his body, and his hands were filled big sheets of white poster boards.

"What are you doing, Bobby?" my mother said and pointed at the boards.

"This is for after dinner," he said. "Instead of playing games."

"Well, if it's for after dinner, we don't need it here now," she said.

"I'd been meaning to talk to you anyway," I said as he came in, remembering Mr. Mason. Who, now that I thought about it, hadn't showed up like I asked. At least while I was there.

Bobby was the only medical member of the family who didn't have a big practice and a big bank account. A nurse practitioner, he ran the community clinic and had recruited my dad and Riya to help out at it on their days off.

"And you can talk *after* dinner, too," my mother said.

"Hey, Mama," Bobby said and went over and kissed her. "Stop fussing. I'll put this stuff right over here." He headed to a corner of the dining area.

"Nope. Not in my kitchen." She shook her head. "Put them in the mudroom."

"Yes, ma'am," he said and winked at me. "Hey, Maisie. Riya." He nodded his hellos. "And who is this?" He looked at Rory.

"My friend from New York," I said.

"Oh, okay," he said. I was sure somehow he already knew she was the one with the bloody shoes.

"Put that paper up," my mother said again. "It's time to start cooking."

"I'm going! I'm going!" He chuckled.

"My brother Bobby," I said to Rory as if she hadn't figured that out. "I'm going to talk to him about Mr. Mason."

"I've heard that the ice cream shop is really booming," he said, coming back from the mudroom. "And all I hear over at the clinic is how genius your glass wall is."

"Thank you," I said proudly, folding one arm in front of me, one behind me, and taking a bow. "We've been pretty busy with my delicious, delectable frozen concoctions and all of this hot weather."

"So proud of you, sis," he said.

"And if you've heard we are busy," I said, "why didn't you drop by and lend a hand? It is still a *family* business."

"I heard you had Aunt Jack helping out," he said with a big grin on his face.

"You're not funny," I said.

"I'm not trying to be." He shrugged. "But I knew you had hired help. Very smart, Win, instead of trying to rope family into it."

"That's not a nice thing to say, Bobby," my mother said. "No one has ever tried to 'rope' anyone into working there. Everyone in the family loves our ice cream shop."

He held up his hands. "Didn't mean it like that." He knew better than to start our mother fussing about something.

"What are you up to, Bobby?" my mother asked.

"Nothing," he said. He raised his hands higher, showing his innocence.

"I mean with the poster boards," she said.

"Oh," he said and glanced toward the mudroom. "I'm organizing a protest against Rhys Enterprises. An out-of-state company coming in and trying to gentrify Chagrin Falls."

Robert Bantham Crewse, the brother next to me, was an activist. He would advocate for any and every cause he felt passionate about. No matter their station in life, he helped everybody. That was how I knew I could count on him to help me with Mr. Mason.

"I wanted to know if you guys are in," he asked, rubbing his hands together.

"I'm in," Maisie said.

"What does this protesting consist of?" I asked.

"Signs, marching, chanting—making ourselves an immovable barrier. The usual."

"Oh my," I said. "You were born in the wrong decade."

"It's never a wrong time—or decade—to exercise one's constitutional rights."

"When is it?" Maisie asked.

"Tomorrow night," he said. "I just need to know who is in so I'll have enough signs."

I wasn't sure what we were going to be doing tomorrow night. I was sure we wouldn't have solved the murder by then, so we'd probably still be busy chasing down clues.

But I couldn't tell him that. Bobby was a tattletale. Everyone knew better than to tell him anything you didn't want the adults to know. Even as adults, he'd tell everything he knew, and although it was usually my father and grandfather he'd spill to, and they already kind of knew what I was doing, I couldn't take a chance on him finding out. I didn't know who else he might tell.

"I'm not sure if I can go," I said.

"Why?" he asked.

"Because I have company," I said and pointed to Rory. It was the best reason I could come up with.

He stuck his hands in his jeans pockets. "Okay, come if you can." He looked back toward the kitchen. "What kind of ice cream you bring?" He didn't wait for me to answer. He walked over to the fridge and opened the freezer door.

"Does he think protesting will help?" Rory asked.

"He's always doing something for some cause," I said. "I don't even know how he thinks Rhys Enterprises will see him."

"Or that they will care," Riya said.

"I think it's a good idea," Maisie said. "It might help save the building I want from turning into a mall."

"Yeah, so getting back to the mall and Rhys Enterprises, what's next?" Riya asked again.

"Shhh!" I said, locating my brother, making sure he was out of earshot. "I don't want Bobby to know what we're doing."

"Hey, everybody!" It was my two oldest brothers, James Jr. and Llewellyn, Lew for short. They both had on shorts and polo shirts. One pink. The other one lavender. Lew carried a board game under each arm. "We found this guy outside. Anyone know him?"

It was O.

What was he doing at my family's family night?

"Of course we know who he is," my mother said and went

over and looped her arm around O's, steering him over to the table. "He's a friend of Win's."

My brothers both looked at me questioningly. These were the guys that piled into a car with my dad and played stakeout whenever I had a date with a boy from school. I put up both my hands. "He's a friend of PopPop's, too," I stated in my defense.

"Who's a friend of PopPop's?" My dad walked into the kitchen.

"O," I said.

"Oh," my dad said and grinned. "And where is my dad? He invites people and doesn't show up?"

"He's coming," my mother said. "But I invited O."

I saw Maisie grin out of the corner of my eye and she nudged Riya. Riya seemed lost, she didn't seem to get the joke.

"The more the merrier," my dad said. "I'm sure we have enough food."

"What are you cooking, Mr. Crewse?" Maisie asked.

"You'll find out soon enough." My grandfather came in through the mudroom. "Everyone has to cook in order to eat."

"I've got a protest planned," Bobby said, announcing it to the newcomers. "I'm looking for volunteers. Even bought some poster boards so you guys can help me make some signs." He eyed our mother and dug his hands down into his pockets. "After dinner of course."

"I brought Monopoly games over to play after dinner." Lew pointed to the island counter where he'd placed them. "One is the Game of Thrones edition, the other is the Ultimate Banking edition. It doesn't use money, only credit cards."

"What are you protesting now, Bobby?" James Jr. asked.

"Building of the mini mall on the triangle."

"The one that Zeke Reynolds was killed over?" PopPop added.

"Aren't you trying to solve that?" Lew asked and looked at me. I'd gotten advice from him when Maisie and I were trying to solve the last murder.

I made a face at him. I didn't know he knew. Then I glanced over at my mother. Why was I trying to keep something secret that she knew about?

"We're thinking of investigating the people at the SOOCFA meeting," Maisie said. She had no discretion.

"Why?" PopPop asked. He probably had the same mindset as my mom. None of the shop owners would have done it.

"Because Zeke Reynolds was messing with our livelihoods." Maisie's voice was already in protest mode.

"Thought you were working at the ice cream shop," Lew said.

"I am. But I also run my garden. And I hope to buy the building next to it." She nodded. "We were thinking of looking into the people that were there that night because those owners probably didn't know about the plan to put up a mall. Hearing about it might have angered them enough to kill him."

"So that would include you," James Jr. said. He had a sparkle in his eye. My brothers liked to tease Maisie as much as they did me.

"It does not." She rolled her eyes.

"Who does it involve?" PopPop asked.

"O had suggested we look at the landowners of the block of buildings that Rhys Enterprises wants to buy," I said.

"And?" he asked.

"Don't yet know how that's working out," I said. Now everyone was going to know we weren't real good at the whole sleuthing thing. "The only people who were there that were affected shop owners had already sold their properties."

My brothers chuckled.

"Maybe you should just stick to making ice cream," James Jr. said.

"Because she makes awesome ice cream, don't you, Pumpkin?" My father's words didn't help me to gather which side he was on.

"She does," PopPop said. "But she's got my vote as a sleuth, too. Caught the last one, didn't she?"

It was nice to have PopPop's praise. It meant a lot to me. I stood there smiling, enjoying it, and didn't notice my mother and O coming to stand on either side of me.

"I told you, Win," O whispered in one ear, "you should leave this alone. It could be dangerous."

"You remember what happened last time," my mother whispered in my other ear. "This time you might just be the one who gets killed."

chapter

THIRTY-SIX

My mother was acting like a Ping-Pong ball, and she was making me dizzy.

Flipping on me. One minute she wanted me to help Rory, the next, warning that I could be the next one who turned up dead.

She'd probably do a triple somersault when she found out what we'd decided to do.

But we planned on being smart about our decision to talk to the Dixby sisters and if we decided to talk to Veronica again. We were going to make sure we did it in a public place and together.

It was quite disquieting to know that danger, in our little village, lurked around every corner and could have its sights trained on just about anyone.

The morning after Family Chef Night, I woke up early, ready to get the day started. And so did Rory.

"Morning," I said as she stood in my bedroom doorway. She'd gone back to sleeping on the couch. "I didn't wake you, did I?"

"Nope. I'm ready to do this. We're still going to talk to suspects today, right?"

"Interrogate them, as Maisie would say. And yes. We still have the sisters and a revisit to the assistant."

"Good." She rubbed her eyes with her fingers. Her hair still in twists. "The sooner we do, the sooner I can get out of here."

"You tired of me and my hometown?" I gave her a puppy-dog pout face.

"No," she said. "Tired of being embroiled in another murder."

I knew exactly how she felt.

First stop of the morning was, as always, my PopPop's house. I'd already made up my mind that five a.m. wasn't too early to start our questioning, and my grandfather was a good person to start with.

"PopPop," I said. He'd been hopping around the kitchen fixing coffee for Rory. He liked that she liked his brew.

"Did you know Mayor Kevin Greer is buying Amelia Hargrove a book truck?"

He looked at me over the rim of his cup. He'd sat at the table across from me. Rory sat between us.

"My food truck guy told me," I offered since he didn't say anything.

"Are we back on that?"—his response.

"What?" I said.

"You thinking the mayor killed Zeke Reynolds."

"I never said that." At least I didn't think I'd said it out loud. "I'm just saying that's a big deal to do for someone who you're not dating."

Rory sipped her coffee and watched us like she was at a tennis match.

"Kevin is married to Faith," PopPop said.

"I know," I said. "But why else would he want to make up to Ms. Hargrove for her having to sell her shop?"

And, I wondered and hoped I hadn't said aloud, why else would the mayor want to placate Amelia Hargrove if he wasn't feeling guilty? Guilty, in my opinion, about being a part of the mall debacle and maybe getting her tangled up in a murder.

PopPop made a big deal of swallowing his coffee before he spoke. "Chuck Manuto? Is that who told you this?"

"You know him?" I asked.

"Not personally," he said. "He's been wanting a spot on North Main for years. Kevin thought he was shady, never would let a deal for him go through."

"How can the mayor stop real estate transactions?" I asked. "Wouldn't that be illegal or something?"

"Kevin got reelected time and time again because people like him. They trust him." He stared down at his coffee. "He makes them feel like he knows what's best for the village."

"Like building a mall on the triangle?"

"Didn't he tell you he didn't have anything to do with Rhys Enterprises coming in here to disrupt us?"

"Yes," I said. I hated keeping up the disagreement with my grandfather. "He did, but—" I quietly protested.

"Look," PopPop said, like he wanted to end our conversation. "I'd believe Chuck killed that guy before I believed Kevin did it." He stirred his coffee although I figured it must be getting cold. "And I'd be careful about digging around in people's personal business because that's how innocent people get hurt."

If that hadn't come from my grandfather, I would have thought it a threat. But I knew he was just looking out for me.

Walking down the hill after morning coffee with PopPop, Rory and I were silent. I didn't know what she was thinking about. But, after what PopPop had said, I was thinking about Charles Randolph Manuto.

He'd been wronged by the mayor of Chagrin Falls. He wanted to be a part of the business community and he'd been denied a place on North Main Street.

But how would he exact revenge on Kevin Greer by killing Zeke Reynolds?

I wasn't sure. That was something I needed to think about.

The day flew by, creating ice cream flavors, serving customers. I had no time to think about murder. Maisie and my mom got in after ten, an hour before we opened. PopPop had taken his place at his regular booth soon after we'd left his house. He'd come with a thermos full of backup coffee. Rory had pitched in to help me make ice cream, and we laughed and talked about old times as I made up another batch of the mango sorbet and the mint mojito coffee. They'd both been a hit and had sold out quickly.

The first time I took a breather and looked up, Aunt Jack was coming in. She'd been there the day before only on my request and the store's need, not that she was officially on—as an employee— but she was family and, like Bobby and I had talked about, the shop always welcomed help from family.

"I told Wilhelmina not to come in today," Aunt Jack announced as she huffed her way in the door. I raised an eyebrow. "She worked late yesterday. Thought I'd take her place today. Give her a break."

I didn't say anything. I was too busy to process all the wrong in what she'd done.

The next time I looked up it was two thirty and Riya was rushing in the door.

Out of breath and flushed, she leaned over the counter. "You haven't questioned anyone yet, have you?"

"No." I chuckled.

"Whew!" she said. "I didn't want to miss that."

"When are we going to question them?" Maisie said. When it came to murder investigations, she always had her radar on.

I shrugged. "I don't know. The sidewalk sale is tonight. Maybe we can do it then."

Maisie shook her head vigorously. "Too many people will be around. We should do it now."

"Now?" I glanced up at the clock. "I don't know. Aunt Jack told Wilhelmina not to come in, and knowing my mother, she's got a class this afternoon."

"We get lunch, don't we?" Rory asked.

I laughed. "We do." I bit my bottom lip and glanced around the shop. The afternoon crowd wouldn't start til after four. I knew the two of them could handle it. "Okay," I said. I reached back to untie my apron. "Who should we start with?"

"The Dixby sisters," Maisie said without hesitation.

"You think?" Riya said. "I was thinking we should talk to Veronica first." She was back to that.

"We already did," Maisie said.

"I know." A pout puckered up Riya's lips. "I missed it."

"The Dixby sisters are the holdouts and have a good motive," Maisie said. "That makes them a good place to start."

"They'd try death by coffee," Rory said. "Not a gun."

"They have a gun collection." Maisie didn't agree with Rory on that point. "They're expert marksmen—"

"Wait. Wait. Wait. They're expert marksmen?" I asked.

"They couldn't be the star attraction as sharpshooters in a carnival if they weren't," she said.

"I never said they were the *star* attraction," Riya said. "But I guess they probably are. Expert marksmen. Isn't that what a sharpshooter is?"

"Without them, the whole vertical mini mall deal would be a bust," Maisie said, a curt nod in affirmation.

"They were already holding out," I said. "They didn't have to kill him to stop it. They just had to keep up with what they were doing."

"You think that those two old ladies are the ones that did that whole wrestle Zeke down thing, take the gun and shoot him?" Rory asked. "The way you enacted it in Riya's kitchen?"

"Maybe so." Maisie shrugged.

I didn't want to mention that I had put my food truck guy on the list. No way we could go all the way to North Olmsted and get back on our "lunch break."

"Okay. The sisters it is," Riya said. "I guess if we find they did it, no need to go back and talk to Veronica. They seem like good suspects."

"And why now do you think that?" I asked.

"Well, because Zeke Reynolds might have been harassing them. Trying to wear them down. Make them sell. That would have been stressful for them, I'm sure. In my medical opinion, it is possible for stress to cause a person to act irrationally."

"And kill someone." Maisie finished the thought as if she had enough medical knowledge to concur.

"So what are we waiting for?" Rory asked. "Let's go get 'em."

W hat are we looking at?" Riya asked.

Maisie and I had stopped dead in our tracks when we got to the large window in front of the Juniper Tree.

"A conspiracy," Maisie said.

"What kind of conspiracy?" Riya stared into the window to try to see what we were seeing.

"I think she means Amelia and Veronica," I said.

"Strange they're sitting there together," Maisie said. "Very strange."

"Isn't Amelia the one who's dating the mayor?" Rory asked.

"I think so." I shrugged. "My PopPop doesn't think so."

"He just said that the mayor was married," Rory said. "I never heard him deny he was having an affair."

I hadn't thought about it that way.

"And didn't Veronica go and talk to the mayor the other day?" Riya asked.

"Yep," Maisie and I said at the same time.

"They're probably planning on how they'll spend the kick-back Riya's uncle Garud was talking about," Maisie said. "And how not to go to jail."

"He's not my uncle," Riya said. "And I thought we came to question the Dixby sisters. Shouldn't we concentrate on one suspect at a time?"

"We have to take whatever opportunity presents itself in solving this," Maisie said, as if she'd been doing this for years. "Follow the clues."

I'd heard that from her before.

Maisie tapped her finger on the glass. "They could, right over a cup of coffee—"

"Bad coffee," Rory chimed in.

"—be figuring out right now, how to push the mayor out of the deal." She narrowed her eyes. "Maybe even how to push him out of a fourth-floor window. *Splat!*" She gave the nonpresent mayor a push. "Kill him dead."

"That's redundant," Riya said.

"What if it's a bigger conspiracy than that?" Rory said, adding to Maisie's story.

"How?" Maisie asked. She was all ears.

"They're in the coffee shop." Rory waggled her eyebrows.

"And?" Maisie's ears perked up.

"With the Dixby sisters . . ." Rory's brows waggled some more as she pulled Maisie in.

"All of them were in it together!" Maisie bought right into Rory's speculation. Excited, her eyes got wide.

I rolled mine. "They wanted different things," I said.

"It doesn't matter." Maisie stepped up on the stoop, ready to go in the door and confront them all. "Two of them wanted Zeke dead for love. Veronica," Maisie recalled, "said she wished Zeke was dead because of a *lovers'* quarrel." Maisie held one hand out, palm up, like she was weighing the option. "And Amelia"—she lowered her hand like it was getting heavier—"was willing to sell her business, did sell, possibly for the love of a paramour. But it seems it was because of some kind of deal with Rhys so she could get a kickback to help her *lover.*"

We listened to her deduction.

Still holding out the one hand, she stuck out the other. "The Dixby sisters wanted Zeke dead to stop him from buying up their property." She smacked her hands together. "Either way," she said, clasping them and giving them a shake, "they all wanted him *dead.* Conspiracy." She nodded. "Conspiracy of the fourth degree."

Whatever that meant . . .

"Excuse me." It was Ivan Rynok, part owner of the art gallery. He came out of the coffee shop, holding his cup up in the air to keep from spilling its contents all over Maisie. She'd been blocking the door and he ran right into her.

"Sorry!" Maisie said.

"It is okay," he said, his accent barely there. "And hi to you." He directed his greeting to Rory. "Thought you were coming back to the gallery to buy a painting."

"I did come back," Rory said. "You were closed."

"Oh." He nodded. "We have a lot of packing up to do and are getting ready for the sale."

Maisie had been wiggling ever since he'd bumped into her. He and his wife were also on our list, and I could tell curiosity had her itching and there were questions inside of her that were bouncing around trying to get out.

"You sold your store?" Maisie's first, I'm sure, of many questions came bursting out.

"*Da*. We did." Ivan took a sip out of his cup. "Time we got out." He coughed into his hand. "Time to be moving to bigger and better things. We have big plans. My wife and I."

And seeing Veronica made me think of something she said. "I heard Zeke Reynolds came to the gallery," I said. I might as well get my questions in, too.

"He was an art lover." He waved his hand. A shiny diamond-encrusted pinky ring glittered in the sunlight.

"And a tough businessman," Riya added.

"He was. *Da*. At first. When he went against his company to complete the mall deal. But then——"

"Wait." Maisie frowned. "He went *against* his company? You mean Rhys Enterprises?"

"*Da*. He pushed for that mall. At first. Thought he'd get in on the ground floor. Turning the village around."

"There's nothing wrong with the village," Riya said. "It's the best place around Cleveland to live."

"He thought it would be better with a mall." Ivan drank from his cup. "Me and my wife didn't care. We are leaving anyway."

"If he wanted the mall——"

"At first," Ivan corrected.

"At first." Maisie went along with the correction. "If Zeke Reynolds wanted the mall at first and that was going against his company, then that would mean they *didn't* want the mall?"

"They did. They changed their mind." Ivan waved his ring-clad hand back and forth, aiding in the confusion he was sprouting. "But now, another company will take over."

"Take over to build the mall?" Maisie said.

"Da!" He seemed to like the idea.

"How do you know that?" I asked. "How could you know?"

"Because they sent me a check!" he said. "And a letter."

"A letter saying they are building a mall?" Maisie asked.

"Of course not. It said that they had taken over the account from Rhys Enterprises." He held up his cup in salute. "You come to the gallery, we'll see if we can't get you a good deal, no?" And with that he left.

"I don't believe him," Maisie said. "Do you believe him, Win?"

"Why wouldn't you believe him?" Riya asked.

"Because that would mean that Veronica was lying when she said that someone from Rhys was coming to take over for Zeke."

"And so was Uncle Garud," Riya said. We all looked at her. "But why would they lie?"

"Murderers always lie," Maisie said.

THIRTY-EIGHT

So if we're going in, who are we going to talk to?" Riya asked. "The Dixby sisters or Amelia and lying Veronica?"

We had yet to go inside, our plans for questioning the twin baristas thwarted when Ivan came out.

"I vote for the Dixby sisters," Rory said. "I've seen their temper firsthand. They get angry and fight back."

"And they own guns," Maisie said.

"You're obsessed with them and their guns," I said.

"Because Zeke Reynolds was killed with one," Maisie said.

"Did Lin or your grandmother find the gun from the restaurant?" Riya asked.

Maisie shrugged. "I don't think so."

"Then maybe we should talk to Veronica," Riya said.

"My mother said everyone around here owns guns. They bought them from the Dixby sisters."

"Aaannndddd we're back to them," Rory said.

"Doesn't look like we have time to debate anymore," I said. "Look!"

Veronica and Amelia had stood up, ready to go.

"We should hide," I said.

"We should question them," Maisie said.

"Not both together," Riya said. "We won't get a straight answer."

"Here comes Veronica!" I called out. And we made a run for it. We ran past the Juniper Tree and toward the corner. We needed to duck out of sight.

"C'mon," Maisie said. "Let's go in here."

We all looked up at the sign and then over at Maisie.

"We have to get out of sight," she said. "There's nothing like hiding in plain sight."

So we entered the Around the Corner Bookshop, owned by the soon-to-be-present Amelia Hargrove, and tried to hide among the rows of books.

"Just act nonchalant," I said as we rushed in the door. The bell jangling announced our arrival. Luckily no one paid any attention to us.

"Now what?" Riya asked.

"After Amelia comes in, we'll sneak out," I said, my voice low. The rows of books were parallel to the door and we could peek through the shelves and watch as she came in.

"Maybe we question her while we're here," Maisie said, wandering out into an open area.

"Shhh!" we all told her and I grabbed her arm and pulled her back. Just in time, it seemed.

"I can't believe it." Amelia walked in the door, her cell phone up to her ear. "Yes. I just talked to her. And it seems like stopping Zeke Reynolds is not stopping the deal."

Her voice was shaky and it sounded as if she may have been crying.

We looked at each other, eyes wide.

"I don't want to give up my shop. I don't want a stupid food truck with books. This place has always been . . ."

Her voice trailed off as she went toward the back of the store. I presumed to her office.

"Oh wow," I said. "Did you guys hear that?"

"Maybe I'm beginning to agree with Maisie," Riya said. "Maybe there was a conspiracy."

MAISIE LAGGED BEHIND us all the way back to the ice cream shop.

She still wanted to go back and talk to the Dixby sisters. I told her we needed to get back to the store.

Maisie was right, though. At some point we were going to have to question the Dixby sisters. Things kept coming up about them and they were the only ones we hadn't talked to. They hadn't been at the SOOCFA meeting, but they met other criteria Maisie had set forth. They didn't want to sell and they knew how to handle a gun.

But that was going to have to wait for another time.

As we neared the ice cream shop, I noticed someone sitting on my Grandma Kay's bench. He waved when I got close enough to be recognized.

"Hi, Mr. Mason," I said. "I was getting worried about you. Did you come by to get some ice cream?"

"Oh, I forgot," he said.

"C'mon," I said, walking past him and holding the door open. "Let's get you a scoop."

"I came for you to help me," he said. "Can you help me?" He followed me into the store.

"Sure, Mr. Mason," I said, thinking I already had plans to do that. I should have mentioned it to Bobby at Family Chef Night the night before. It had slipped my mind. "What do you want me to do?"

"There's a big black hole."

"A black hole?" I asked. "What is that?"

"I want them back."

"You want what back?"

Riya came over and smiled at him. "Here, sit down," she said, and took his hand. "Let me take a look at you."

He grinned so wide all three of his teeth were showing.

"You feeling okay?" she asked.

"Just worried about that black hole. I think that's where everything is," he said.

"Does his speech seem a little slurred to you?" Riya asked me.

"I don't think so," I said. I knew she asked me because I knew him better than she did, and knew what was normal for him. "He sometimes talks like that. But I did notice he wasn't using his right side the other day when I saw him. Kind of dragging his leg."

"I didn't notice that when he walked in just now." She stuck out two fingers. "Can you give my fingers a squeeze, Mr. Mason?" she asked. "Squeeze as hard as you can."

He did as she asked, all the while grinning.

"Can you push my fingers away?" she asked and he did. "Seems like he's okay now," she said. She looked at me then glanced up at the clock. "Maybe I should take him over to the clinic and check him out."

"Good idea," I said. "You think it'll be okay, though, if I give him some ice cream first?"

Riya looked at Mr. Mason and nodded. "I don't think it'll hurt. Might do him some good. Bring his blood glucose up. Can you give him some water, too? All this heat, he might be a little dehydrated."

"Okay," I said. "I'd meant to tell Bobby I wanted to get him to the clinic. I'm glad you're taking a look at him."

"No problem," she said.

I went in the back to get Mr. Mason some ice cream and a bottle of water. I noticed that Aunt Jack had been eyeing me the whole time. She followed me into the back.

"You were gone longer than an hour," she said.

"Did I say I'd only be gone an hour?" I asked. I didn't remember saying that, but maybe I had.

"If you're back," she said, "I'm leaving."

I glanced at her as I pulled a bottle of water from a case I kept stored in the pantry. "Okay," I said. "I had thought about doing some kind of special to draw people in during the sidewalk sale. But I've been so busy running around."

"The what?" she said.

"The flyer in the window," I said. "The bookstore and a couple of other shops are having a fire sale."

"I didn't hear about a fire."

"Me either, Aunt Jack, it's just what they're calling it."

"You don't expect me to stay, do you?"

"No," I said.

"And you do plan on paying me for the time I've spent here, right?"

I hadn't thought about that.

"Of course," I said.

"Good," she said, then looked as if she wanted to say something more but Maisie walked in.

"The protest is tonight," Maisie said. "I almost forgot all about it. Bobby just texted me." She held up her phone.

"I was thinking about participating tonight." I repeated what I'd just told Aunt Jack.

"I thought we might go to . . . you know." She looked at me and then Aunt Jack.

Aunt Jack looked at us, and it took her a minute to realize that Maisie didn't want to say whatever she had to say in front of her.

Aunt Jack put up her hands. "I'm out of here. I don't want to know anything about what you two are up to." She grabbed her purse off the back wall rack and left, going through the store to leave by the front door.

"She probably already knows," I said. We both chuckled. "So what were you trying to say?"

"I was saying that we should go to the Juniper Tree."

"I was thinking the same thing," I said.

"You were?"

"Yeah, I don't want to overlook them, even though I don't know how much I agree with them being the killers."

"So when are we going to talk to them?"

"I don't know," I said. "You're going to protest with Bobby, Riya is going to take Mr. Mason over to the clinic and check him out, and we might get busy if their sale brings more foot traffic."

"The protest isn't until later," she said.

"Where is it?"

"On the block where Rhys Enterprises wants to buy."

"Is anyone from Rhys going to be there?" I asked. Didn't seem like it would do much good if the company they were protesting against wouldn't know they were doing it.

"I don't know. Veronica said someone from the company was coming to take Zeke's place, but I don't know if they arrived yet or not."

"Yeah, but Ivan said that a new company was taking over." We looked at each other unsure what to do. "Well, anyway, I can't go. Aunt Jack left and my mother would be here by herself. The ice cream store has to come first."

Maisie gave me a pained look.

"We might have to admit defeat on this one, Maisie. This might be one that *we* won't be able to solve."

chapter

THIRTY-NINE

Riya left with Mr. Mason. She said she'd check him out and see to him getting back home. I wasn't even sure where that was. She said she would try to find out.

Not long after my mother said she was tired and ready to go, although she did say she would be stopping by at Around the Corner Bookshop to see what she could pick up.

But as it were, foot traffic turned out to be no more than the usual number of feet that went through that time of the evening, so again I left running the shop to Candy and Wilhelmina and headed out with Rory. The two of them headed toward the sidewalk sale, and Rory and I stopped by my house. We found Rory's catalogue raisonné on the front stoop. It was a good thing my elderly landlord hadn't seen it. She would have swooped it up, and we might not have ever gotten it back.

I was tired, it had been a couple of taxing days, but I didn't want to be the reason that Rory missed out on having something of value to take back with her.

She told me on the walk over, she'd called and gotten an increase on one of her credit cards and wouldn't have to dig into her savings to buy the painting she wanted.

I wasn't so sure if financing such a purchase was a good idea either, but I wasn't one to talk, I had taken out a huge line of credit to redo the ice cream shop. My grandchildren would probably still be paying on it long after I was gone.

But if business kept at the pace it was going, we just might be able to pay off that loan sooner than anticipated.

The block where the proposed vertical mini mall was to be built looked beautiful. By the time we got there dusk had set in, and the candles they had used to line the sidewalk glowed cheerfully. There were bright lights sparkling in the windows of the stores and someone had a speaker going, playing soft music that wafted up and down the street just like the small crowd of people.

All year Chagrin Falls has visitors from Cleveland, and its suburbs come in to see our waterfall and to browse our shop-lined streets. I didn't think that there were a lot of people from anywhere else, but our citizens had come out to support the nonfire fire sale.

"You want to stop and look in the bookstore?" I suggested. It was the first store in the block.

"No," Rory said. She swiped a wave of her red hair out of her face. "I just want to get to my picture before anyone else does." She held up the catalog.

"Okay," I said. "Too bad you didn't have a chance to study it before we got here."

"It's okay," she said. "I'll see what I want and then slip out to the restroom and consult it. It'll be more efficient that way, anyway. I'll know what I'm looking for."

As we passed the Juniper Tree I noticed Bobby and Maisie inside. There were a handful of people with them, all with signs, but there didn't seem to be any marching or chanting going on. After Rory got her picture, I would have to check in with them and find out what was happening.

"Hello."

I had turned my head to look into the Juniper Tree window and when I turned back I almost ran into Uncle Garud.

"Hello," I said.

"What are you doing out here?" he asked. "Trying to cause more trouble?"

"Have I caused you trouble?" I asked.

"Where is Riya?" he asked.

"I don't know," I lied. I didn't know what he was up to. Riya had said he was shady.

His suit seemed to be even less fitted than any of the others I'd seen him in. His bow tie was untied and laid around his neck. Tonight his smile looked sinister.

"Have you seen the new representative from Rhys Enterprises?" he asked.

"Bronwyn," Rory said, "I'm going to go on ahead."

I tried signaling her with a look not to leave me but she didn't seem to get it. She turned to walk away.

"I have to go with my friend," I said to Uncle Garud.

"Oh no," he said. "I have something you need to do for me."

"Do for you?"

"Yes. Come with me," he said.

"No," I said. "I have to go with my friend."

He grabbed my arm. "I want to know which one of you told," he said. He spoke close to my ear, and I could feel his warm breath bristle the hairs on my neck.

I pulled my arm away like Riya had taught me and stepped back from him. There were too many people out for him to try to do anything to me, I was sure, but his actions frightened me nonetheless.

"I am not going to lose out on this because of you," he said.

"I don't know what you mean," I said. "But you need to leave me alone."

"Where are your friends now?" he said.

I walked away from him, my heart beating a little faster than it had been. I just wanted to get away from him.

The outside of the gallery had tables lined with small prints and paintings. There were paintings in the window and hanging on what looked like a clothesline. Bright, white Christmas-like lights hung everywhere.

I wiggled through a crowd congregated at the front door and went in to find Rory.

"What's wrong?" Rory asked. She had her catalog tucked away under an arm and was eyeing a picture of a swamp and a weeping willow tree. Maybe I looked more shaken than I thought.

"Nothing," I said. "It's just Uncle Garud . . ." I let my voice trail off. I still couldn't figure out what he wanted.

"What?" she asked.

"I don't know. He seemed to be accusing me of something. Grabbing my wrist, trying to get me to tell him who'd done something."

"Did what?"

"I don't know." I shrugged. "I'm okay." I swallowed hard, trying to calm my nerves. I looked around the gallery. It looked just as stuffed with artwork as it had been the first time we visited. The only difference was that there were customers mingling around and food was set out. "Did you find what you were looking for?" I asked.

"I think I did," she said excitedly. "I was just going to find a bathroom and see if I can find it in my catalog." She pulled it out from under her arm. "The gallery actually has a catalog of their offerings, too." She had it clutched in her hand.

"Oh good," I said. "You can compare."

"Right. And negotiate."

"Yeah, right. If they are a little high," I said, "you can show them the information you got in the mail."

"Exactly," she said. I could hear her breathing heavily from the anticipation. "But I don't think I have to worry about that." She pointed to the price tag on the picture. "Look."

I took a look. "Oh," I said and smiled. "Fire sale prices."

"Yes!" She beamed. "Looks like I'm going home with a Florida Highwaymen painting." She wiggled and giggled. "I'm going to study their catalog, too, see what they have."

"In the restroom?" I asked.

"Yeah," she said. "I won't be too long."

I wandered around the gallery. I walked past Ivan and could hear him say they were moving the gallery to California. Yep, they had sold out. And maybe next year, standing in the same spot, I'd be in the first mall Chagrin Falls ever had.

Unless those Dixby sisters held out.

For some reason I found that funny.

"Have you seen Mr. Mason?"

I turned to find Riya standing behind me.

"No," I said. "I thought he was with you. Why are you here?"

"He *was* with me," she said. "And I'm here because he came in here."

"Oh," I said. "I haven't seen him. Did he check out okay?"

"Yeah," she said. "High blood pressure and maybe a little malnourished from having such bad teeth. I think he might have had a TIA. I need an MRI to know for sure."

"All those abbreviations don't mean a thing to me. Are you concerned he might pass out or have some kind of attack or something?"

"No," she said and shook her head. "He was fine until we passed this place."

"What happened?"

"He wouldn't leave. Kept pointing at some picture in the window saying it was a black hole." Riya shook her head. "He was pretty upset about it and then he came in here."

"He asked me to help him with a black hole earlier," I said.

"Apparently he's fallen through a black hole," Riya said. "Because I can't find him anywhere."

"Well, it's not that crowded," I said and looked around. "Maybe he left and went home."

"Maybe," she said. "I wanted him to go and take some tests tomorrow so I was trying to find out where he lived." She looked around the gallery. "He sure is a sneaky old man."

"At least he's not shady," I said.

She looked at me, her head slightly tilted. "No, that would be Uncle Garud," she said. "I just saw him, too. Outside."

"So did I," I said. "He grabbed my arm, wanting to know who told on him."

"Told what?" Riya asked, frowning.

"I don't know," I said, rubbing my wrist, remembering how he'd grabbed me. "He was acting crazy. It kind of scared me, but I remembered that little move you showed me to pull my wrist out from someone's grasp."

Her frown faded and I saw a wave of anger cross it.

"He was trying to hold on to you? He is crazy," she said, hissing out the words. "Stay here, I'll be back."

"No!" I said, trying to stop her. I knew that look. There was no telling what she might do.

I needed to go after her, but I didn't want to leave and not let Rory know where I'd gone. Stopping Riya might not be a quick excursion. I turned to find her, remembering she'd said she was going to duck into a bathroom to peruse the two catalogs. I didn't know where the restrooms were.

That was when I saw Mr. Mason. He had a painting in his hand and he was headed out through the back of the store.

"Shoot!" I said.

I looked the way Riya had gone and back to Mr. Mason. She

could be charged with felonious assault if I didn't get to her. But at the prices these paintings were going, Mr. Mason could be charged with grand larceny.

Riya's thing was a family affair. I decided to go after Mr. Mason. He needed my help more than she did. I took off after him.

chapter FORTY

Past the showroom area was a small hallway with the restroom, probably where Rory was, but I didn't take the time to stop. Beyond that was a workroom. It was long and cluttered. Frames, canvas and the smell of acrylic pants and turpentine filled the area. Some finished paintings were stacked along the walls and it looked as if someone had been working on a painting or two that were perched on easels, but I didn't stop to look at that either.

When I caught up to him he was going through the back door and it looked like he had picked up another painting.

"Mr. Mason!" I said. He looked back, I waved, but he either didn't recognize me or was too intent on getting away with his crime to take the time to respond to me.

I followed him out the back and found him by a dumpster on the other side of the alley that ran behind the stores. He was trying to put the pictures in it.

"Mr. Mason!" I said and ran over to him. "What are you doing?"

"What is going on out here?"

I turned to see Baraniece Black coming toward us.

"Oh shoot, Mr. Mason," I said, "we're in trouble now."

"I know you," Baraniece said, pointing her talon at me. That must have been her signature line. "Do you know him?" she asked me.

"Mr. Mason? Yes, I know him and I am so sorry," I said and tried to tug the paintings from Mr. Mason's hands. "He got ahold of these and I was trying to get them back."

"Get them back?" she said. "I'll get them from the little thief. Step aside."

She said it with such force that it shook me.

"He didn't mean any harm," I said, feeling protective of him. "I'll get them from him. Just let me get them."

"Hey, why are you back here?"

"It's the red ball," Mr. Mason said. "Back in the alley."

Rory had come out the back door and crossed the alley. "I thought I saw you come back here, but I wanted to check . . ." She took the situation in, it seemed, for the first time. "Why are you guys back here with those paintings?"

She looked to me for an answer, it seemed, avoiding Baraniece. "Mr. Mason *accidently*"—as I said it I looked at Baraniece—"took them. I was just giving them back." Rory looked down at the paintings as I tried to tug them from his hands again. He wasn't having a problem with weakness because I couldn't pry them from his hands.

"How about if I buy them," Rory offered. The idea seemed to just come to her and she seemed very careful with her words, barely looking at Baraniece.

"I don't know that you can afford them," Baraniece said.

"Can we make a deal?" Rory asked. "How much do you want for them?"

"Two thousand dollars," Baraniece said.

"For the two?" I asked.

"Each!" she said.

"Fine," Rory said and looked at me. "You two go around the front. I'll pay for these and join you."

"No," I said. "I'm not letting you pay four thousand dollars for these paintings. Mr. Mason didn't mean to do any harm," I said. "We can give them back."

Baraniece raised an eyebrow. "I can get them back from him if necessary," she said, her arms folded across her torso. She was tapping her foot.

"It's not necessary," Rory said. Her eyes seemed to plead with me. "Take the paintings and go."

"Rory!" I protested.

"Please," Rory said, and for the first time it seemed that I heard agitation in her voice. "Please, just go."

"What is wrong here?" It was Ivan. He yelled from across the alleyway. "Are you okay, sweetie?"

It was turning into a backyard party. Only not a fun one.

"Nothing's wrong," Baraniece said. "We were just conducting business."

"In the alley!" he said. "Lately, you have begun to worry me." He waved us in with a hand. "Please. Everyone. Come back inside."

"C'mon," I said to Mr. Mason. "Let's go back inside."

He shook his head and seemed to tether himself there next to the dumpster.

"Fine," I said. "You stay here, we'll go and buy these paintings and then you can throw them away."

"It's a black hole," Mr. Mason yelled as we walked away. "I won't cut off my ear!"

"He is crazy," Ivan said.

Rory eyed me and I could tell something more was going on than what I knew, but before we could get in the door Baraniece stopped. "I think they know," she said suspiciously.

"Know what?" I said.

"Know what?" Ivan echoed my statement.

"She does." Baraniece pointed to Rory. "And he does, too." She looked back at Mr. Mason.

"What do they know?" I asked again. I was totally confused. "Rory"—I turned to her—"you know something? Because I don't know what she's talking about."

"No," Rory said and shook her head. She licked her lips and I could have sworn I saw her bottom lip tremble. "I don't know anything except I want to buy his paintings." She flapped an arm toward Mr. Mason.

He had stopped trying to throw them in the dumpster and was standing there holding them.

"You are overreacting again, sweetie," Ivan said, his accent heavy and gruff.

"We can't let them go back inside," Baraniece said.

"And we can't kill them," he responded.

"Wow," I said. "Where did that come from?" I held out my arms. "I said he was sorry. Mr. Mason is just going through something. We're getting him help."

Baraniece looked at Rory. Rory lowered her eyes.

"See, she knows," Baraniece said.

"Rory," I said. "Do you know something? Something that would make this woman want to kill us?"

She looked up at me, then over at Mr. Mason.

"Mr. Mason doesn't mean a black hole like space, he means Van Gogh," Rory said.

"Are those paintings by Vincent van Gogh?" I asked. "Is that why you were willing to pay for them? They have to be worth more than that." I swung around and looked at Mr. Mason still holding on to the paintings.

"They're fakes," Rory said, like she was happy to say it out loud. "Mr. Mason, it seems, is a recognized artist. I looked him up when I was in the bathroom because he was in their catalog."

"Oh," I said. "They were trying to sell his work." I looked at Baraniece. "That you painted?"

Now I understood. Mr. Mason knew those weren't his works. He wasn't too out there after all.

"So why did you offer to pay for something that was fake?" I asked. "Especially so much."

"So we could get out of here." Rory glanced at the door and groaned like she'd given up trying to get through it. "Their Florida Highwaymen are fakes, too."

"Ohhh," I said again. Things were beginning to clear up for me. "You found that out from your catalogue raisonné?"

"Ha!" Baraniece let out a nervous laugh. "You have one of those, too. When did we get so many art fanciers in little ole Chagrin Falls?" She swiped a hand across her forehead. "I can't take it!"

"Too?" I mumbled, my mind churning.

"We have to leave, my dear," Ivan said. He grabbed her elbow, but it seemed she didn't want to budge. "We should go now."

"We can't. They know."

"I only know because you told me," I said sarcastically. Although, unlike Rory and Mr. Mason, I didn't care that they were forging paintings. "But we can . . . Wait . . ." I tilted my head. "Too? You have one, too." I looked at Rory. "Didn't you say that Becky girl, the one that helped you get the catalog thingy, said you were the second person to order one of those for this zip code?"

Rory nodded.

I looked at Baraniece then Ivan. "Did you guys get one, too?" I looked at Rory again, this time with a scowl on my face. "But why would they need one, right?" I reasoned. "They would know the location if they owned the painting. They wouldn't need one of those catalogs, would they?"

Rory shrugged.

"Why did you say you couldn't kill us?" I asked Ivan.

"It is an expression," Ivan said. He tugged on his wife. "We can go now. I will tell everyone that the sale is over. And we can go."

"And what about them?" she asked.

"Baraniece!" he said, seemingly exasperated. "You just can't kill everyone."

She pulled a gun out of the folds of her kimono.

"Oh my!" I jumped, nearly out of my skin. "What the heck!"

I had flashbacks. Back to that stairwell when Althea Quigley tried to stab me to death.

"Baraniece, sweetie," Ivan said. "It's too many. How will we explain?"

I couldn't believe what he was saying, and I couldn't figure a way out. He blocked the path to the door out, and she blocked the way back in.

"She was in the alley," Baraniece said, pointing the gun at Rory. "Her and that mop of hair."

"The alley?" I repeated. Then my mouth dropped open. Everything I'd heard along the investigation came flooding back.

Oh, why in the world would I do another investigation!

My voice shaky, I turned to Rory. I needed her to help me understand why I was about to die. Again. "Veronica said that Zeke Reynolds was supposed to come over here that night. To buy art." In my periphery, I could see Baraniece grip the gun tighter. "He didn't buy any art, did he? Because he knew they were forgeries."

"Fakes," Rory said. She didn't seem as frightened as I was. Her voice was calm—matter-of-fact. Maybe she was going into shock again. Because certainly, her voice had to belie the fear inside of her.

"Zeke Reynolds was from Florida." My eyes were wide. "He would have known about the Florida Highwaymen, you think, Rory?"

"I don't know," she said. Her eyes had gone blank and were staring off into space. I needed her to snap out of it. Maybe we could make a run for it, but not if she was playing the role of a zombie.

"Rory!" I said. "Rory!" This time I stamped my foot and flinched. I wanted to get her attention, but I didn't want to scare Baraniece into pulling that trigger.

Rory turned and looked at me.

"Amelia told me he'd been in Chagrin Falls for a week," I said. "Veronica said he'd been over here a few times. He ordered the catalog, came over to check out what they had, just like you did, and . . ."

"I think we should go," Rory said.

Like we could do that . . .

"*Prekrati!*" Ivan said. He put both hands on his head, covering his face with his arms.

"I can't stop," Baraniece said. "They don't understand."

"They don't need to understand," he said.

But she paid no attention to him. "He just wouldn't go away," Baraniece said, her voice and the hand that was holding that gun trembling. "We told him we were leaving. He already had our deal. Signed. Money transferred. But he didn't care. He just wanted to turn us in."

"Let's go, Baraniece."

"No!" she squealed. "We can't leave them. They will tell."

"You can't kill all of them," Ivan said, as if it really was an option.

"He'll never know to tell." She pointed the gun at Mr. Mason, saying, I guess, she could spare his life, but not ours.

My mouth got so dry, and my knees started to buckle. I closed my eyes, not wanting to see any of what was going to happen. All of this sleuthing stuff was going to get me killed.

Then I opened my eyes. Baraniece had told on herself. If I had just gone after Riya instead of Mr. Mason, maybe none of this would have happened.

"Riya!" I shouted, surprised she'd appeared just when I had thought of her.

Riya had come out of nowhere. She high-kicked Ivan off his feet and out cold to the ground. She swung around and with her left hand she pushed the gun Baraniece was holding, and with her right hand she punched her in the face. I could see only the whites of her eyes and the crimson red of the blood trickling out of her nose as she started to go down. Then, with both of her hands, Riya twisted the gun out of the painting faker's already limp hands.

"Oh my lord," Rory said, panting, as she leaned up against the building. "You are a superhero."

Epilogue

D on't tell me. Don't tell me." Maisie covered her ears and shook her curls. "How could you solve the murder without me?"

"I didn't solve it," I said. "Baraniece spilled the beans all on her own."

"She just came up to you and said, 'I killed Zeke Reynolds'?"

"Practically," I said. "She was an art forger."

"Faker," Rory said. "There's a difference."

"Baraniece and her husband, what's his name?"

"Ivan," I said.

"Ivan," Maisie repeated. "I never would have thought that Zeke was killed for any other reason except he wanted to put a vertical mall here."

"Or because he'd had a spat with Veronica," my mother said. "A lover's quarrel."

"Veronica as a suspect was filled with so much gossip that it was hard to prove. None of the stuff, except for the argument, was true."

"Lin found the gun," Maisie said.

"Where was it?" I asked.

"In the kitchen," Maisie said. "In almost the same spot where they always kept it."

"See, we were chasing her around for nothing," I said.

"I don't think we would have ever figured this one out."

"So that means we shouldn't ever try again."

"Oh, God forbid," my mother said, clutching her chest. "I don't want to hear any more talk of murder."

"What I want to hear again is how Riya took that gun away from the crazy faker lady." Maisie jumped up and started doing karate chops through the air.

And that was how it went. We were back at the ice cream shop, and once we thought we had talked about it enough, customers started coming in and asking more questions about it.

The question we got the most? Was Riya really a doctor or was that just a front for her real job—a CIA operative.

Like Riya, Baraniece Black had a problem controlling her temper. By the time Baraniece and her husband, Ivan, came to, Detective Beverly and his team had arrived and they were waiting for the FBI. Apparently it was a special unit for art crimes, but they had already been alerted. It seemed that Zeke Reynolds had left a message standing in that alleyway before Baraniece had caught up to him.

That was why they had stopped the art exhibit at the visitors' center. For some reason they thought the call had been about one of those paintings.

And the mall idea was a bust. Cue the applause.

Everyone, except for Uncle Garud, was happy about that. I

never found out what he wanted that night outside of the gallery when he grabbed my arm and accused me of doing who knows what, and I was fine not knowing and happy to steer clear of him. But whatever he wanted, it had to do with the mall coming and now that wasn't going to happen. So technically, he couldn't have any beef with me. I had nothing to do with that decision. The new company didn't want their mall in a place where someone would possibly murder their company's representative and wasn't sending any of their people up (that's why Bobby's protest didn't happen, he was waiting for someone from the company to see that they had grievances).

It was the first time in my life that I was okay with someone saying something bad about my hometown.

I did hope that Chagrin Falls wouldn't get a bad rap out in the world, because in my eyes, and even with Rory trying to lure me back to the Big Apple with promises of grandeur, it was still, in my heart and eyes, the best place to be.

My family was sad to see Rory go, and I believe if we had better coffee in our little village, she might have stayed. Not quite sure what she was going to do when she got back to New York and to work, though. She had to go back and tell them she hadn't convinced me to return, and she had to return to a job that didn't make her happy. There was going to be a lot for her to figure out.

I told her, as we hugged our goodbyes, she should do the things that made her happy. It was why I made ice cream.

Speaking of people getting to do the things that made them happy, Mr. Mason might have a second chance at that.

It turned out that he had a niacin deficiency and it had left him—well, confused. To top it off, the MRI showed that he'd had a TIA—a transient ischemic attack, or ministroke. It resolves itself within twenty-four to forty-eight hours, so I was told, but can lead to a real stroke. Bobby and Riya said they would make sure Mr. Mason would get the care he needed, and in time, he could go back to his normal activities. Like painting.

It was a good feeling when Rory and I tracked down some of his paintings before she left. She took one home and told me she was hanging it in her living room. She even paid him for it.

Aunt Jack didn't stay long. Thank goodness! (Oops, I hope I didn't say that out loud!) Nice for her, her internet man came looking for her. Begging her to come back to North Carolina with him. Telling her how much he needed her. He sounded like one of those old tracks that my Grandma Kay used to listen to.

O took me out to dinner. I was reluctant to go. I didn't want to give him any ideas, but I figured it would be nice for a moment to sit back and relax. One of my mother's parking lot moments without the parking lot. He said he probably needed to spend more time with me to keep me out of trouble. I told him, I don't need any help staying out of trouble. I just need help in keeping trouble from finding me.

Acknowledgments

Writing is not a solitary activity. At least not for me. There are so many that support me, read for me, encourage me. Some like Kathryn Dionne that have been with me since I started this journey. I couldn't ask for a better writing partner. She has the patience and creativity that I rely on to get my next story out. I always say I couldn't do it without her, and that's the truth.

And then there's my South Euclid-Lyndhurst Library crew. Just their presence helps get me motivated. Thank you, Laurie, Nicole, Molly, Rose, Connie and LaBena.

My Berkley team has made me feel right at home. I love them. So helpful and supportive. Since the release of my first Ice Cream Parlor Mystery book, *A Deadly Inside Scoop*, I have gotten so many compliments on what they helped me pull together. People are saying they are seeing it everywhere, and all seem to love the cover, agreeing that it is fun and cute and makes them want to pick up the book. And of course without their help, my story wouldn't be as good. So thank you, Dache

Rogers and Elisha Katz, cover artist Vi-An Nuygen, and Jessica Wade and Miranda Hill for making me and my book look good.

My agent, Rachel Brooks, and BookEnds Literary Agency are the best, I am so happy and lucky to have them by my side.

Crewse Creamery
ICE CREAM RECIPES
❧❧❧

For these recipes, you don't need an ice cream machine. But if you do use one, be sure to follow the manufacturer's instructions. And if you don't have one, remember to use whipped cream to create a better texture. It'll take a little longer for your mixture to freeze properly, but it'll be fine. Just check on it every couple of hours and give it a good stir.

Here are a few other tips before you get started:

TIP #1: When it comes to the milk you add, embrace the fat content. Low-fat products don't freeze as well, don't taste as good and give the ice cream an icy texture. Always use heavy cream, whole milk or half-and-half.

TIP #2: If you use an ice cream maker, never pour your warm (or even room-temperature) base into your ice cream machine. A base that isn't chilled prior to going into your ice cream maker won't freeze. The colder, the better!

TIP #3: Don't overfill your ice cream machine. Remember, liquids expand as they freeze, and if your machine is filled to the top, it will end up spilling over the sides. Fill it no more than three-quarters of the way full.

TIP #4: Don't over churn your ice cream. The ice cream will start to freeze as it churns in your machine, but it won't freeze to the right consistency. Churning too much will cause your ice cream to have an icy texture. Churn just enough until the mixture is thick, about the consistency of soft serve, before transferring it to the freezer.

Rory's Mint Mojito Coffee Ice Cream

2 vanilla beans or 2 teaspoons vanilla extract

2 cups heavy whipping cream

2 cups whole milk

1 cup sugar

⅓ cup ground decaffeinated coffee beans

1 bunch fresh mint leaves, torn

⅓ cup white rum

If using beans, with a knife, halve vanilla beans lengthwise. Scrape seeds into a medium-sized pot. Combine cream, milk and sugar and heat until sugar dissolved. Add coffee beans and mint leaves. Stir together. Cover pot and steep for forty-five minutes.

Strain liquid mixture and discard coffee beans and mint leaves. Place mixture over medium heat and bring to a boil. Take off heat and allow to cool.

Cover and refrigerate until chilled, four to five hours. Add rum once chilled.

Using the ice cream maker, add the chilled mixture according to the manufacturer's instructions. Churn until it is the consistency of soft serve. Place in covered freezer-proof container and freeze for at least two hours.

Enjoy!

Aunt Jack's Peppermint Candy Ice Cream

2 vanilla beans

2½ cups heavy cream

1½ cups whole milk

1 cup sugar

¼ teaspoon salt

2 teaspoons peppermint extract

8 large egg yolks

½ cup crushed candy canes or star mints

With a knife, halve vanilla beans lengthwise. Scrape seeds into a large heavy saucepan and stir in heavy cream, milk, sugar and salt. Bring mixture to a boil, stirring occasionally, and remove pan from heat. Add peppermint extract.

In a large bowl lightly beat egg yolks. Add hot cream mixture to eggs in a slow stream, whisking, then return custard mixture to pan. Cook custard over moderate heat, and do not let it come to a boil. Stir constantly until mixture reaches 170°F.

Pour custard through a sieve into a clean bowl and cool. Chill custard, its surface covered with wax paper, in refrigerator until cold, about three hours.

Add cold mixture to ice cream maker and proceed according to manufacturer's instructions. Just before ice cream is set, add crushed candy and continue mixing until combined.

Place ice cream in an airtight container and freeze until fully set, at least two hours.

Enjoy!

Win's Easy Summer Mango Sorbet

1 cup water

1 cup sugar

¼ teaspoon salt

4 mangoes, peeled and diced

2 teaspoons freshly squeezed lime juice

2½ tablespoons vodka or tequila (optional)

In a small pot, heat water, sugar and salt until sugar is melted.

Peel and dice mangoes and place them in food processor (discard seeds along with peels). Add lime juice and sugar water. Blend until smooth. Pour into a medium bowl, cover and refrigerate until completely chilled, at least two hours.

Before putting mango mixture in ice cream maker, add liquor if using. Mix according to the manufacturer's instructions.

Transfer mixture to a covered freezer-safe container and freeze until firm, at least six hours.

Enjoy!

Wall Street Journal bestselling author ABBY COLLETTE loves a good mystery. She was born and raised in Cleveland, and it's a mystery even to her why she hasn't yet moved to a warmer place. She is the author of the Logan Dickerson Mysteries, the southern cozy mystery series featuring a second-generation archaeologist and a nonagenarian who is always digging up trouble. She is also the author of the Romaine Wilder Mysteries, set in East Texas, which pairs a medical examiner and her feisty auntie who owns a funeral home and is always ready to solve a whodunit. Abby spends her time writing, facilitating writing workshops at local libraries and spending time with her grandchildren, each of whom is her favorite.

Abby is a member of Crime Writers of Color, and the Sisters in Crime national, regional and guppy chapters, and a member of the Alpha Kappa Alpha Sorority.

CONNECT ONLINE

AbbyCollette.com

Ready to find
your next great read?

Let us help.

Visit prh.com/nextread